BIRD'S FLIGHT

BIRD'S FLIGHT

AUDREY MURPHY

Audrey Murphy

iUniverse®

BIRD'S FLIGHT

iUniverse books may be ordered through booksellers or by contacting:

iUniverse
1663 Liberty Drive
Bloomington, IN 47403
www.iuniverse.com
1-800-Authors (1-800-288-4677)

ISBN: 978-1-4917-5096-4 (sc)
ISBN: 978-1-4917-5097-1 (hc)
ISBN: 978-1-4917-5098-8 (e)

Library of Congress Control Number: 2014918992

Printed in the United States of America.

iUniverse rev. date: 2/03/2015

Many thanks to my husband, Mike, and my sons, for their support while I was writing Bird's Flight, and also to my friend, Rhonda, for her honest critique.

Chapter 1

Anchored into the rigid Missouri soil were two corroded pipes, and from them hung a weathered sign that read: "Greenstone – Population 754." Each generation died, but their offspring kept that number true enough. As a young boy, I thought I'd never get away from that place.

Partridge is my surname. That's right, as in "partridge in a pear tree." And according to Grandpa Partridge, I'm of Irish descent, and that's why I'm tall and have a chiseled jawline that angles to form a somewhat pointed chin. He said my light skin, straight, black hair, and blue eyes make me a ringer for an Irishman too. I guess that's why Grandpa Partridge felt the need to tell me about my heritage.

Grandpa said that the man who would become his great-grandpa, Tyrell, left Ireland when a fungus ruined the single crop the Irish depended on for food: the potato. During what was called the Irish Potato Famine, the British offered no help to feed their Irish subjects, who were starving. Tyrell was among thousands of Irish who immigrated to America around 1847 on a steamboat that took them to New York. He settled in Manhattan, along with a community of his countrymen; he paid a landlord rent for a single unsanitary, rundown room, and he became a dockworker. Tyrell married an Irish girl in the community, and they had one son, *my* great-grandpa, Joseph, who at age nineteen, around 1886, left New York to pursue work in Missouri mining coal, a fuel that was in demand for running trains. He arrived by rail in Saint Louis, Missouri, and then traveled to Greenstone in northern Missouri, where coal was plentiful. He became a coal miner, a trade his son, my grandpa, would learn and pass on to his male heir.

Ty is my given name. Never been fond of it, but at least Dad didn't impose *Tyrell* on me, trying to hold onto his Irish roots. As a boy, though, anyone close to me called me by my nickname, Bird.

My folks, Marta and Charles, grew up together and got married in Greenstone. They raised me and my younger sister, Allison, there, and I knew for certain that that's where they'd die.

Grandpa Partridge started working as a coal miner when he was only fifteen, and he would put in six days a week for Mr. Arthur Shott, who took over Shott Coal Company in Greenstone, Missouri, after his father, Wilfred, died. When Arthur died, his two sons took over the business, and Grandpa worked for them till he was too old to handle a pick or carry a bucket of coal. Grandpa Partridge implanted the idea in my dad's mind that being a coal miner was his destiny too. And my mother followed in her mother's footsteps and worked as a waitress in the same restaurant Grandma Morgan had. My folks' lives were carbon copies of their parents' lives. They thought Allison and I should fall in line too. I disagreed.

Another thing I disagreed with was the town's name, Greenstone. It wasn't a place that flourished; it was the most backward, dried-up place I could ever have imagined. Even the town's only tree, a weeping willow, was testament that nothing and no one could overcome that town's force of gravity.

We had Burt Brown's Grocery, a family-operated store. An orange sign advertising the business hung by a chain above the entrance and was the only speck of color on the building's weathered-gray slate siding. Inside, the smell of pigs' feet and snouts hung ripe in the air, 'cause the unwrapped delicacies were displayed on ice in a wooden, glass-enclosed case. A sign that I'm sure Burt's son, Jack, had made dangled from the ceiling in red letters that read: "Meat Department." The greasy odor of lard floated through the air in Mrs. Brown's bakery section, where she kept watch, shooing flies from her uncovered pastries, wrapping each customer's selection personally.

Then there was Dollar Shop. Talk about covering the bases. That old wooden floor that creaked when I walked on it had shelves of cleansers, light switches, towels, sheets, baby diapers, toiletries—you name it, everything from *A* to *Z*. Yet the only thing I ever bought there was Bazooka bubble gum that came in a comic wrapper. It was rock-hard and took twenty chews to soften, but I loved it.

We had Jenk's Pharmacy, run by Martin Jenks, who filled prescriptions, rang the register, and closed up shop by hanging a "Pharmacist back in fifteen minutes" sign on the door when he had a delivery. Jenks's wood clapboard siding on the pharmacy wouldn't hold paint long. Unlike most of the other business owners, Jenks liked bright colors. One time, he painted that pharmacy kind of a purplish-red color. Mom called it *magenta*. I used to get a kick out of trying to guess what color paint he'd choose next.

Then there was Doc Arnold, who leased space from Jenks for his family practice. The waiting area, consisting of three chairs and one exam room, was separated from the pharmacy by a curtain that hung from the ceiling to the floor. A "No Appointment Necessary" sign was taped to the accordion-like partition where Doc Arnold examined patients.

Sussman Bank was next door. Folks cashed their paychecks and had savings accounts there, but loans were handled at Sussman headquarters in Wakefield, Missouri, a one-hour drive from Greenstone.

To pique our curiosity about the world at large and satisfy us in the entertainment sense, we had a beat-up movie theater called Motion Picture Palace. It may have once been a palace, but when I was a young boy, it had seen its day and then some. None of the old, red-velvet seats had less than two broken springs. The trace of blue paint on the concrete floor must have dated back to George Washington's time, and the sticky soda and bubble gum, some of which was mine, made the soles of my sneakers adhere to the floor. The movies we watched had been shown earlier in large cities; they got tossed our way when they were cheap to rent. But in the Motion Picture Palace, I wasn't Bird Partridge, a "going nowhere" guy; I was a lawyer, detective, or scientist, trying to set things right.

Since I didn't often have fifty cents to buy a movie ticket, I mostly hung out with friends or rode my bike on the gravel roads, getting a wave from local drivers who inched along. I figured those narrow, bumpy roads had to connect with better paved ones somewhere. There had to be towns and cities where people didn't crawl their way through life.

As a freshman in high school that August of 1964, I did have a special hangout. Above the entrance to the building, a weathered, red-and-white striped canvas awning hung unsteadily from the cracked mortar, and a red neon sign in the picture window flashed on and off like bursts of lightning, advertising the business, Pop's Pop. And though it was a shabby building, like the rest in Greenstone, for me, that soda-fountain shop was the highlight of the town, and old man Bradford, who insisted that everyone call him Pop, sold the best cherry cola I've ever had. He didn't skimp on the cherry syrup, and I liked the cylinder-shaped glasses he served the cola in.

Lined up along his black Formica soda fountain bar were chrome-legged stools with red leather seats. Matching tables and chairs were scattered about on black-and-white tiles that made a checkerboard floor, and the cracked plaster wall behind the bar was a shrine to rock 'n' roll artists. Pop told me that of all the pictures on that wall, Elvis's was his favorite, 'cause he pulled himself up out of poverty and became the King of Rock 'n' Roll.

"Bird, anybody can come up in the world if they work hard and don't give up," Pop said while we sat sipping our cola and shooting the breeze one day. After that, Elvis's picture was my favorite too. And though I didn't expect a life like Elvis's, I knew I wanted more than Greenstone had to offer.

Even though I didn't much take to advice from adults in Greenstone, I could tell right off that Pop wasn't like the other folks who lived there. I wanted to believe what Pop said was true, but with Dad's insistence that I become a coal miner, I felt like a fly on a sticky trap; I knew all the hard work I could muster wouldn't release me from my sure fate. I was down in the dumps from Dad's preaching about mining, and Pop could sense I was blue. He asked me why it looked like my best friend just died, so I told him.

"Bird, your dad's wrong to try to brainwash you about that God-awful job. The pay's poor, and the hours are long. All that comes from mining is a broken-down back and lungs full of coal dust. I'm proof of that. Figure out what you want and go after it. Don't let nobody or nothing hold you back."

Though I didn't realize it that day, that old soda-fountain shop and its owner were going to impact my life in a way I could never have imagined.

I looked at my watch and saw what time it was. "Gotta get going, Pop. Dad's due home from the mine, and Mom will be home from waitressing at the diner."

I'd been given a few chores to do: milking our cow, Brownie, and slopping the hogs, and I wanted my folks to see me in the act of carrying them out. That way, I got a lighter hammering when Dad started in on me about "acting more like a man." Besides, if I didn't get home before my dad, he'd ask Allison where I was. I figured I'd get more than a lecture if he found out I'd been with Pop, so I peddled that old bike of mine fast as I could to get home.

Chapter 2

While movies at the Motion Picture Palace had helped me imagine being something other than a miner, Pop planted the seed that stretched my imagination to a possibility I hadn't considered. That seed was planted the first time I saw what Pop called the "jitterbug."

Like usual, me and a bunch of the kids were hanging out at Pop's Pop after high school let out for the day, having a cherry cola, me chewing my bubble gum, trying to get it wedged in the space between my front teeth. Pop started talking about back in the day when he was young and did the jitterbug.

"We danced wild back then, even did acrobatics. I'd face my partner, grip her waist, and she'd jump up at the same time I lifted her, swinging her legs up and forward so they formed a *V* at my waist. Then she'd swing her legs back, away from my waist, and I'd throw her straight up in the air. That was a barrel of fun."

All of a sudden, he got up from his barstool, dropped a quarter in the jukebox, and grabbed Emma Jean Wilmyer, who was fourteen at the time, same as me.

That fast music started and Pop said, "Emma Jean, you're about to have more fun than you've ever had before."

Pop's movements were quick and freewheeling. Emma Jean tried to copy his bouncy steps that looked like he was hopping from one foot to the other, but she couldn't. She had never danced before, and when he turned her in circles, she got so off-balance, I thought she was going to fall. She was tall for a girl and solidly built, and Pop knew he didn't have the strength to lift her, but his steps were quick, and Emma Jean got winded trying to keep up with the old guy. Us kids watching laughed till we couldn't get *our* breath. When the music stopped, Emma Jean flopped down on a barstool.

We all clapped and yelled, "More, more!" Pop said we should be participants, not spectators. He said he wasn't able to do the acrobatic moves that he had done in his youth, but he offered to teach us kids what he said was a tamer version of jitterbug called East Coast swing. A bunch of us said we'd show up every afternoon for lessons at Pop's Pop. Some of the guys and gals didn't keep their word, though; they only showed up once or twice a week, but I didn't miss, not even once. We'd push the tables and chairs up against the wall, and we had ourselves a pretty decent dance floor.

After three weeks of lessons, Pop told me I had the potential to become a "darn good swing dancer."

The few times my folks inquired as to what I did after school, I said I hung out with friends awhile and then went home to take care of my chores. I think my folks were too exhausted when they got home from work to press me about where my friends and I were hanging out. Dad's usual routine was to change out of his mining clothes and then catch a few winks in his chair while Mom made supper. Since my folks had no clue I was at Pop's soda-fountain shop, I was able to take each afternoon dance lesson Pop offered, and I still had time to sit and talk with him before I had to get home.

One day, Pop told me how he used to be a "hot item" on the dance floor, how he never sat out a dance 'cause the ladies about fought over him. When he told me that, the twinkle in his eyes gave him a mischievous look, a look I didn't expect from a guy as old as him. And his thin, white hair, wrinkled skin, and brown age spots seemed like a disguise, that the real Pop was hidden by those markers of age.

"I competed once. Won too," Pop said, and he pointed to the wall behind the bar. "See that trophy up there?"

Two gold metallic dancers were atop the tall column of the trophy; a gold metallic "#1" was mounted onto the base.

"Won that a long time ago in Wakefield. When I was your age."

Even if Pop hadn't had the trophy on display, I would have believed him.

"Bird, you're rough around the edges 'cause you lack the know-how for the steps, but your feet are quick, you're coordinated, and you catch on fast. There's talent waiting to be drawn out of you; I'd stake my name on that. Why, I can see you someday dancing on stage."

Then Pop asked me that important question that teased my mind and set me on course for my chosen career. "You ever thought of becoming a professional dancer?"

I hadn't. No one had ever suggested that I could become anything other than a coal miner. So, like a lighthouse, Pop's question illuminated a path I hadn't considered.

Pop kept giving me more difficult moves to learn, and every time I mastered what he asked of me, he showed me another move that challenged me more. With each new step Pop added, I pushed myself to work harder. I was determined to not let him down, determined to build up my self-confidence, so I could believe in me, like he did.

Chapter 3

I walked into Pop's Pop after school let out that afternoon in February of 1965. I was the first of Pop's swing-dance students to arrive. Pop was sitting on a barstool watching his old dinosaur black-and-white TV that sat on the soda-fountain counter. He was adjusting the rabbit ears to get better reception. The static cleared, and the screen showed a bunch of college students carrying signs opposing US involvement in the Vietnam War. I sat down on the barstool next to Pop.

"Wow, look at all those protestors," I said.

"Those North Vietnamese shouldn't force Communist rule on South Vietnam, but those young kids got a point. This war's costing young American soldiers their lives. How do you feel about it, Bird?"

As far as I was concerned, Greenstone, Missouri, was good for nothing, except mining, but there'd never been anyone shot there. How could I wrap my head around the massive killing that took place in a war? I didn't know how to answer.

"The other kids are here for your lesson, Pop; can we get started?"

He turned off the TV. "Sure. Can't solve the world's problems, anyhow."

In the past, I had hated starting back to school to hit the books again. But that August, beginning my sophomore year at Greenstone High School was easier to endure. I knew after school, I had dance lessons to look forward to.

By October, I was dedicated to swing dancing, and Pop and I had grown close. I could talk to him about anything, things I wouldn't have talked to my folks about. I'd tell Pop my plans for performing on stage, saving money, and someday having my own dance studio. How after I accomplished those things and found my future wife, I'd expect him at the wedding. Pop smiled, but the fire in his mischievous eyes was no more than a flicker.

Though I didn't know how I was going to make it happen, by the end of my sophomore year that May of 1966, I was more determined than ever to have a dancing career. It didn't matter how many times I had to repeat a dance step Pop showed me; I did it until I got his approval. And even when he said, "Perfect, Bird," I'd practice it half a dozen times more. It got to the point that Pop's dance lessons were more than lessons to me. He'd drop a quarter in the jukebox, and I'd pretend I was in a dance contest like Pop had been in. My partner and I would outdance the other competitors on that checkerboard floor at Pop's Pop. When the dance finished, I imagined the crowd clapping and cheering for us as we were handed a first-place trophy like the one Pop had.

I knew what I wanted out of life. I wasn't going to live out my days as a coal miner. Professional dancing was my ticket out of Greenstone to a new way of life that would give me recognition for something I loved to do. My folks didn't have a clue that I was dancing, and that's the way I wanted it. My sister, Allison, knew, but she'd been sworn to secrecy. I was sure I could count on Allison as long as Dad didn't interrogate her concerning my whereabouts, so I always got home before my folks got off work. When I had to tell my folks that dance was my chosen career, they'd have to accept it. I wasn't going to back off.

Chapter 4

I had finished my junior year at Greenstone High School. The only kids who continued to show up for Pop's dance lessons were Drew Proffit, Sally Jo Merkel, Patti Baker, and Emma Jean Wilmyer. Pop knew hands down that Emma Jean had become the best dancer of the three girls, so he made her my permanent partner. Drew got Sally Jo, who wasn't near as good, and Pop partnered up with "Two Left Feet" Patti, who couldn't keep beat with the music to save her soul.

With my birthday on the twenty-first of May, I hadn't yet turned seventeen. I'd been on summer break for *one* day when Dad approached me after supper with his "opportunity's knocking" speech. I should have seen that coming 'cause Grandpa Partridge had forced Dad to quit high school to become a coal miner—and Dad had been sucking in coal dust ever since.

Many of the guys my age wanted to fill in that summer at the current underground coal mine being worked. They figured they might as well fall in line with their folks' wishes and follow in their fathers' footsteps. When one of the full-time miners got laid-off due to an injury or one of them took their hard-earned bit of vacation, those were opportunities for a guy my age to fill in and get training. That made them eligible for a full-time job when it opened up.

Like my dad and Grandpa, many of those guys my age wouldn't finish high school; they'd work a mine till every bit of coal was removed, then work the next one and all the mines that were opened up thereafter till their backs broke down; then they'd retire and die of old age. But some weren't so lucky. During retreat mining, as much coal as possible was mined from the pillars supporting the roof as the miners backed out of a room in the mine. Sometimes, the miners didn't retreat fast enough, and the roof would collapse, burying them with rock that fell from the coal seam above them.

Dad, hell-bent on getting me in as a fill-in at the mine, had started talking about the prospect when I was fourteen. His persistence had been like a bad case of poison ivy that kept multiplying and irritating me over the years, but I knew I'd never give in. I wanted no part of mining.

"Time to step up and be a man," Dad said. "Can't expect me and your mother to keep you forever. We've got your sister to look after too. One of the full-timers got hurt, and they need a fill-in at the mine. I spoke up and said you'd do it. This is your chance."

That one of the miners got hurt was hard luck for him, but I felt it was a bigger disaster for me.

"I'm not mining; I told you that before. You have no right to tell me how to make my living." I stormed out of the house and slept at Drew Proffit's house that night.

The next morning, I made sure my folks got off to work before I showed my face at home. When I entered the kitchen, my sister had her back to me and was washing breakfast dishes. She was only two years younger than me, but with her long, brown hair that hung down to her waist and her petite shape, she looked much younger. Allison turned around and smiled that shy way, like she always did.

"Don't you dare tell Mom and Dad I'm taking dance lessons with Pop," I said.

Allison said she wouldn't, but no way could I be sure of that. She was always one to fall in line.

Chapter 5

I could barely eat at mealtime, 'cause that's when Dad lectured me about stepping up and taking the fill-in job at the mine. But I didn't give in; I refused. That I didn't want anything to do with mining fueled Dad with anger. He referred to me as "useless and lazy." I remember wishing I didn't have to sit at his table, feeling like an imposition, another mouth to feed. Dad had a black-and-white philosophy about what constituted a man. I knew if he found out about me dancing, I'd be in a gray area. The future I wanted wasn't in Greenstone, and my resolve to leave was now even stronger. I hoped that my sister, Allison, would get away too, that our parents, that town, wouldn't pressure her into compliance. But I was kidding myself; Allison never had any backbone. She was part of the clan of conformers, indoctrinated with ideas most folks in Greenstone had.

During that summer break from high school, I met Emma Jean at Pop's Pop for a three-hour dance lesson every weekday morning after Mom and Dad left for work. In an attempt to account for how I spent my days, I took on scraping and painting the exterior of the house, but it was taking longer than it should have 'cause of my dance lessons. One day, Dad approached me after he got home from work.

"Bird, you're not making much progress. When I was your age, I'd have had this house painted by now."

"My shoulder's been aching, and yesterday was too hot; I had to take breaks."

"Boy, you're what we miners call soft and lazy."

My chores of feeding Brownie, our cow, and slopping the hogs gave accountability for how my time was spent too, but none of the work I did appeased Dad. He was still angry about me not taking the fill-in job at the coal mine. But I didn't care. The bottom line was I made it to Pop's dance lessons on weekdays, and 'cause Mom spoke up for me, I got to "hang out" with friends on weekend evenings, which was code for practicing swing dance at Pop's Pop. My relationship with Dad had deteriorated more 'cause I wouldn't give in to his pressure to work the coal mine. By owning up to my love of dance, I would have caused myself more grief, so I continued to keep my folks in the dark.

Chapter 6

Pop had helped Emma Jean and me work up a dance routine, and he'd been driving us hard to get the kinks out. One night on the weekend, after Emma Jean and I were done practicing, wringing wet and falling-down exhausted, Pop surprised us. He gave each of us an honest-to-God pair of dance shoes.

"Get these babies broken in," Pop said. "Bring them to practices and wear them inside, but don't use them as street shoes."

Day after day and weekend nights, Pop had Emma Jean and me practicing the same routine over and over. Each time we did it, he'd bark out something that needed improvement. My feet burned, new blisters formed on top of old ones, and a dull pain pulsed in my legs. Finally, he'd say, "That's enough." Then Emma Jean and I would limp out of Pop's soda-fountain shop.

Not trying to second-guess what criticism Pop would come up with next, Emma Jean and I kept putting in our practices. One night after we finished an intense practice on the routine, it became clear why Pop had been working us extra hard.

"That's enough. You're ready," he said.

"Ready for what?" Emma Jean asked, before I got the words out of my mouth.

"There's going to be a dance contest in Wakefield, June 8," Pop said. "It's a bigger town, one hour away. That's where I won my trophy."

I'd heard of Wakefield but hadn't been there. "You think we're good enough to compete?"

"Yep, sure do. I think you and Emma Jean will take first."

Pop turned his attention to Emma Jean. "Saw your mom yesterday in the grocery store. She said you've been giving your brother, Nate, dance lessons. I'm glad you've been up-front with your folks about dancing."

Emma Jean got all puffed-up with pride. She threw her head back, tilting that turned-up nose of hers to due north, that strawberry-blonde ponytail of hers swinging like a horse's tail swatting flies. You'd have thought President Lyndon B. Johnson had just paid her a compliment.

Then his eyes turned to me and narrowed, became slits. "Unlike you, Bird."

"What do you mean?" I said, though I knew what Pop was getting at.

"Bird, don't play dumb. Your folks don't know you've been dancing."

"Pop, it was the only way."

"Son, you had to know that one day things would come to a head. I'll take care of the entry fee and get you to the dance contest in Wakefield, but you *must* tell your parents you're going to compete. They need to know how you feel about dancing. Understand?"

I knew Pop was right. I was at a crossroad; I had to make a decision. I could press on, see if I could make a career out of dancing, or I could forget the notion and settle for a lifetime of mining, and I knew I wasn't doing the latter.

I nodded my head to affirm. But I didn't know if I could tell my folks.

Chapter 7

Two days went by, and I'd thought a lot about the talk with Pop. The deadline to enter the dance contest was approaching. I knew if I let this opportunity pass me by, I wouldn't get another one, and Emma Jean wouldn't either. Pop would be finished teaching me, and I couldn't blame him. More than anything, I wanted that first-place trophy.

Though the wrapper looked the same, the me inside changed that Monday, June 3. Pop had known what was right for me even in those first few months he'd given me lessons. He'd seen the real me, the me I might never have discovered without his guidance. Pop was right to give that ultimatum. If my life was going to turn around, I had to speak my mind to my folks. They had to understand how important dancing was to me. They had to understand that the competition in Wakefield could open up a new future for me.

I had put up with Dad's bullying since high school let out for summer vacation, listening to his humiliating remarks about me never amounting to anything, about me being lazy. I couldn't swallow any more food or shaming remarks that Monday night at the supper table. Enough was enough. I wanted my shot at a different kind of life.

"I'm not going to be a miner, Mom and Dad. I know what I want out of life, and it doesn't put black dust in my lungs or make me old before my time. I don't mean to be a burden to either of you, and I won't. You've both worked hard to raise Allison and me; I appreciate that. But I want a different kind of life. After I get my high-school diploma, I'll get out of your hair."

Dad gave me a hostile stare. "And then what are you going to do to earn money, Mr. Wise Guy?"

"I'm going to dance. I'm good at it. In fact, Emma Jean Wilmyer and I are going to be in a competition in Wakefield on the eighth. Pop, the man who owns the soda-fountain shop in town, has been teaching us East Coast swing dancing. He's going to take us."

Dad's face was flushed with anger. "Pop? Dance? That's why this house isn't painted yet, isn't it, Bird? You weren't hanging out with friends. You have some gall telling me what you're going to do. Don't take me for a fool, boy."

"Well, you got everything figured out, except I *was* with friends, dance friends. I could have gotten more done on this house, but I'm not apologizing for that or for dancing either. Pop should have become a professional dancer. But he didn't, 'cause he never left this dried-up pit, good for nothing but mining. My dance teacher thinks I have talent, that I can become a professional dancer. That's what I want, and I'm going after it."

"You're going after it." Dad laughed, but it wasn't a jovial laugh. "You'd better get that nonsense out of your head. What the hell's the matter with you? You're a dreamer. A good-for-nothing dreamer."

"I'm going to win that competition in Wakefield, and after I finish my senior year of high school, I'll get out of your house. I'll make my way to a bigger city where I can have a dancing career."

Dad got up from his chair and grabbed me by the collar of my shirt, his face ablaze. "Boy, now you listen to me."

Allison pushed a lock of her brown hair away from her face, a face with small features, so unlike mine. It was tensed with fright, and her hazel-colored eyes expressed the terror of a small child who felt threatened. She slipped out of her chair—I'd have bet her slight body was trembling—and went to her room. And that fueled my anger; Dad's bullying tactic had frightened her. My eyes held steady on his; I knew what I wanted to do, but there was my mother to consider.

"Charles, let the boy be," Mom said. "Maybe he will, maybe he won't have a dancing career, but Bird's been a good son. He's not a drunkard like some of the other young men around here, and he hasn't gotten any girlfriend pregnant either."

Dad threw a look Mom's way. His anger vanished and was replaced with bottomless hurt. He let go of my collar. But then his focus returned to me, and his face was again on fire.

"Sure as hell would rather have you tip a few cans of beer as to dance around like some ... well, you know. You even like girls, boy?"

"Enough! I've never asked you for anything, Charles. I've hired myself out to wait tables, cooked for you, cleaned, and raised two children. I've lived in this small, broken-down house and worn homemade clothes till they were ragged. But I've not complained. If you don't quit speaking poorly about Bird, I'll take him and Allison and we'll leave. Don't know where we'll sleep tonight, but I swear we'll leave."

"Marta." Dad's voice was little more than a whisper, and that hurt look returned to his face. I'd never heard Mom speak to him that way before. Never. Dad went off to be by himself in the bedroom. He stayed there the rest of that night.

"Mom, I'm sorry. I didn't mean to cause trouble."

"Bird, there's nothing for you to be sorry about. Your father's pig-headed, just like his father was before him. But he loves you, Son. You have to believe me, 'cause that's the God's truth. Your father believes menfolk around here are raised to be miners. Coal mining is all Charles has ever known."

Mom's eyes were bloodshot, and for the first time, I noticed how wrinkled she looked for someone thirty-three. I'd never thought about why my folks married so young, but now I knew; I was the cog in the wheel that had steered her future.

"Your father's doing the same as his did, trying to make sure you can keep a roof over your head. Charles never questioned his father when he was told to take a job at the mine. My folks had six of us to raise, and Charles's folks had seven. Neither of us finished high school; we had to work, and half of our paychecks went to our folks until we married."

Though I wished she'd had a different life and knew she deserved better, I'd never heard Mom let on about regrets till that day. I tried to remember a time when she was dressed up and had makeup on but couldn't. I felt a sense of loss for her, for what she could have had under different circumstances.

"I wish you had nice things, Mom."

"Don't worry about me, Bird; I let myself go down this path. This town, this life, isn't for you; if dancing is what you want, go after it. I'll pick up extra hours at the restaurant and put some money aside. It won't be much, but when you're ready to leave Greenstone, it'll help. Just don't rub your father the wrong way with your mouth anymore. Let me see to him. He'll never understand your choice to leave Greenstone and pursue dancing, but I'll make sure he doesn't try to stop you. And one other thing: promise me you *will* finish high school."

"I promise." I went outside and sat on the porch step. It was a lot for a guy my age to deal with, knowing I had put a wedge between Mom and Dad, knowing what Dad thought of me had gone from bad to worse. But the thought that my mother was probably sitting alone in the living room crying was the worst of all of it.

Chapter 8

My folks left for work, and I came out of my room. Allison was in the kitchen washing breakfast dishes. "Going to see Pop," I said. I didn't have to say why. Though she didn't let on, I knew my sister had listened in on the rest of Dad's flare-up the night before.

"Bye," she said.

Mornings, Pop's Pop didn't get much business. Heck, Pop was lucky to have two customers drop in before noon, even on weekdays. Occasionally, a couple of the store employees on that little strip, which everyone called "downtown," came in for a cola to get caffeinated before they started their workday. But when I arrived, there were no customers, and Pop was sweeping, though it didn't appear there was any dirt on the floor. I guessed that was Pop's way of burning nervous energy.

"Hi, Pop. How's it going?"

"Bird, what brings you by so early?"

Pop's expression didn't look questioning. We both knew the entry-form deadline was approaching for the Wakefield Dance Contest. He stopped sweeping and rested the broom against a table.

"About that dance in Wakefield—I'm in. Talked to my folks. Told them I was going to be a dancer, not a miner."

Pop patted me on the back, but his face was sober, and he was quiet for what seemed like a full minute before he spoke.

"Bird, you took a big step, committed yourself. I'll do everything in my power to help you realize a dancing career, but whether you make it or not rests on your determination, your talent."

"What's wrong? You don't seem happy for me."

"I am, but there's somethin' I need to 'fess up to. I gave you kids swing-dance lessons 'cause I had a plan in mind. Your first attempt to dance was proof you had the same raw ability I'd had at your age, and I knew your folks were hell-bent on you being a miner, like mine were when I was a kid. That made you the guy I needed to achieve my goal. My dad's temper went red-hot when he found out I'd gone to the Wakefield Dance Contest. Said dancing didn't put food on the table. Said he'd throw me out of the house if I didn't straighten up. Mary and I were excellent dancers; we should've had a different life. But I was a kid and gave in; I became a miner, and regret's festered in me ever since. You were my last chance to stand up to the townspeople in Greenstone. Sons of miners shouldn't *have to* follow in their dad's footsteps. You'll win the dance contest in Wakefield, Bird, and escape the misery I've known. You'll have your chance at a dancing career. We'll show 'em!"

It wasn't more than seventy degrees that fourth day of June, and Pop wasn't exerting himself, but he took out his handkerchief and wiped his brow. I had believed he was full of life, when in fact, he was struggling to finish an unhappy existence the best he could. Pop's anger about being held back from pursuing a dancing career had tortured him, and I was the vehicle he'd chosen to accomplish something he'd thought about for a long time—a way to "show 'em."

"Bird, hope you don't hold my reason for teaching you to swing dance against me. I need you to understand; I've grown fond of you and think of you as my son."

Pop had given me hour upon hour of his time. And if I did make a go of dancing as a career, I knew I had him to thank. Still, finding out his motive for teaching me to dance made me feel like a naïve knucklehead. I'd thought Pop's only goal was to gain my friendship. But the fact remained, I believed Pop when he said he loved me like a son. The truth was he had been more of a father to me than my own. And another truth that hit me was that Pop wouldn't have had to "fess up" to anything, and then I wouldn't have been the wiser. Still, the one man I had trusted in Greenstone to be straight with me hadn't been.

An awkward silence set in. Pop's hunched stance looked more pronounced, and his aged face had turned tissue-paper white. Finally, I found the words I felt I needed to say, though other words were on the tip of my tongue. "Consider the slate wiped clean."

Pop took out his handkerchief and blew his nose. "Thank you, Bird. I used your given name on the entry form. Thought Ty was more professional. That okay with you?"

"That's fine."

"Good. I'll get the form in the mail today."

I turned away and headed toward the door.

"Hold up a second, Bird. Got something for you and Emma Jean."

Pop went in the back room and returned with two boxes that were yellowed with age and had a musty odor. "Here, I think these'll fit you and Emma Jean. Mary and I wore them when we won the competition in Wakefield. Thought they might bring you good luck."

I didn't open the boxes in front of Pop. I went home and sat on the front porch and held them on my lap, digesting what I'd learned. Pop wasn't full of life like he'd pretended, and he had also deceived me on another count, acting like his desire to teach me to dance was an unselfish one. A truth had been shoved in my face; Pop wasn't who I'd thought he was. And like when

I was six and saw Mom Christmas Eve night, putting presents under the tree for Allison and me, my eyes had been opened to something I didn't want to see.

Finally, I lifted each costume out of its box. They were the fanciest, most sparkly clothes I'd ever seen. Sunlight made the red sequins on the costumes glisten. I should have been grateful that Pop had given them to Emma Jean and me to wear at the Wakefield Dance Contest, but I wasn't.

Chapter 9

Emma Jean and I had practiced with Pop three hours each morning, Monday through Wednesday. His critique was that our steps weren't energetic enough, our arms weren't fully extended, and our facial expressions needed to show more enthusiasm. By the end of our practice on Thursday, my stomach was doing flip-flops. I believed that Emma Jean and I didn't have a prayer's chance of winning the dance competition in Wakefield and that I was going to end up being a miner.

"Enough," Pop finally said. "No practice tomorrow; you need a break before the competition. Be here at 8:30 sharp Saturday morning. That'll get us to Eddie's Place by 9:30. When we get there, you'll practice your routine once, then rest. The competition begins at 10:00. One other thing: that ballroom in Wakefield has a wooden floor, and they'll have it powdered to make it slick. When you take your practice, pay attention to the way the floor feels. If you slip during your performance, it'll cost you a deduction in points and most likely the contest."

Emma Jean didn't speak. That she was on the verge of crying was obvious. She waved good-bye and hurried out the door.

I looked Pop in the eyes and spoke the dark thought in my mind, the same thought I was sure Emma Jean was having. "We don't have a chance in hell of winning."

Pop was silent, like he was soaking in what I'd said. Then he spoke. "Bird Partridge, you listen to me: you're the best dancer I've ever set eyes on. I was good, but I didn't have your style. If you keep your head screwed on straight—and that's something you have to do, 'cause Emma Jean looks to you for strength—then that trophy's yours. Step up and get this contest won. Don't let self-doubt get in the way. Otherwise, you'll disappoint the one person it hurts worst to disappoint—yourself."

I didn't figure it out until some years later, but what I came to believe about that pep talk Pop gave me was this: those words had nothing to do with Pop's original motive for teaching me to dance; his only concern was that I achieve my dream.

Chapter 10

With no dance practice, my legs were rested, but my mind was exhausted from running through the dance routine over and over, each time remembering one more of Pop's tips. There was so much to get right in order to be the total package. Time didn't pass fast enough for me that Friday, and when I went to bed, I watched the hour hand land on every number.

At 7:30 a.m., I got up, showered, and ate a few spoonfuls of cereal.

When I walked in Pop's Pop at 8:25, Pop had that broom in his hands, like he did every morning.

"Have a seat; just cleaning up a bit."

Seeing Pop sweep was normal, but I'd never seen him moving that broom so fast, with no care taken to sweep the dirt in a pile. I remained standing, shifting my weight from side to side about as fast as that broom was moving.

Emma Jean arrived at 8:30. She was picking at the skin on her lips, but she looked more rested than me.

"Let's get going," Pop said.

Nobody said a word, until we pulled into the parking lot of Eddie's Place.

"Now here's how it is," Pop said, turning to face Emma Jean and me in the backseat. "I trained you, and I know what you're capable of. When we leave this swing-dance competition, I'll have two winners riding back with me to Greenstone. As soon as we're inside the ballroom, change into your dance shoes and run through your routine."

We got out of the car, and my first impression was that Eddie's Place looked like it belonged in Greenstone. The building, shaped like an *L* lying on its side, had tufts of moss growing between the splintered, once-white boards, and remnants of black stubble clung for dear life to the front door, where gray duct tape sealed a broken pane of glass.

We were two steps in, and cigarette smoke hung like fog and made my eyes water. A piece of dark-brown paneling was missing behind the bar, exposing red paint on the wall beneath, and some of the dingy ceiling tiles were gone, exposing the original ceiling. Rowdy drunkards seemed to be in a competition with the blaring jukebox, and the billiard balls banging together sounded like gunfire. The place was a dump.

Pop led Emma Jean and me past the noise of the tavern, where there was a door that gave us entrance to the ballroom, and inside that room was another world. Chandeliers hung from the high ceiling, and the ivory-colored wallpaper was filled with gold-framed portraits of famous dancers. The room buzzed with young gals and guys dressed in coordinated, glittery costumes.

Emma Jean and I put on our dance shoes, and Pop had us take our practice. When we finished, Emma Jean excused herself to go to the restroom.

"Mr. Ty Partridge, when Emma Jean comes back, you two walk over to the judges' table. I want you to see that first-place trophy that's gonna be yours. When they call you and Emma Jean out on the floor to perform, remember there's only one thing that can defeat you."

"But I'm the son of a miner. What made me think I could do this?"

"Stop doubting yourself," Pop said. "You've got more than enough ability to win this contest. Before the music starts, clear your head of everything except the performance. Then keep tempo with the music, and give Emma Jean a good lead into every dance move you do."

A man dressed in blue jeans and a plaid shirt stepped onto the dance floor and introduced himself as George. He announced that all competitors should come to the judges' table. He told us that each couple performing would dance for the duration of two and a half minutes to the same music. Then George asked that one contestant from each couple draw a number out of a hat. That determined the order in which each of the thirteen couples would dance. I told Emma Jean to try her luck. She drew number eight. Thank God she didn't draw number thirteen; that would have been bad luck.

Rows of folding chairs were lined up on opposite walls, bordering the wooden dance floor. Two signs designated the contestants' and spectators' sections. George told everyone to be seated and called the first couple to dance out to the floor. And the Wakefield Dance Contest began.

Watching the first couple dance, I decided I was either pumping myself up by finding phantom errors, or Pop's hard-nosed critiques of Emma Jean and me had made me a capable critic. I had deducted two points out of the ten each judge could give for a perfect score. When the three judges held up their scorecards, they agreed with my assessment. I made sure Emma Jean understood the deductions, so we'd sidestep the same mistakes. Still, I knew that score of twenty-four would be hard to beat.

Emma Jean and I watched each of the next six couples (those who had drawn the second through seventh dancing slots). The couple who danced fifth was awarded twenty-six out of the thirty points possible from the judges. They had the highest score at that point—a score I knew would be hard to beat. I looked across the room at the spectators' section where Pop was sitting. He looked worried.

"Couple number eight, take the dance floor," George said.

The palm of Emma Jean's hand was sweaty when I took hold of it to escort her to the dance floor. And couple number five's score of twenty-six had my stomach churning. But then I remembered what Pop had said: *"You've got more than enough ability to win this dance contest."*

"Emma Jean," I said, "trust me; we've got this." To this day, I don't know if she believed me or if she was being polite when she smiled. In fact, I don't think I believed it myself.

I held Emma Jean in closed position, and we both tried to act as poised as we could while waiting for the music to start. The red sequins on that black, high-collared shirt Pop had given me rubbed against my jawline and made me itch, and the black pants, striped with sequins down each side, were two inches short and revealed my white socks. But when the music began, I blocked out the discomforts of that ill-fitting costume, and I was Bird Partridge, *the dancer,* performing for my audience.

We finished our routine. Many of the spectators, including Pop, gave us a standing ovation, but I didn't know if our best effort was enough to match a score of twenty-six, much less beat it. Even if we got lucky and pulled a better score, there were more dancers left to perform. When Emma Jean and I walked off the dance floor, Pop's pride in us was apparent; his smile stretched from ear to ear, and for the first time, I felt a sense of worth, a sense that Bird Partridge had accomplished something.

The first judge held up his scorecard; Emma Jean and I received nine points. The second judge revealed his score, also nine points. But when it was the third judge's turn to show her scorecard, she tapped her pen on the table, adjusted her glasses, and then fixed her eyes on us competitors seated across from her. The first judge cleared his throat. Judge three stopped tapping her pen and gave him a harsh look. With pursed lips, she scribbled and held up her scorecard. Judge three gave Emma Jean and me ten points for our performance. Emma Jean and I jumped up from our seats and hugged each other. With a score of twenty-eight and five more sets of dancers, I hoped that none of the other couples could pull a better score.

The first of the remaining five couples, the contestants who danced ninth, performed advanced moves, but they showed no hint that they were enjoying themselves. The female's drawn lips made her look like she was sucking on a lemon, and the male's emotionless expression made him appear disconnected from his partner. I turned to Pop for his assessment. He shook his head ever so slightly to indicate a negative appraisal.

After each of the judges held up their scorecard, twenty-one points was the couple's score. I breathed a sigh of relief. Emma Jean let out a giggle.

The contestants dancing tenth took the floor. Both were tall and slender. The girl, blonde and well-endowed, had mile-high legs that she was showing plenty of. The guy had raven-black hair and what I guess girls would call sex appeal. Their blue-and-gold sequined costumes were expensive and certainly not hand-me-downs. As they waited for the music to begin, they were composed, like they had competed many times before. A knot formed in my chest.

The beginning of their dance was energetic, and their bodies were in perfect sync with each other and the music. Their teeth were the straightest I'd ever seen and white as milk. Their nonstop smiling looked both natural and exciting. A small, deflated voice in my head told me, *"They're the total package."* They finished a neck wrap, and then the guy sent his partner back out and set up a tunnel. That's when it happened. The girl's right foot got tangled with her partner's left when she ducked under the tunnel, and down she went. The couple regained their composure and finished the routine, but I knew the judges would deduct points. The judges' combined points added up to a score of twenty-two. That blunder cost couple number ten the contest.

The eleventh couple was up. The girl was a head and a half taller than her partner. Each time the short guy turned the girl, his arm ruffled her hair, flinging it across her face, and the girl got off balance. The incompatible dancers received a score of thirteen points.

The couple dancing twelfth gave a performance that never surpassed a beginner's level. Their routine bored the audience, bringing little applause. The judges' combined points gave the dance couple a score of nine.

With the last dance couple left in the competition, I was feeling pretty comfortable—no, cocky would be more accurate. *They drew number thirteen. That's an unlucky number,* I thought. I felt Emma Jean and I had that first-place trophy won. I made eye contact with Pop, smiled, and gave him a confident nod. He frowned.

The music started, and everyone's attention turned to the dance floor. Couple thirteen did two push steps and then performed a move I'd never seen. The guy supported his partner by placing his hands on her waist. She thrust her legs upward, inverting her head down toward the floor, and the guy caught the girl on his thigh when gravity brought her down. That's when I wished I'd have watched them take their practice.

Each step was crisp, each move entertaining and expressive. The spectators' applause was loud, at least as loud as it had been for Emma Jean and me, and dance couple thirteen had many in the audience on their feet too.

The first judge held up his scorecard; he gave couple number thirteen nine points. The second male judge scored likewise; that's when Emma Jean started crying and picking at her lip. Then the lady judge scratched her head. I knew if she wrote a ten on her scorecard, there'd be a tie-breaker dance. Emma Jean was a bundle of nerves; I knew she couldn't dance again.

The lady judge adjusted her glasses and tapped her pen. Couple thirteen already had eighteen points. That the lady judge had poked around the same way before giving Emma Jean and me a ten had me worried. She fiddled with her glasses once more before writing on her scorecard, and then she held her card up. She gave couple thirteen nine points. I jumped up, grabbed Emma Jean, and gave her a big kiss on the cheek.

"Dance couple number eight, Emma Jean Wilmyer and Ty Partridge, come to the judges' table to receive your first-place trophy," the announcer said.

In that moment, I'd swear my feet left the dance floor, and I floated up to those chandeliers in that ballroom; suspended above all those other dancers I'd competed against. I felt like a king on his throne. *No way am I going to be a miner!* I thought.

I looked over at the spectators' section, relishing the taste of victory, and saw Pop standing and applauding. And I sucked in a deep breath, trying to imagine my new life, as *"Come to the judges' table to receive your first-place trophy,"* danced in my head. I took Emma Jean by the hand and we started walking toward the judges' table. I stopped and whispered what I needed to say to her. We turned back to get Pop. He deserved to be at that table with us.

That Saturday, the eighth day in June of 1967, I left Greenstone the son of a miner, but I returned from the dance contest in Wakefield as a changed person. By crossing paths with Pop, I had learned to have faith in myself. I was going to be a professional dancer.

Chapter 11

Emma Jean and I continued practicing swing dance at Pop's Pop. Every time Pop dropped a quarter in the jukebox, I was transported to a magical place. My life as Bird Partridge, the son of a coal miner, didn't exist; I was a dancer, a great dancer, performing for an audience. And my confidence gained by winning the Wakefield Dance Contest had spurred my determination to get out of Greenstone, Missouri, to somewhere I could make a career out of dancing.

Dance contests in Greenstone were nonexistent, and those in other parts of Missouri were few and far between. I was getting antsy, wondering how I would move forward toward my goal of dancing professionally. But then in March of 1968, Pop approached me with an opportunity that I was sure would help me reach my goal.

"Bird, there's a swing-dance contest scheduled in Saint Louis, Missouri, on May 10. I want you and Emma Jean to enter it."

"What about the Wakefield Dance Contest in June?"

"There's no prospect for a dancing career in Wakefield, but there is in Saint Louis. If you and Emma Jean won the Saint Louis contest, that'd be proof of your ability, proof you can cut the mustard. You two might get hired for a stage performance there. That's what you want, isn't it, Bird?"

"Yeah, that's what I want."

"Check with Emma Jean and let me know if she wants to compete in Saint Louis," Pop said. "If she does, I'll get the entry form filled out and send in the entrance fee."

Emma Jean said yes. I figured like me, she loved swing dancing and believed that winning the contest in Saint Louis would be our ticket out of Greenstone.

Pop told Emma Jean and me what he expected of us if we wanted to be serious competitors. "I want you to perform the routine you did at the Wakefield Dance Contest, but we'll add two moves to enhance the difficulty level. Two couples at that competition performed moves I want in your dance routine. One is a tunnel; the other I don't know the name of, but I watched how it was done. The guy held onto the girl's waist, supporting her as she thrust her legs upward, putting her into an inverted position. As gravity brought the girl's body down, the guy caught her on his thigh."

"Pop, the tunnel is something Emma Jean and I can master, but that lift dance couple number thirteen did at Wakefield looked tough to execute." What I was worried about was the fact that Emma Jean carried more weight than I cared to have land on my thigh.

"Doubting your ability again, Bird? You and Emma Jean can do both moves. And you will."

Chapter 12

Saturday, May 10, Pop drove Emma Jean and me to 3610 Grandel Square in Saint Louis, Missouri. We parked in a large lot and went inside Grandel Theatre Hall. A sign in the entrance read "Saint Louis Swing-Dance Contestants, Follow the Arrows on the Floor." The arrows led Pop, Emma Jean, and me to a room three times the size of the ballroom at Eddie's Place in Wakefield, Missouri. A paper banner that read "Swing Contestants Check-In Here" was taped to the drawn red-velvet drapes on the stage at the end of the room. Three women were seated behind a table set up on the wooden floor in front of the stage, and three long lines of dance contestants had formed in front of the table. We picked the shortest line.

A dance couple wearing fuchsia-colored costumes that looked to be new stood in front of us. The girl's eyes were caked with makeup, and unlike my buzz cut, the guy's hair was shoulder-length. Emma Jean and I were wearing our red-and-black costumes we'd worn at the Wakefield Contest. I had let the hem out of my pants so my white socks didn't show.

I expected to be standing in line a long time to get checked in, but soon, Emma Jean, Pop, and I were next.

"Names, please," the woman sitting behind the table said.

"Ty Partridge and Emma Jean Wilmyer," I said.

The woman found our names on the list and checked them off. "You're dance couple number thirty-two," she said, and handed Emma Jean and me two sets of numbers. "Peel the backing off and stick one number on the front, one on the back of your shirts before you dance. Contestants' seats are those off to my right; spectators' seats are to my left. When the announcer calls for heat number four, go out onto the dance floor."

"Pop, there's a lot of dancers here," Emma Jean said.

"Yeah," I said. "This whole setup is different than the contest at Wakefield. That woman at the desk said we're dancing in heats."

"After I sent in the entry form, I received information explaining how this swing contest is run," Pop said. "The judges pick a dance couple as the winner of each heat. After the preliminary winners are chosen, they'll be called back out to the dance floor to give one last performance, and the judges will choose the couple who wins the first-place trophy."

Pop walked with Emma Jean and me to the contestants' seating area. He peeled the backing off of our dance numbers and we stuck them on our shirts. Contestants and spectators were standing around chatting.

"Don't see anybody taking a practice, Pop," I said.

"Me neither. Guess they do that different in Saint Louis too. Remember, you and Emma Jean are in the fourth heat. When it's your turn to dance, concentrate on your performance. Don't think about the other competitors, the judges, or the spectators."

Emma Jean and I sat down, and Pop went across the room to the spectators' seating area.

The lines of dance contestants dwindled, then became nonexistent at the check-in table. The ladies at the table picked up their lists and moved to the spectators' seating area. Two different women and a man sat down in the chairs behind the check-in table.

A man holding a microphone walked over and stood off to the right side of the table. "May I have your attention, please? All contestants and spectators, be seated."

Every seat was filled in the contestants' area.

"I'm Fredrick Fornsworth, your host and announcer for the Saint Louis Swing-Dance Contest. I'm pleased to announce our distinguished judges for today. In the first seat to my left, Maureen Albright. Next we have Clarence Stedman, and in the third seat, Cynthia Markel."

There was a round of applause, and Ms. Markel blew the announcer a kiss.

"Let's get this competition started," Mr. Fornsworth said. "In fairness to the participants, the same medley of musical selections will be played during each of the four heats. This will give our judges ample time to evaluate all the couples. Now, swing-dance couples with numbers one through ten, please come to the dance floor for the first heat."

A man showed each of the couples to an assigned area on the dance floor, staggering them so that all couples were visible to the judges, and then the music started.

Dance couple number one had timing problems. The lady was the culprit. Like Patti Baker from Pop's swing dance lessons, she couldn't keep beat to the music.

Finally, the medley of musical selections stopped.

Only one of the ten couples' performances had impressed me in the first heat, couple number four. They had incorporated a tunnel, like the one Emma Jean and I had in our routine. It was executed well, as were the other dance moves they did, and couple number four appeared passionate about dancing.

The announcer said, "Dancers from heat one, be seated. The judges will tally their points and have scores for the first ten dancers momentarily. Ten points is the maximum each judge can give a couple. A score of thirty is possible."

Mr. Fornsworth remained next to the judges' table awaiting their decision. After a few minutes, Ms. Markel, the third judge, got up from her seat, approached the announcer, and smiled as she handed him a sheet of paper.

"I will announce the dance couple with the lowest score first and proceed in ascending order. The last couple I announce will have the highest score and will be the winner for heat one. Couple number one has a score of six points. Couple number eight, seven points. Couple number five, nine points. Couple number three, ten points."

On and on the announcer went. All I wanted to know was who won the first heat.

At last, the announcer said, "And couple number four, the winners of heat one, had a score of twenty-three. Couple number four will be a finalist, competing for the first-place trophy today."

There was a loud round of applause for couple number four.

In the second heat, contestants with the numbers eleven through twenty danced. Couple number twelve won with twenty-five points. The third heat had only nine contestants. Couple number twenty-three won with twenty-seven points.

"Contestants in heat four, numbers thirty through thirty-nine, come to the dance floor," the announcer said.

Emma Jean and I, along with nine other couples, were shown to our assigned spot on the dance floor. The music began, and all went well the first third of our performance, but then my eyes began to wander. Couple number thirty-three, in front and to the right of Emma Jean and me, had gotten my attention. They were doing choreographed moves I'd never seen before. Leading his partner sideways in front of him, the guy put one hand on either side of the girl's waist and led her into a cartwheel. Then, after doing a basic step, the guy broke hold with his partner, bent over and touched his toes, and the girl flipped over him.

Great! They're acrobats, I thought.

From listening to the medley in the previous heats, I knew we were in the last third of our performance. I led Emma Jean into the new tunnel Pop had put into our routine. It went okay, like the rest of our moves had, but I knew we weren't as polished as couple number thirty-three. I led two whips next, then set up to put Emma Jean in a neck wrap. I followed with the hully gully. That's when Emma Jean accidentally stepped on my foot. While we didn't miss a beat, I knew the judges had seen her misstep.

I made eye contact with Emma Jean and led her into the move couple number thirteen from the Wakefield Dance Contest had performed. *Our turn to be acrobats now,* I thought. I took hold of her waist, and she flung her legs upward. At that point, everything was fine. But when gravity brought Emma Jean down and I caught her on my thigh, her landing wasn't graceful. The music ceased, and our performance was finished. I turned to the spectators' seating area. The expression on Pop's face told me what I already knew; Emma Jean and I hadn't shown the dancing skills we were capable of.

"Dance contestants in heat four, be seated," The announcer said. "The judges will tally points and have scores for you momentarily."

After a few minutes, Ms. Markel got up from her seat and handed the announcer the judges' scores.

"The scores in ascending order are as follows: couple number thirty, fifteen points. Couple number thirty-eight, sixteen points. Couples thirty-four and thirty-five each have nineteen points. Couple number thirty-nine, twenty points. Couple number thirty-one, twenty-one points. Couple number thirty-six, twenty-two points. Couple number thirty-two, twenty-three points."

"That's us. We lost," Emma Jean said. Her eyes filled with tears.

I put my arm around her and looked over to the spectators' seating area. Pop was hunched over and appeared to be looking down at the floor.

There were two couples left vying to be the winner of heat four.

"Couple number thirty-seven has twenty-five points," Mr. Fornsworth said. "Couple number thirty-three has twenty-seven points and is the winner of heat four."

There was a round of applause for the winning couple. *Wish that was for Emma Jean and me,* I thought.

"The preliminary winners that will compete in the final dance-off will be the following," the announcer said. "Heat one, couple number four. Heat two, couple number twelve. Heat three, couple number twenty-three, and heat four, couple number thirty-three. There will be a ten-minute intermission before the dance-off for the first-place trophy."

Emma Jean and I walked over to Pop, seated in the spectators' section.

"I didn't deserve to win," I said. "I wasn't focused; I was watching the other dancers. And I did a lousy job of catching Emma Jean from that aerial."

"You're too hard on yourself, Bird," Emma Jean said. "We both made mistakes. I stepped on your foot."

"Don't either of you beat yourselves up," Pop said. "This is my fault. You needed more practice."

"Can we stay and see who wins the contest, Pop?" I said.

"You bet."

The intermission over, the announcer, Mr. Fornsworth, took the floor. "Spectators take a seat, please, and the following finalists: couples number four, twelve, twenty-three, and thirty-three, come to the dance floor."

The four couples in the dance-off were all excellent competitors. But couple number thirty-three who had distracted me as Emma Jean and I competed against them won the Saint Louis Swing-Dance Contest. And they deserved that first-place trophy.

Chapter 13

After getting my high-school diploma that May of 1968, I moved out of my parents' house but not out of Greenstone. Pop offered me a bed, food, and a small wage for helping him run his soda-fountain shop, and I gladly accepted. Mom worked extra at the diner and kept Dad in the dark about her stopping in at the soda-fountain shop to give me money. I saved what she gave me and what Pop paid me for helping out at Pop's Pop. It wasn't a lot of money, but I figured it put me closer to my goal of getting out of Greenstone and pursuing a dancing career. What big city Emma Jean and I would seek out to find employment dancing on stage was up in the air. Even though Emma Jean and I had won the Wakefield Dance Contest at Eddie's Place, that small Missouri town didn't provide any opportunity for us to find employment as dancers. But I wasn't giving up; Emma Jean and I would become better swing dancers. We'd enter more dance contests and win; then prospective employers would hire us for stage performances.

I'd been living with Pop a little over a year. It was apparent that his health was deteriorating. Not only was his memory giving him difficulty, but I'd have sworn that loose red-and-white striped canvas awning on Pop's Pop and Pop's stooped back were competing to see which could hold on the longest before collapsing. I did more and more of the cleaning and worked the soda fountain, and Pop eventually asked me to balance his checkbook. His desire to dance was strong, but his body was getting frailer. He got winded giving dance lessons to those of us who still showed up, and then he'd sit on a chair looking sad and frustrated. Sometimes Pop's train of thought clouded, floating on an uncertain course, or left him altogether. When that happened, Sally Jo Merkel giggled. One day, Pop told Drew and Sallie Jo he couldn't be their dance teacher anymore. I was glad; it killed me when Sallie Jo made fun of him.

Emma Jean and I continued practicing at Pop's Pop, pretending Pop was still teaching us. Though Pop seemed to enjoy this, his memory lapses got worse, and sometimes, even the day of the week eluded him. Emma Jean played along, but Pop's confusion grated on her.

Emma Jean took a job at Dollar Shop and stopped showing up for dance practices at Pop's Pop. I'd seen her out with John Johnston, a miner three years older than us, and decided to go in Dollar Shop and ask her what was up. She showed me her engagement ring and said she was pregnant. It's not that I was ever attracted to Emma Jean, but we'd danced together so long, I'd taken for granted that she loved dancing the way I did, that she believed the same as me, that dancing would be our ticket out of Greenstone.

I broke the news to Pop. Though his addition and subtraction in his checkbook wasn't always accurate, he soaked in what I told him about Emma Jean just fine.

"Emma Jean. What was she thinking, Bird?"

"Don't expect she was thinking, just falling in line."

Pop sighed like he was tired and closed his eyes. I thought he had drifted off to sleep, but I was wrong. His eyes opened. "What a shame. Threw her chance away. Well, what's done is done. Now, here's what we gotta do. We gotta get you to New York City."

"New York City?"

"There's more opportunity to perform on stage there, Bird."

"Without my dance partner?"

"They'll pair you with a young lady at auditions."

"But I haven't danced with anyone but Emma Jean."

"There's that self-doubt trying to worm its way back into your head," Pop said.

Not having Emma Jean as my dance partner was awful enough, but there was something else I was feeling punk about. Besides my savings from working at Pop's Pop and the money Mom had slipped me, I figured Emma Jean would kick in money to help get us out of Greenstone to a large city, where a dancing career was possible.

As if my concern about money was in bold print on my forehead, Pop said, "Don't worry. I got your airfare covered and enough cash to keep you for a month. You'll find some kind of job to keep you afloat till you get hired as a dancer."

"But, Pop—"

"There's no *but* about this. Didn't push you to leave Greenstone sooner 'cause, well, I was thinking of myself again, Bird. I hate to see you leave, but now it's time. You'll be okay."

Indecision about leaving Greenstone visited me. A career in dancing was what I wanted, and escape from a life as a miner was within my reach. But Pop was old and had no one else to look after him, and we were family. The bottom line was, I hated to leave for the same reason Pop hated to see me go. Part of me was sad; the other part wanted to run up and down Main Street shouting out the news of my departure.

Chapter 14

The next two weeks, Pop pulled himself together and planned for my move to New York City. He checked airfares and found that the cheapest flight was out of Wakefield Airport, a one-hour drive from Greenstone. He booked my flight and then taped a note with my departure date and time on the refrigerator. Pop knew his memory wasn't what it used to be.

He told me how he'd heard taxi fare was expensive in New York City, how taking the subway or bus was cheaper. He reminded me to look for work as soon as I got there. After Pop had given me all the advice he could think of, he pulled a roll of bills out of his pocket. Then he took my hand and placed the wad in my palm. At that point in my life, it looked like a lot of money.

I stared at it. *How can he spare that?* I thought. And the answer came to me; Pop was digging into his life's savings. I wanted my shot at professional dancing, but I knew he couldn't afford to give me that much money.

"Thanks, but I can't take this, Pop." A bitter taste worked its way up my throat. I swallowed and forced it back down.

"Don't argue with me; put that money in your pocket. You're leaving tomorrow. And don't think you're taking anything from me, Bird; I'm giving it to you," Pop said that June day in 1969. "I worked that coal mine till my back couldn't take anymore, and my wife, Mary, ran the soda fountain by herself till I retired from mining. We were frugal and saved our money. Our only child, Emily, was smart enough to get out of Greenstone after she graduated from high school. She took a secretarial job in Wakefield. Her mother and I gave her enough money to sustain her till she could stand on her own two feet. Emily calls once in a while, but she hasn't been back since Mary passed."

That was the first I knew that Pop had a daughter, and I couldn't help but ask, "Why's that? Wakefield's only one hour away."

"Emily got settled in Wakefield and then asked Mary and me to move there. Mary was ready to go, but I dug my heels in. Nobody wanted to buy this old soda-fountain shop, so I said we'd have to stay. Less than a year later, Mary died of a heart attack. Emily always hated Greenstone. Told me I should've gotten her mother out of here, that staying took Mary to her grave early. After Mary was gone, I was more frugal than ever. And what you need to understand is that I think of you as the son Mary and I should have had. Giving you enough for a one-way ticket out of Greenstone and a little to start you off in New York City brings me more joy than you can realize."

With the business of planning my move out of the way, we celebrated Pop's birthday.

"How many candles should be on this cake I bought you?"

"Eighty-one, Bird. I'm an old man."

My curiosity about his age satisfied, I felt the need to ask what his first name was. I couldn't leave Greenstone without knowing.

"Robert," Pop said.

We ate chocolate birthday cake and laughed about Patti Baker being Pop's partner at dance lessons. "Think she'll ever be on beat, Pop?"

"Wouldn't count on it." Then his eyes got wet. "Bird, I need to say something. You going to New York City is the best birthday present I've ever gotten." When he said that, I got wet eyes too.

The time Pop and I spent together was an important marker in my life. Even though I owned memories I had made with him, I wanted to know more about his life before we met. We sat at his soda-fountain bar sipping cherry cola, me nudging him to reminisce about the years when he and Mary danced. Pop sounded thirty years younger as he spoke about winning the first-place trophy in Wakefield and how after he and Mary wed, they'd close the dance down at Eddie's Place on weekends. Before I knew it, it was 9:00 p.m., Pop's bedtime. As he walked away from me, his short-lived youthfulness was gone; his gait was unsteady and slow. I could feel the finality of my leaving taking its toll on him. I headed for my room; a small suitcase was on my bed.

Chapter 15

I heard the coffee pot percolating in the kitchen that morning. My guess was, like me, Pop hadn't slept a wink. The clock on the crate I used for a nightstand read 5:00 a.m. I got a quick shower and made my way to the kitchen, where Pop had a sweet roll and cup of coffee waiting for me. He sat opposite me on one of the cane-backed chairs, drinking his coffee and resting his left forearm on the old oak kitchen table. Neither of us said a word.

At 5:30, Pop took his car keys off the hook next to the light switch in the kitchen; we were out the door and on our way to Wakefield Airport. He turned on the radio, and though I didn't care to listen to the news, it was better than silence. Pop had told me the drive to the airport was just over an hour, but the highway seemed to stretch on and on, like it had no ending. In truth, I wanted Pop's memory to slip up so he'd get us lost. Part of me wanted to be back in Greenstone sitting on his red-leather bar stools. But at 6:45, a sign came into view that said "Wakefield Airport," and my hope sank. I remember how I almost said, *"Take me back to Greenstone,"* instead of, *"There's the sign for departures."*

Pop pulled into a drop-off parking spot. We hadn't talked about whether he'd go into the airport to see me off, but I thought it best he chose not to. I started to open the car door but stopped and turned to face him. There was a smile on his face, but his eyes looked wet and sad.

"Write and let me know what flying's like, Bird."

"I will." I was searching for the right thing to say to express what Pop meant to me. A mix of joy and sadness flowed through me. I wanted my chance at a dancing career, but the realization came to me that once I got on that plane leaving for New York City, I'd *never* go back to Greenstone, *never* see Pop again, *never* make amends with Dad, Mom, or Allison. *Never*—such a dead-end word. Somehow, I got out the following words: "Pop, you mean the world to me. I'll never forget you, Robert Bradford. You gave me the key to my future by teaching me to dance."

"Back at you, Bird. And with your talent, I'd bet my last dollar on your success."

What Pop said should have made me feel better; I guess to some degree it did, but for the most part, I felt sad. And the uncertainty of what lay ahead in New York City concerned me.

"You're the best, Pop. About my folks, my sister."

"I'll tell them you said good-bye and that you'll miss them. You ought to drop them a line now and then, Bird, let them know you're okay."

"Yeah, I will; I'll write you too. I promise. Let you know how I'm doing, ask for your advice from time to time."

"You don't need my advice anymore. Now, you better get going."

I got out of the car and grabbed my small bag from the back seat. Before I entered the terminal, I turned around and saw that Pop hadn't left. I gave him a wave. Part of me still wished that Pop and I were sitting in his place sipping cherry cola.

Chapter 16

Inside Wakefield Airport, people were bustling about, wheeling luggage or pulling cranky children by their hands to hurry them along. Behind me, I heard a beeping sound. I turned around to check out what was making that racket. A man in a small, motorized cart gave me an angry look and waved me out of his way. I hugged the right side of the walkway and quickened my pace to get to the boarding area.

A little old lady, clutching her boarding pass, was sitting by herself. I sat down next to her, and she started up a conversation. She said her name was Emma, but that she liked to be called Em. She told me she was going to visit her grandson Harry and maybe her son Harold.

"Harold Senior is a lawyer. He moved to New York City after Harry got a stockbroker job in Manhattan. Harry's called me once a week since he moved, but my son doesn't speak to me," Em said.

I asked, "Why?"

"Well, after my daughter-in-law, Mary Margaret, died, he met up with that gold digger Kasey. Harold Senior threw a fit when I tried to stop him from marrying her. After she got her name on the house title and he bought her a Cadillac, she divorced him. That's when Harold stopped talking to me and wouldn't let me visit Harry. When my grandson got old enough to figure things out for himself, he visited me. Before he moved, that is. It'll be good to visit with my grandson, but I don't expect my son will agree to see me. I shouldn't bother you with my troubles."

"You're not bothering me at all," I said.

Poor Em had more to unload, and she did. She went on and on about her broken family situation, and I listened.

My seating section was called for boarding. I gave Em a smile, thinking I was taking leave of her, but she got up and shuffled in right behind me. I stopped at row fourteen and put my carry-on in the overhead compartment.

Em pushed in the handle on her small, wheeled suitcase. "This is my row too."

"Let me get that," I said, then put her tote in the overhead.

Em sat down in seat A next to the window; I sat down in seat C. The silver-haired lady lowered her head. She looked shamefaced, like she wished she hadn't unloaded to me. I wanted to tell Em that I knew what it was like to be shunned by your own flesh and blood. But I couldn't do it. Guess my hurt was too fresh, my mind too fixed on the uncertainty of what lay ahead for me.

"Sounds like your son should have listened to you," I said, trying to start a conversation.

Em turned and made eye contact with me. In a weary voice, she said, "I need to nap." She snapped on her seat belt, closed her eyes, and turned, putting her back to me.

Everyone boarded, and the seat between Em and me remained unoccupied. She had the solitude she needed, and that empty seat afforded me privacy as well.

A woman's voice that had a comforting quality to it came over the intercom. "Please direct your attention to the stewardess standing in the aisle while she demonstrates how to fasten your seat belt."

The voice explained the procedure while the stewardess, with her graying hair pulled up into what looked like a dirty snowball, went through the motions. I buckled up, and at that point, everything was fine by me.

But then the voice said, "Now the stewardess will demonstrate what to do if a drop in cabin pressure occurs."

Drop in cabin pressure? I thought.

While the now not-so-soothing voice continued, the stewardess with the dirty-snowball bun went through the motions of demonstrating. "The oxygen mask will automatically drop from the compartment above you. Place the mask over your nose, and then secure it by pulling on the elastic straps on either side. Once your mask is secured, assist your children with theirs."

That's when things heated up. I was young, alone, and flying for the first time; that my breathing could be jeopardized hadn't occurred to me.

There was a pause, and I thought the instructions coming through the intercom were finished. But I was wrong.

"The cushion on your seat can be removed and used as a life preserver," was her follow-up. The grand finale then came with, "Please note the exit locations in case we must evacuate the plane." That's when I looked over at Em and wished she'd talk to me.

The engine started, and the plane moved down the runway. I gripped the armrests and focused on the magazine, *TWA Skyliner,* in the back pouch of the seat in front of me. The plane built up speed, then started its ascent. With the third lift, the sweet roll and coffee I'd had for breakfast threatened to make a second showing. I grabbed the magazine and held it under my mouth. The flight attendant with the dirty-snowball bun must have heard me retch. She came bustling down the aisle and handed me a vomit bag, hand towel, and disinfectant wipes. The plane stopped climbing, and I stopped retching, the contents of my stomach still intact. The flight attendant asked me if I was okay. I said yes. She left me with the "vomit kit."

Now that the plane was flying level, a younger stewardess rolled a snack cart down the aisle. I took a Seven-Up and a bag of chips. Em, her back still toward me, didn't acknowledge the stewardess. I drank the soda, hoping to settle my stomach, and kept the bag of chips for later.

Exhausted from not sleeping the night before but unable to doze, I played possum, like I thought Em was doing. After what seemed like forever, the pilot announced that we were going to land. Em put her seat in the upright position and sat up, but she didn't speak. I held onto the armrests and my stomach too, during our descent. Once we were on the ground, the pilot taxied the plane to a stop, and a few minutes later, the "Release Seatbelt" sign came on. I stood up, got Em's suitcase down from the overhead compartment, and popped the handle up so she could roll it. "Hope things work out, Em," I said.

She gave me a faint smile and then rolled her small, wheeled suitcase out to the waiting area. I was right behind her. A slim man in a suit walked up to her, gave her a hug, and kissed her on the cheek. That Em hadn't said good-bye before we parted ways left me feeling kind of bummed. But her grandson, Harry, looked happy to see her, and though her son Harold hadn't shown, I hoped he'd come around. My feet were back on the ground; for that, I was thankful, and I hoped things would work out for me too.

Chapter 17

LaGuardia Airport was buzzing; everyone seemed to be in a hurry. I sat down at a waiting area to look at the written instructions Pop had given me. After landing in the borough of Queens, I was to get a taxi at the airport, 'cause Pop said I wouldn't have my bearings and know how to get around. Then he said to ask the "cabbie" to take me to a cheap apartment I could rent in Queens. I located an airline employee and asked where I could catch a cab. He pointed to an exit sign and said, "Out that door and to the left is a taxi stand."

When I stepped outside, buses were lined up along the curb. A capital Q preceded a different number on each one of them. I guessed they were all going to some place in Queens, but to where, I had no idea. In fact, I had no idea where I wanted to go, so I stuck to the instructions Pop had given me.

A black, checked stripe ran the length of each yellow Checker Cab, and "NYC TAXI" was printed on the side of each one. With their motors humming, they reminded me of bumblebees ready to attack.

A chubby man leaning against his cab saw me approaching and hurried up to me. "Taxi, sir?"

"Yes," I said.

The cabbie took my bag and opened the back door for me. After tossing my luggage in the trunk, he scurried to the driver's seat.

"What's the address?" The cabbie said, talking to me through a glass partition. He sounded like a clothespin was clipped onto his nose, and he had that look someone has when they'd rather not be doing what they're doing.

"Don't have one. Just take me to a cheap apartment in Queens."

The cabbie grunted and took off. Everything was fine by me till we got on the highway and he started weaving in and out of traffic. You'd have thought the devil himself was chasing us. The probability of being injured was more real than when I was flying, and the Seven-Up I'd had on the plane was teasing my bladder. Horns were blaring, hand gestures flew, and I knew even if I could afford a car someday, I'd never want one in New York City. No way was I driving in that traffic.

The cabbie pulled up to the curb, slammed on the brakes, and said, "We're here."

To my right was an old, brick apartment building five stories high. The cabbie got out, retrieved my bag, and then opened the door for me.

"Jackson Heights neighborhood," the cabbie said. "Subway's close; the Roosevelt Avenue hub takes you to Seventy-Fourth Street and Broadway to the seven train, IRT Flushing Line." He stuck out his cupped hand.

I handed him a twenty and paused, waiting for change. The cabbie smiled, got in his cab, and took off. Gripping the bag that contained my earthly belongings and holding back the contents of my bladder, which felt like a dam ready to burst, I hurried into the apartment building. Just inside the front door sat an untidy man behind a desk that was covered with once-edible food and a stack of newspapers.

"I need a bathroom," I said.

"No public restrooms here, boy," the scruffy-looking man said.

"But I want to rent an apartment, just need to use a bathroom first."

"Well, should have said so. Back there." He pointed over his left shoulder.

My apartment needed a thorough scrubbing and a fresh coat of paint. The kitchen had a single sink with one cabinet beneath it, and a small stove and refrigerator. An island with two barstools separated the kitchen from the living room/bedroom, where a Murphy bed that I'd also use as my couch was stored vertically against the wall. And a little bathroom and closet were at the end of the room. I wasn't used to anything fancy growing up in Greenstone, Missouri, so the apartment suited me okay. But Pop's estimates for expenses were low. The money he'd given me didn't even cover my first month's rent. I had to give the apartment manager most of the money Mom had slipped me from working extra at the diner too. A roof was over my head for one month. Two hundred and seventy dollars I'd earned working at Pop's Pop and some coins, tip money from Mom's waitress job, had to keep me till I found a job.

After unpacking my belongings, I went to the lobby, where I'd seen a payphone. A phone book was attached by a chain. Using the yellow page listings of dance theaters, I started at the beginning and began calling. I didn't know any dance except East Coast swing. Other dances were foreign to me, and it wouldn't have mattered if I'd been skilled at them. I couldn't get an audition for any stage performances. I hadn't studied under a noteworthy instructor, and I had no dance performance experience. I didn't have the "credentials" to be a member of a dance troupe in New York City. Neither Pop nor I had had a clue about how things worked in the Big Apple.

I didn't have formal swing-dance instruction, but Pop had taught me well. I figured an owner of a dance studio had those credentials that seemed so important. With my financial situation, I couldn't pay for dance training, but I figured if a studio owner hired me to teach swing, I could study under him or her, and then I'd be qualified to be a member of a swing-dance troupe. I had called every dance studio listed in the yellow pages, except one. I dialed the number of The Silver Slipper located in midtown Manhattan, hoping to get an interview with the owner.

"The Silver Slipper, Ms. Slovinskia speaking."

"Hi," I said, noticing she spoke with an accent. "My name's Ty," I said, figuring my nickname, Bird, would label me as a hick. "I'd like to speak to the owner of the studio, please."

"I am the owner, young man; do you wish to enroll for dance lessons?"

"No, I'd like to apply for a job as a dance instructor."

"I have an instructor, and I teach as well."

"But if you had *another* instructor, you could handle more dance students," I said. "If you saw me dance, I know you'd hire me."

"What renowned dance teacher have you studied under, and where have you performed?"

"I haven't had formal training, but I've had instruction in East Coast swing, Ms. Slovinskia. I won a swing-dance contest in Missouri."

"You have no dance reputation, and your skills are limited to East Coast, only?"

"Yes, but—"

"As I said, I do not need another instructor at this time. And if I decide to hire one in the future, they must have formal instruction and be versed in all the dances I teach at my studio. I do not wish to train you. I'm sorry; good luck to you," Ms. Slovinskia said.

Utilities for my apartment in Queens, food, and transportation would use up the rest of my money in no time. I had to find a job or I'd end up living on the street. Ms. Slovinskia's stubborn attitude about not wanting to train me wasn't going to discourage me. And in some way, she struck me as being likable. In part, it might have been that I liked her accent, but more importantly, the fact that she wished me good luck, instead of hanging up on me, like the other studio owners had, was encouraging. *If she sees me dance, she'll change her mind,* I thought.

I followed the cabbie's instructions and took the train at the Roosevelt Avenue Subway Hub near my Jackson Heights apartment. It took me to Seventy-Fourth Street and Broadway, like the cabbie said it would. There, I boarded the number-seven train, the Interborough Rapid Transit Flushing Line, which took me to the Times Square Station Complex next to and beneath Grand Central Terminal. I got off and asked a middle-aged guy that got off at the same stop how I could get to The Silver Slipper.

"Don't have time, buddy," he said abruptly.

Then I approached an elderly woman as she walked past me. "Can you tell me what train I should take to get to The Silver Slipper?"

She asked me the address, and I showed her what I had written down from the phone book at my apartment building.

She pointed at a directional sign that read "Woodlawn, Bronx" and told me to board the number-four train at that platform. "At the first stop, exit the subway and turn right. The Silver Slipper will be about a half a block ahead on your right."

I got to the platform and waited for my train. The doors opened, and I moved with the flow of people to enter.

The train stopped, and people hurriedly exited. I kept pace with the crowd and climbed the steps. My feet hit the sidewalk, and I made my way to my destination, The Silver Slipper, at Lexington Avenue off Fifty-First Street.

It was a red-brick, two-story building, among others that were much larger. I could tell by the number of people I saw rushing about that midtown Manhattan was a busy shopping area. I grasped the silver handle on the doorknob and opened the fancy black door with the name of the dance studio, The Silver Slipper, written in silver letters. A petite woman with her dark hair pulled up in a bun greeted me.

"Good afternoon, young man. I was just coming to lock the door for lunch break. Do you wish to sign up for a dance class?"

"Uh, no. I want to apply for a job as a dance instructor, Ms. Slovinskia," I said.

"How do you know my name? Wait, your voice sounds familiar. Did you call this morning?"

"Yes, but I thought if I *showed* you what a good dancer I am, you'd change your mind."

"What is your name, young man?"

"Ty."

"Ty, on the phone you told me you have no formal dance instruction, and furthermore, your dancing skill is limited to East Coast swing," Ms. Slovinskia said. "My reply is the same as it was this morning. I do not wish to hire another dance instructor, and if I choose to in the future, they must have formal training."

"But—"

"I'm sorry; again, I wish you luck finding employment. Without the proper credentials, you will not get hired as a dancer. Where are you living?"

"Jackson Heights," I said.

"If you can't find employment in midtown, try Flushing in north-central Queens. Main Street has a lot of retail businesses as well as restaurants and bars. Now, I must lock the door and eat my lunch; my students will be arriving soon."

I left, feeling like I wanted to crawl in a hole and die. If I couldn't be a dancer, what would I do? *How stupid to think I could have a dancing career in New York City,* I thought. My world had been turned upside down, and misery swallowed me. I took the number-seven train to downtown Flushing to search for a job, *any* job. A guy from Greenstone, Missouri, didn't belong in midtown Manhattan; it was too highfalutin for me. If I didn't find work, I knew the money I had left wouldn't last long, and then I'd be living on the street.

The sidewalk was pulsing with people, some a nationality I'd never seen before. A guy with olive skin and long, black hair held up his hand, his forefinger and middle finger forming a *V*. He hurried past me, the strings of multicolored beads hanging from his neck making tracks through the blood-red words, "Love, Not War," on his T-shirt.

Not having any know-how about cooking, I passed up restaurants, and the shops where I inquired about a job had no openings. Then I came upon Smack's Bar. A sign was in the window: "Help Wanted." I went in to apply for the job, again using my given name, Ty, to introduce myself. The owner interviewed me on the spot.

"Ty, everybody calls me Smack. The job I need filled involves serving food, busing tables, and cleaning."

Smack gave me a look-over. "You're not twenty-one, are you?"

"No, sir."

"You can't serve liquor, then; the bartender will take care of that. The shift I need filled starts at 5:00 p.m. and goes till we close at midnight, then you clean the place. Pay's $1.85 an hour, and customers leave tips. I need somebody who'll work five days a week. Want the job, Ty?"

"Yes, sir."

"Be here tomorrow at 4:00; Frankie'll show you the ropes before your shift begins."

I bought a ham and cheese sandwich at the deli across the street from Smack's Bar, then walked to the subway hub and took the seven train back to my apartment. While eating the chips I'd received on the plane and my sandwich, I wrote my folks and Allison to let them know I had made it to New York City and had an apartment in Queens. Then I wrote Pop a letter too, and told him some lies. I said flying was great and that I'd found myself a job at a dance studio.

Chapter 18

That December of '69, the postman knocked on the door of my Jackson Heights apartment in Queens and had me sign for a registered letter. The government had conducted two draft lotteries for the Vietnam War, and I was among those men being called for military service.

I took the required physical and passed, but I was diagnosed with night blindness and failed the eye exam. In my next letter to Pop, I told him I'd have served my country if I had been given a clean bill of health, but I was happy my pursuit of a dancing career on stage wouldn't be interrupted. As always, I wrote him about my dance instructor's job, saying my students thought I was top-notch and that I was sure my experience teaching at the studio would help me get hired for a stage performance soon. But in truth, I had been to numerous dance studios and not one owner would hire me. Still, I kept up my charade; how could I disappoint Pop, the one person who'd had faith in me?

Pop sent me many letters in return; each one contained encouraging words like, "I'm so proud of you." Once in a while, he'd send a check to help me out, and then apologize for not being able to send more. Pop's handwriting became more difficult to read, and though he'd never let on about his health, I was worried about him. I'd sent letters to my parents and Allison but hadn't gotten any response. I figured Dad's wrath at me for leaving Greenstone was the reason. Pop was all the family I had contact with, and the certainty was that one day his letters would stop, and then I'd have no thread left connecting me to Greenstone. I understood missing Pop, missing those I used to call family. But I missed the quiet streets of Greenstone and the friendly folks there too. Even in my apartment complex, the other tenants didn't wave or say hi. And the widespread crime in New York City was something I wasn't used to, either.

By this point, I blended in at Smack's Bar like the woodwork. I was quiet, hardworking, and it seemed that the owner, Smack, liked me, but the feeling wasn't mutual. Too many pretty, young girls were dropping in the bar to see Smack. He'd take them back to the storage room and then they'd leave, but one night, one of the girls came in looking like she'd been crying, sat down at the bar, and asked for Smack. I'd seen him go in the bathroom, so I knocked on the door and told him some girl was asking for him. When Smack got to the bar, he grabbed the girl's arm and yanked her off the stool. Then he walked her to the door, reached in his pocket, and slipped her something.

It was a Friday, past midnight, and after being told half a dozen times that the bar was closed, the last of the drunken slobs waddled out. I locked up and started cleaning in the dining area. Smack was sitting at one of the tables, conversing with a well-dressed guy who had a pockmarked face. My employer was sucking the last bit of his steak off the bone. I'd never heard anyone make that kind of smacking noise; for that matter, I'd never seen anyone strip a bone slick like he did.

After pocketing my tip, I cleared dirty dishes from another table. Smack was still talking in a low voice to the same man. Something soured my stomach that night, something besides that nauseating sound Smack's mouth made when he ate. He was getting young girls hooked on heroin, then forcing them to work as prostitutes to support their habit. The price negotiated for the heroin, the man with the pockmarked face gave Smack a package, and then left. My employer was more than a slob; he was a criminal.

I finished cleaning as fast as I could. At 1:00 a.m., I was out the door, walking at a brisk pace to catch the subway back to my apartment. To discourage a thief from robbing me, I kept my hand in my pocket and poked my comb against the lining. Back then, the change customers left me as tips meant I could survive in the Big Apple. I'd made it to New York City, but I felt more out of place there than I had in Greenstone.

Chapter 19

I got up the following Monday morning, determined to change my situation. I didn't want to be associated with that lowlife Smack anymore. I guess that old saying, "If you lie down with dogs, you get up with fleas," had been ingrained in me by my mother.

I didn't have to start work at Smack's Bar till five p.m., and I decided to approach Ms. Slovinskia, the owner of The Silver Slipper, about a dance instructor's job one more time. There was something about her that I had liked, a kind of bond that I'd felt when I spoke to her on the phone the previous June about hiring me as a dance instructor. And then, when I showed up at her studio to ask her for a job again, I'd felt the same way. I didn't understand why I felt a connection with Ms. Slovinskia. But I knew I couldn't stand to work at Smack's Bar anymore.

I caught the train at the Roosevelt Avenue Subway Hub by my Jackson Heights apartment, which took me to Seventy-Fourth Street and Broadway, then boarded the number-seven train IRT Flushing Line. At Grand Central Station, I transferred to the Woodland number-four train and got off at the Lexington/Fifty-First Street station in midtown Manhattan at 8:20, hoping to talk to Ms. Slovinskia before she started her first dance lesson. I climbed the steps of the underground subway station, my feet hit the sidewalk, and I made my way to my destination, The Silver Slipper. A bike courier with a package to deliver sped past me.

The door was locked. I looked through the front window of the red-brick, two-story dance studio and couldn't see any lights on. I thought I had hit an off day when the owner, Ms. Slovinskia, wasn't open for business. I leaned against the black door with the words *The Silver Slipper* written in silver and closed my eyes, thinking about my previous failed attempts to get the owner to hire me, thinking if The Silver Slipper was closed, I had spent my hard-earned money in vain again. I heard humming and opened my eyes. Ms. Slovinskia was holding what looked to be a small pastry bag, and she was smiling at me.

"Those blue eyes and dark hair. You, I could not forget. Morning, young man. I have to say you are persistent, coming here again, but as I told you before, I have no job for you. You lack training, and I can't afford another instructor anyway. I'm sorry."

Ms. Slovinskia unlocked the door, and I followed her into the foyer. "But ... you don't understand. My job at the bar is awful, worse than that. I'm a talented swing dancer; I've been taught by Pop, I mean, Mr. Robert Bradford. Please, can't we work something out?"

"What do you mean?" Ms. Slovinskia said.

"It's true I don't have formal dance training, but I know swing. I want to study under you and become a swing-dance instructor. I'll clean your studio, run errands, whatever you need help with, I'll do it. Please, let me dance for you. You'll see."

"Very well, the tall, handsome young man can dance for me. My instructor will be here momentarily. You will show me this talent you think you have."

A few minutes later, the most beautiful girl I'd ever seen came down the steps that led to the second floor.

Where was she before? I thought.

She was tall, almost as tall as me. She had warm brown eyes, long, dark hair, and a smile that made me lose my thoughts.

"Good morning, Alexandra," Ms. Slovinskia said. "This young man—ah, your face I remember, but not your name."

"Ty," I said, hoping to sidestep my last name, till the studio owner saw me dance.

Ms. Slovinskia smiled. "Last name?"

"Partridge, Ty Partridge, ma'am."

"Ty, this is my instructor, Alexandra Carbone." Then to Alexandra, she said, "He claims he's a *talented* East Coast swing dancer. Take the floor as his partner.

"We shall see, Ty," Ms. Slovinskia said.

Alexandra nodded and smiled at me as she went to the center of the dance floor. I followed, and then took her in closed dance position, my right hand to her waist, my left hand holding her right hand. She rested her left hand on the upper part of my right arm, and something happened that never had when I was paired with my former dance partner, Emma Jean; my bicep twitched. Alexandra's pouty lips parted and arched into a smile, and I'm sure my face flushed. I averted my eyes and watched Ms. Slovinskia put a record on the record player.

I listened to the music and got the beat, then led Alexandra into the basic six-count East Coast swing step, a triple-step count of one and two, three and four, and a rock-step count of five and six. With my left hand to her right, I turned her out with an inside underarm turn.

The music was a piece I wasn't familiar with, and it changed from a medium tempo to a fast one. *Concentrate*, I thought. Not only did I have to show Ms. Slovinskia that I knew many swing-dance steps but that I could lead a girl I'd never danced with before. And my style had to impress her too. Alexandra was about my height, and I was being careful that all of my arm movements cleared her head.

Next, I led she goes/he goes turns, first turning Alexandra outside. Then I crossed under our connected hands and turned to my left to face her, and on count five and six we did our rock-step. With my left-hand lead, I brought Alexandra towards me and placed my right hand on her right shoulder. I led a push-step to nudge her back and move us apart. With my right arm, I slid down her right arm, until our hands met. Then I brought her to my right side to a Sweetheart Wrap and led her across, in front of me, to begin a tunnel. As Alexandra began to enter the tunnel under my right arm, the music stopped. We stopped dancing, but my heart kept racing. And I knew physical exertion wasn't the cause.

"I have seen enough. You are gifted, young Ty. Perhaps we can come to some agreement," Ms. Slovinskia said. Then she turned to Alexandra. "I will be in the office with Ty. When the students arrive, begin without me. I won't be long."

"Nice to meet you, Ty," Alexandra said. She didn't sound like a New Yorker. I liked the way she stretched the long-*i* sound when she pronounced my name.

The studio owner took me to a small room in the back with two folding chairs and a desk. Pictures with younger versions of Ms. Slovinskia as a ballerina, posing with trophies she'd won, covered the walls.

"You teach ballet?"

"Not to worry, young Ty; when I came to America, I studied dance at the university. I am versed in ballroom, swing, contemporary, many dances. My first love was ballet, but do not be mistaken: I am an accomplished dance teacher, an artist, and a capable woman who has run this studio for many years without interference from any *man*. Under my direction, Alexandra has learned many dances and has become a skilled instructor. I can teach you to be a capable instructor too. But if you do not wish to study under me, then say so."

"No ... I'm interested. But just in swing."

The dance teacher tossed her head back, pursed her lips, and frowned.

"Young man, you have no appreciation for elegance. I will not put you in leotards, if you do not wish to wear them. Swing only. Does that suit you?"

"Yes, of course. I didn't mean to offend you," I said, trying to smooth things over.

"Then we shall talk terms," Ms. Slovinskia said. "I do not know what your wage is at that 'worse than awful job' you wish to quit, but I will pay you sixty dollars a week."

There was no way I could survive on that. Though I hated working for Smack, at least tips came with the job. "I'd have to live on the street."

"Not to worry. I give you room and food besides. When I came to America, I had little money in my pocket. You will survive. Do you accept my terms or not?"

"Yes, thank you, Ms. Slovinskia."

"You will call me Nadia. Now come; we will see how Alexandra is doing with the beginners' waltz class."

I followed Nadia out of the office, back to the ballroom. "They are learning the basic box step," she said.

The men were standing on the perimeter of the ballroom; the ladies were standing in two lines on the dance floor.

"Now that the gentlemen know their footwork to lead the box step, I will demonstrate the ladies' footwork," Alex said. "As I did with the gentlemen, I will turn my back to you to make it easier for you to mimic my steps. I will also be demonstrating the 'rise,' in my steps, the upward stretch of my body, and 'fall,' the bending of my knees and ankles. This gives the waltz elegance. The woman must follow the man's lead and will therefore be stepping on the opposite foot the gentleman steps with. Watch. Ladies step back on their right foot on count one, bending at the knees for the "fall." On count two, their left foot steps back and to the side as they "rise" on their toes. On count three, the right foot closes to the left and she again bends at the knees to show the "fall." To finish the other half of the box- on count one she steps forward on her left (again showing the "fall"), count two she brings her right foot forward and to the right, "rising," and finally, on count three, her left foot closes to her right to complete the box. Now, practice the box-step pattern with me as I call out the steps."

I watched Alexandra repeat the box-step pattern four times with the ladies.

Turning to face the women, she said, "Now I will mirror the steps by facing you. Though I will be stepping on the opposite foot that I call out for you to step on, this will allow me to watch you as you do the box step."

Alexandra repeated the footwork for the box step over and over. Though some of the women looked clumsy in their attempts, Alexandra kept smiling. *She's really a nice person. So patient,* I thought.

Finally, she said, "Men, come out on the dance floor, pick a lady for your partner, and introduce yourselves."

Every man had a partner, except one, a short guy with a big belly. Alexandra became his partner.

"Eugene's the name, Alexandra."

"Nice to meet you."

"I'm going to show you the proper closed dance position for the waltz," Alexandra said. "Gentlemen, face your partners and follow my instructions. As leaders, make sure you remember the rise and fall to make the dance look graceful.

"Put your right hand just beneath the lady's left shoulder blade, keeping your arm at a ninety-degree level to your body. No droopy arms.

"Eugene. Place your right hand beneath my shoulder blade, please," she instructed.

"Now, gentlemen, raise your left arm, allowing the woman to rest her right hand in yours. Ladies, put your left hand on the man's right shoulder and look over it. Posture is important; everyone stand tall. I'll call out the gentlemen's footwork; remember, ladies, your footwork will be the opposite, and as I said, the gentleman *always* leads and you follow. We'll practice without music."

Alexandra's partner, Eugene, was out of step and he trampled on her feet, but she didn't get annoyed; she kept smiling and said to him, "You'll get it."

Nadia began clapping out the beat with her hands. "Students, let me see that rise and fall. Very good posture, Alexandra. *Sir,* what are you doing?"

All of the men stopped and looked at Nadia.

"Partner of Alexandra. The waltz is done in three-quarter time, and your steps *must* form a box.

"Watch as I help Alexandra's partner," Nadia said to Ty.

Nadia walked toward Alexandra and her dance partner, Eugene. "My dear, I will work with this student. Float around the room and check the other students."

In an hour, the box step and a lady's turn had been taught. With it being only the students' first lesson, I was sure most in the class would be competent waltz dancers after they finished the remaining lessons of the course. I was also certain that Eugene would need to repeat the class.

The second class scheduled at The Silver Slipper that day was ballet. All the little girls showed up in their tutus, and yes, the few little boys who had signed up tiptoed around in their leotards. I stood off to the side, watching Nadia and Alexandra give the lesson, feeling like a fish out of water. As I watched Alexandra working with those young kids, I saw the same patience she'd shown to the man with the big belly taking her waltz class, and I knew that her beauty went deeper than her skin. She was a kind person who loved her work.

With ballet class finished, in came the third class, eager to learn East Coast swing dancing.

"Ty, now you must earn your keep," Nadia said. "This is their first class. Teach the basic six-count step: triple-step, triple-step, rock-step, and count it out for them, one and two, three and four, five and six. Make it clear that the man starts with his left foot, the woman with her right, and that the man always leads and the woman always follows. If there is time, I will tell you what to teach next. Be clear in your instruction and firm, or your students will not learn. Like you, Alexandra came to me as a swing dancer, but I shaped her into an excellent instructor, one knowledgeable of many dances. Knowing the steps and being able to teach them are two different things. I will watch as you teach and help you."

Nadia stood next to me, interrupting me in midsentence to interject suggestions, while Alexandra and I demonstrated the triple-step, triple-step, rock-step. But even with Nadia hovering and Alexandra melting me with her smile, when my first class of students left that day, they all knew the basic swing step. And the icing on the cake was when Alexandra gently touched my arm and said, "Good job."

The studio owner locked the door after the third class left and announced it was lunch time. To my surprise, Alexandra joined Nadia and me for sandwiches in the apartment upstairs. That's when Alexandra told me she'd been living under Nadia's roof for more than a year.

"The first bedroom at the top of the stairs has the master bath; that is my room," Nadia said as we ate at the kitchen table. "Alexandra has the second bedroom down the hall. The living room is at the end of the hall. It has a sofa that pulls out into a bed. That is yours, Ty. You will share the hall bathroom with Alexandra. This will be no problem?"

"No, sounds fine," I said, sure that the bathroom situation would be a problem.

CHAPTER 20

I'd been at The Silver Slipper a little more than two years, but working with my dance partner, whom I had come to call Alex, had made the time fly by. On May 21 of 1971, I celebrated my twenty-first birthday, and Alex made me a chocolate cake with chocolate icing. By this point in time, Nadia had me versed in every swing move she knew, and Alex and I were teaching the most advanced moves and sequences I could ever have imagined. And though I had originally opted to bypass ballroom, ballet, and contemporary dance, Alex had wanted me to learn them, so I had, and I was a capable instructor of those dances as well. Alex and I had spent hour upon hour teaching together, and we were inseparable friends, but I wanted more; I wanted her to be my girlfriend.

During ballroom dance lessons, I wanted to hold Alex as close as possible. The waltz, in particular, was such a romantic dance that I couldn't help myself. Nadia scolded me for not maintaining the proper frame and posture in closed position. I didn't like keeping a "big top-line," with my arms and elbows out wide, because that put too much distance between Alex and me, and if I tilted my head with my eyes looking over Alex's right shoulder, as I was supposed to do, it meant I couldn't look at her beautiful face. I refused to do that, and that's when Nadia would reprimand me. But I couldn't help myself. Feeling Alex's rhythmic breathing as my right hand rested on her left shoulder blade, and holding her delicate right hand in my left, I imagined she was my Cinderella and I was her prince. That made tolerating the studio owner's negative remarks easy. I felt encouraged that Alex didn't pull back when I had her in what Nadia called an "improper hold," and there were moments when Alex's eyes met mine that it felt like I had the same effect on her that she had on me.

Though I still had no true interest in ballet, every lift gave me the opportunity to have physical contact with Alex, and each time her eyes met mine, I became more convinced that their steadfast hold was more than just artistic drama.

One day, after Nadia finished giving Alex and me a contemporary dance lesson, Alex said, "Ty, I think we should ask Nadia to offer lessons for contemporary dance. I think it might appeal to younger students."

Nadia said okay, but there was one stipulation. The contemporary class had to be scheduled at the end of the day after we finished our currently scheduled classes, and Alex and I had to teach it. That gave me an opportunity to spend more time with Alex and that suited me just fine. And I didn't have Nadia hanging around to hamper my attempts to show the dark-haired beauty that I loved her.

An advertisement that The Silver Slipper was offering a six-week class for contemporary dance drew twelve students. Alex and I held class once a week.

Aside from our obligations as dance instructors, Alex and I had become close friends, of that I was sure. We'd spend hours talking after finishing our work day, and once in a while, I'd ask her out to get a sandwich and soda, which was all I could afford since I was making only sixty dollars a week. She knew I left Greenstone, Missouri, 'cause my dad was pressuring me to become a miner. And I knew she and her dad, Bruno, didn't see eye-to-eye, either, and that's why she had left Saint Louis, Missouri. It was easy for us to talk; we had so much in common. And I hoped my desire to know her in an intimate way hadn't clouded my notion that she wanted to be my girlfriend.

Chapter 21

I wrote to Pop, and though my folks and Allison didn't reply to my letters, I continued to write to them too. Pop's letters to me became more and more spaced out, and his handwriting had worsened to the point I could barely make sense out of what he wrote. I had little hope of scraping up enough money to get back to Greenstone, but I hoped my news about teaching as a dance instructor brought him some joy. At least now I was telling Pop the truth. Though I made it clear I wasn't wearing leotards, I wished I could have seen Pop's face when he read I was teaching ballet. I had told him that I'd audition for stage performances after I got professional dance training, but that would have taken me away from Alex. So that wasn't a topic in my letters to Pop anymore, but Alex always was.

Many times, I thought about the letters I had written my folks and Allison to let them know I was okay, that I was working in my chosen career. I wanted to tell them about Alex, but they didn't write, so what was the use? A man becoming a dance instructor wasn't Dad's idea of a real man, and even though my mother tried to smooth things over when I lived in Greenstone, I thought she didn't find it proper either. And as far as Allison was concerned, she'd follow suit with what my folks told her to do. But I had Pop's letters. To Pop, I was family.

I stepped out to get the mail for Nadia, and the wind was whistling a melancholy tune. I shuffled through the envelopes, and the lot seemed nothing more than a bunch of advertisements pertaining to the studio, till I got to the bottom of the stack and saw my mother's handwriting. Once inside, I put Nadia's mail on the desk and then ripped opened my letter.

> Dear Son,
>
> I've wanted to write, but you and Charles were on bad terms when you left Greenstone, so I felt like I'd be going against my husband if I wrote you back. Then your letters stopped, and I thought either something bad happened to you, or that you were burning mad not only at your father but at your sister and me for not writing. I thought you decided to be finished with all of us. Like me, Allison is a bundle of nerves from not hearing from you, and though he doesn't admit it, Charles is worried too. If you get this letter, please write us that you're all right.
>
> Read all your letters over and over. Allison has too. Left them on the kitchen table, so your dad could read them on the sly. Sounds like you have made a go of dancing. I'm so proud of you.
>
> You're an uncle, Bird. Allison gave birth to a little girl, Drew Proffit's baby, and thank goodness, they've decided to get married. Your sister talks about you all the time. She misses you. Me too. Charles misses you something awful, but he won't swallow his pride and say it. Your family loves you, Bird; that's the God's truth. Please write back. I promise that Allison and me will write back now. Can't say your father

> will. He's a good man, but not one for expressing his love. We'll be looking for your letter.
>
> All our love,
> Mom, Dad, and Allison

I read that letter from Mom over and over, committed it to memory. That afternoon, I collected my thoughts and wrote three separate letters: one to Mom, one to Allison, and one to Dad, which was the most difficult to write, the most difficult to send.

Chapter 22

I was sure Nadia's shrewd nature had pinpointed the reason for my attentiveness to Alex, 'cause the first week of December, our employer surprised us. She gave Alex and me a raise.

"Christmas is coming; you two should exchange gifts," she said. "Besides, you need to go to a movie or out to eat more."

It was the third weekend in a row that I had asked Alex out. We walked to a corner café near The Silver Slipper, and during our meal, we talked about the future.

"I want my own dance studio," I said.

"Me too," Alex said.

"Let's buy one together. What do you say?"

"That'd be great, Ty."

We talked and talked, imagining what our future dance studio would be like. Conversing with Alex was like when we danced to music; we were always in sync. I'd never been that at ease talking with *any* girl before, yet at the same time, I was aroused just watching her full lips form words, and I wanted to express my love for her. I didn't realized how long we'd been at the café till a stout man with a mustache, whom I guessed was the owner, approached us and looked at his wristwatch.

"We close in ten minutes," he said, then pointed. "Server left the bill."

"Didn't notice how late it was," I said. And I hadn't noticed the server leave the bill, either. When I was with Alex, I lost track of time.

It was bitter cold and snowing when we started walking back to The Silver Slipper. I decided to present my feelings for Alex in a way that had only one possible interpretation, that I loved her and wanted her to be my girlfriend. And a positive response is what I was hoping for.

"Let me keep you warm," I said, drawing Alex close to me as we walked. The snowflakes glistened like diamonds on her dark hair. "Do you know how beautiful you are?"

Alex stopped walking. Her wide-eyed expression wasn't what I was expecting.

Doesn't she know I love her?

But then she wrapped her arms around my neck, and we kissed. The exhale of her warm breath tantalized my skin as my lips encased her lower lip, and I knew that when I was financially able to support her, I would ask her to be my wife. From that night on, Alex and I were a couple.

Chapter 23

The first of January arrived; the year was 1972. Alex and I taught dance classes in bell-bottom pants. Though Bird would never have done such a thing, I had decided to let my hair grow to shoulder-length. Nadia said Alex and I looked like hippies with our "unconventional dance apparel," but she allowed it. She had a bigger problem to worry about: her aged body. She no longer moved like a scarf blowing in a gentle breeze; her movements were jerky, stiff, and clumsy. Our employer blamed old dance injuries for her uncooperative body, but the doctor said she had rheumatoid arthritis. Nadia stayed in bed most of the day, and the full weight of running The Silver Slipper fell to Alex and me.

With all my responsibilities at the studio, I hadn't written Pop or my folks and Allison for two weeks. With my last letter to Pop, I had included a photo of Alex and me, taken in one of those booths where you draw the curtain, smile, press a button, and the photo is ready in a jiffy. Pop had written back. His handwriting was difficult to read, but I could decipher enough to know that he was happy I'd found myself a girl and that he called Alex a "beauty." Before Nadia started having problems with arthritis, I'd written my folks and Allison faithfully too.

And though I could tell that my mother had signed *Dad* on the letters she sent me, I was glad to receive them just the same.

The third Friday in January, New York City's temperature dropped, setting a record low, and Nadia's arthritis got worse. Her joints ached constantly, and she was depressed and cranky. In addition to running The Silver Slipper as though it were ours, Alex and I dealt with the household duties too. We fixed Nadia's breakfast, lunch, and dinner and served it to her in bed. I still hadn't written to Pop or my folks and Allison, and I hadn't received any letters from Greenstone either. The way Pop's last letter had looked, I understood him not writing, but I wondered what was up with Mom and Allison.

My hair hadn't grown past my earlobes yet, and I was disappointed when out of the blue, Alex said, "Ty, get your hair cut. We're going to stop dressing like hippies."

I didn't know if Alex was trying to improve Nadia's disposition or if she really thought we'd look more professional. But to please my girl, I got a haircut, and from then on, Alex and I wore what Nadia called "conventional dance attire."

Chapter 24

We were two weeks into February. The cold weather had remained harsh, and Nadia's arthritis wouldn't let up.

It was after business hours; Alex had gone to the grocery store down the street, and I had stayed at The Silver Slipper to keep an eye on Nadia. I stepped outside to get the mail. Among the stack of envelopes was one with Pop's return address on it, but I knew at a glance the neat handwriting on it wasn't his.

I made my way back inside and heard Nadia calling to me from her bedroom. "Ty, my throat's dry; I need a glass of water."

I put the envelope down on the table, my own throat feeling parched. Without responding to Nadia, I fetched the glass of water, hurried to her bedroom, and then held the glass to her lips. I took leave of Nadia without acknowledging her "thank you." Back at the kitchen table, I fingered the envelope, repeatedly picking it up, laying it down.

The door downstairs creaked, like it always did when someone opened it. I hurried down the steps and took the bag of groceries from Alex.

"Is something wrong, Ty? You look awful."

"It's Pop." We climbed the steps and went into the kitchen. I set the bag on the counter, and then Alex and I sat down at the table.

"What's wrong?" Alex whispered.

"Don't know. This envelope came today," I said and picked it up. "It has Pop's return address on it, but he didn't write that."

Alex took the envelope from me and examined the handwriting. "Want me to open it?"

"Okay," I said, certain the letter contained bad news.

Two obituaries were enclosed: Allison Jean Proffit's and her stillborn infant son's, Jacob Drew Proffit. My sister and my nephew had died the eighth of February. The contents of Mom's letter I'd received almost two years earlier revisited me. News that my sister and Drew Proffit had a baby girl and were getting married had made me so happy.

Drew wrote that he and the family knew I'd open the envelope if Pop's return address was on it. My brother-in-law stated he had decided to "inform me" about Allison and Jacob's deaths only because Allison had spoken kindly about me to their daughter Hannah. My failure to write while Alex and I were struggling to take care of Nadia and run The Silver Slipper had caused a problem. My family believed that I no longer wanted any contact with them. And that they hadn't wanted me to attend Allison's and Jacob's funerals made me an outsider.

I got up and began putting the groceries away.

"I can do that," Alex said.

"Thanks. Going out for a while." I grabbed my coat and hat and was out the door. Remnants of ice from a snow the day before were on the sidewalk. Like other New Yorkers, I walked as fast as I could, not allowing the ice to slow me down. The wind struck me. I leaned into it and walked faster, trying to diminish the sting. I walked a long time, hoping to eventually feel numb. But I didn't. Every part of my body hurt, especially my heart.

Chapter 25

I'd been up late the night before writing letters, one to Drew and Hannah, another to my folks, expressing my sorrow about my sister's and nephew's deaths. My mind was a jumbled mess from too little sleep, yet I was sure I'd had a dream and that it was important for me to remember it. I made my way to the kitchen and started a pot of coffee. Two cups later, the cobwebs began to clear, and the silhouette of a building surfaced in my mind. I drank another, hoping to erase the dark and see the structure in detail, and the sensation that I must sort out what the dream meant grew stronger. My recall said it wasn't tall and rejected a skyscraper. Then something distinctive about the building came to me: an old red-and-white striped canvas awning. And I remembered that in my dream, it was giving way.

As was usual every morning, Alex was busy giving Nadia her breakfast and helping her bathe before our nine o'clock dance class started. When she finished, I took her aside, away from Nadia's earshot. "I had an unsettling dream," I said.

"That news about your sister and nephew was hard on you."

"It wasn't about them. There was an awning falling."

"An awning?" Alex said.

"The red-and-white striped canvas one on the front of Pop's soda-fountain shop in Greenstone, Missouri. It was a message, telling me what I need to do."

"What you need to do? It was a silly dream, Ty."

"No, it wasn't. It was a sign; Pop's health has declined more. That's why he hasn't written. I need to go back."

"Go back? Just call him. Why don't you tell the truth, Ty; you miss all of them ... that place; that's why you *need* to go back."

"After Pop's letters stopped, I did call him. There was no answer. I don't want to live in Greenstone, Alex; you and this dance studio are my home. But look how things turned out with Allison and Jacob. I don't want a letter with Pop's obituary to show up after he's been buried. I'm taking the train back to Greenstone."

With the little money Alex and I had saved, she knew two round-trip train tickets weren't in the cards. Besides, there was Nadia to care for.

"You won't come back," Alex said. Then she ran to her bedroom and locked me out. I stood outside her door, listening to her sobbing.

Alex was wrong about me not returning to her, but she was right about part of what she'd said. I did miss them: Pop, Mom, Drew, my niece, even Dad. I wished I had at least told Allison good-bye before I left Greenstone. I couldn't change that. She'd never know how much I missed her. But her brother, Bird, needed to see her grave and grieve for her. And though I thought I had left Bird in Greenstone when I got on the plane for New York City, he was still a part of me. My family had to know that my life was interlaced with theirs, no matter where I lived.

"You're wrong. Open the door and talk to me, Alex."

Old as she was, Nadia had excellent hearing. "Ty, come to my room," she called out as loud as she could. "I want to speak to you."

I didn't want to, but I figured Nadia had heard everything that was said. She knew me. Not just as a dancer. She knew about Greenstone. She knew about Pop, my former dance teacher, my adopted dad. She knew about Allison and my nephew, Jacob, 'cause she'd heard Alex read my letter. Those good ears of hers. So I went to Nadia's room. She had propped her pillow against the headboard and was sitting up in bed.

Nadia patted the bed with her hand. "Come here."

I sat down and began to explain the situation. "I need to see Pop, and—"

"Other family you left behind. I understand."

Nadia's tone made her words seem sympathetic, and when she said she understood, I believed she did.

"And Alex feels you will not return to her. But you will. This is true, Ty?"

"Of course. Yes. How could she even think I wouldn't? I love her."

Nadia shook her head. "I believe you, but Alex must go with you."

"I'd take her, but—"

"You can't afford to. Now, listen to me; the two of you look after me, and you run my business better than I did. You've added classes, and my income has increased. You've both worked hard. I will pay for Alex's train ticket."

"But who'll look after you?"

"Do not worry, Ty; I will handle that. Now, go tell Alex the news."

As I took leave of Nadia, I saw her get in the nightstand drawer; she removed a small, blue book and then reached for the phone. I closed her bedroom door behind me and listened in the hallway. Guess Nadia wasn't the only eavesdropper. Nadia called Margaret, a retired elementary teacher who was one of our long-standing dance students at The Silver Slipper. She and some of the other widowed dance ladies went to get coffee and visited after their lesson. Nadia asked Margaret to stay with her while Alex and I were away. In exchange, Margaret was promised a free six-week session of dance lessons.

I went down the hall to Alex's bedroom and listened. It was quiet. "Open the door; you're going to Greenstone with me. Nadia's paying your train fare, and Margaret from class will stay with her." But Alex didn't open the door.

It was almost nine o'clock. Students arriving for our first dance class were chatting in the foyer. If Alex decided to stay in her bedroom, I knew I'd have to teach by myself. "Class is about to start," I said.

Alex opened the door and gave me that "you're in the doghouse" look. Without speaking, we went downstairs and began teaching. Each time I held Alex in dance position, she felt rigid.

It was lunchtime. As was customary, Alex went upstairs to make sandwiches. I waited for our students to leave and then locked the studio's door. When I climbed the stairs to the apartment, Alex was coming out of Nadia's bedroom, carrying an empty tray. I followed her back to the kitchen. She sat down at the table and began eating her sandwich, but there was none made for me. I got the sliced ham out, made my sandwich, and ate in the office.

Alex and I finished our last class for the day, and she went upstairs. Two students stayed, and I gave them additional help with a new dance move. When they left, I locked the studio door, then phoned Mom and Dad from the office.

Dad answered. "Hello."

"Dad, it's Bird. How have you and Mom been doing?"

"Okay."

"Glad to hear that. Alex and I are taking the train out of New York City the second Saturday in March and will arrive in Saint Louis, Missouri, Monday around seven a.m." I hesitated to see if

Dad would offer to pick us up at the train depot in his old truck, but he didn't. "I'd like to bring my girl by. That okay with you?"

"Well, we'll be here. Stop by if you want," Dad said, then hung up.

Alex and I would need a ride from Saint Louis to Greenstone. I figured there was no use asking my brother-in-law, Drew, to pick us up, since Dad hadn't offered to. That letter I'd received about my sister's and nephew's deaths had made it clear what my family thought of me. So I called Emma Jean Johnston, my former dance partner in Greenstone, and asked her for a ride. She said her husband, John, would pick Alex and me up.

I climbed the steps and reached the landing. The smell of Campbell's chicken noodle soup was floating in the air. Alex passed me, carrying a tray with two bowls of soup, crackers, and two glasses of tea. She delivered Nadia's food, then carried the tray to her bedroom and shut the door. I went to the kitchen, hoping to find my soup on the table, but it wasn't. I took a notepad out of the junk drawer and wrote three words that filled the page: *I love you*. I tore the page out and slid it under Alex's bedroom door. Peanut butter on crackers and a glass of tea was my dinner. Then I retired to the sofa bed in the living room.

I woke up early the next morning; not having eaten much the night before, I was starving. I put on the coffee and started breakfast. Now, I was good with a broom, mop, and vacuum, and I could even unplug toilets or sinks. Cooking, well, that was Alex's department. But I had watched her make scrambled eggs with onion and green pepper. Certain Alex wouldn't be cooking me breakfast, I decided to give it a try. Besides, I thought me cooking breakfast for a change might soften her up. I took the pan out of the cupboard, the one I'd seen Alex use many times, and poured cooking oil into it. With the burner on high, I went to work with Alex's cutting board, then dumped the chopped vegetables in the grease. I cracked open six eggs and began beating them in a bowl. That's when the smell of burnt onion and green pepper got my attention, and I saw a cloud of gray smoke rising from the pan. A split second later, the smoke detector went off, transmitting a high-pitched tone that I was sure would wake Alex and Nadia, if the smell hadn't already roused them. I turned off the burner, removed the pan, and was standing on a kitchen chair removing the smoke detector's battery when Alex came running into the kitchen.

"Ty!"

I got down from the chair, and before I could say anything, Alex threw her arms around me and gave me a kiss.

After Alex calmed down, she made us breakfast. Nadia was upset about the burnt odor hovering in the air, but she was happy that the rift between Alex and me about Greenstone wasn't an issue anymore. Not as happy as me, though.

Chapter 26

A light dusting of snow was falling that second Saturday in March when Alex and I left Manhattan for Greenstone, Missouri. The pure whiteness of it seemed so cleansing, like it could wash away the woes of the world, as Alex and I entered Madison Square Garden perched on top of the underground Penn Station. We made our way below street level through the concourses, then to the train platform on the lowest level, and boarded. Alex put our bag of snacks on the floor, and our train left the station at 7:05 a.m. Eastern Standard Time. With a little over nineteen hours till our transfer at Chicago, Alex propped her head against my shoulder. In a matter of minutes, she was asleep, but two concerns wouldn't allow me slumber: Pop's health and what kind of welcome we'd get from my dad. And in truth, I dreaded the trip.

I wanted to remember Pop the way he was when I danced on that checkerboard floor in Pop's Pop and we drank cherry colas together from his soda fountain. He'd filled my otherwise dull teen life in Greenstone with excitement. Pop was old when I met him, and I'd seen firsthand that he'd had memory lapses. His handwriting in letters he'd sent to me in New York City was more proof of his deteriorating health. That image I'd seen in my dream of Pop's falling red-and-white striped canvas awning haunted me.

I listened to Alex's tranquil breathing and the *clickety-clack* of the rails, and my thoughts concerning my folks burrowed into the core of me too. I went to that place we all have where lies are useless and only truth counts, that place where you answer to yourself 'cause you must. Like a time warp, my adolescence in Greenstone played back to me. Food was on the table, clothes were on my back, and our old house with no air-conditioning was miserable hot in summer, but pleasantly warm in winter 'cause we always had plenty of coal to burn. Harsh words chipped away at me that shot rapid-fire from Dad's mouth, 'cause I wouldn't become a miner. *"You're a dreamer. A good-for-nothing-dreamer."* As I backtracked that road of my youth, I knew those hurtful times had fueled me, driven me to define myself by my own terms. And after I scraped the rough layer away from my life in Greenstone, I thought about some good times too, like when Mom and Dad bought me that old bike parked outside Dollar Shop. Every day for a week, I'd gone by the store to look at it, parked there with a "For Sale" sign attached to the handlebars. Every day, I begged them to get it for me. "My birthday's coming up," I kept saying.

My birthday arrived, and Mom had baked me a chocolate cake. We ate our meal, our piece of cake, and Dad handed me a birthday card. I figured there was five dollars in it, 'cause that was the usual. But there was no money. Times were hard. I said thank you, to be polite.

Dad wasn't one to smile often; in fact, I can count the times on one hand that he did. But that day, he smiled big enough to show the missing space where his eyetooth should have been, and then he broke out into a roaring laugh and said, "Go take a look in the barn."

There was the bike I'd seen parked outside Dollar Shop; a blue bow made from Mom's sewing ribbon was hanging from the pitted handlebars. The fenders, with their blue paint faded from sun exposure, were dented with disconnected tracks, losing their own battle with rust. Dad and I sanded and painted it. That bike meant a lot to me; the time Dad and I spent together fixing it up meant a lot to me too.

Alex shifted in her sleep; her head dropped from my shoulder and then came to rest on my upper arm. Her eyes opened and she sat up. "Can't you sleep, Ty?"

"Haven't yet. Been thinking about Greenstone. Not sure what we'll be walking into. I don't know what shape Pop'll be in. And as far as my folks, I don't expect a good reception."

"Worrying won't help," Alex said, then closed her eyes and rested her head against my arm again.

Sunday at 1:10 a.m. Central Time, our train came to a stop. Alex looked rested, but I'd been on edge, munching on snacks and listening to the man across the aisle snoring. We had a four-hour layover at the Chicago depot before we started on the final leg, five hours and thirty-six minutes to Saint Louis, Missouri.

Our train pulled into the Saint Louis depot at 10:56 a.m., ten minutes behind schedule. John Johnston was waiting for us.

The sound of John's car pulling into my folks' gravel driveway woke me up. Alex and I thanked John for the ride and got our luggage out of his car. I handed him two dollars, not enough, but what I could afford.

Alex and I got as far as the old, wooden steps, the steps I used to sit on when I wanted to mull things over. Dad stepped out onto the porch and held the door open for us. We stepped inside, and there was a moment of silence.

Dad cleared his throat and stuck out his hand "Alex. Thought that was a man's name."

"It's Alexandra. But I go by Alex, Mr. Partridge."

Then Dad turned to me with a somber stare. "Well, she's pretty."

"Yes, she is. And she's smart, an excellent dancer too."

"That so," Dad said.

The crack about Alex's name angered me. It was an example of Dad's rude nature, as was the fact that his greeting to Alex lacked essential words, like "Hello, nice to meet you." I had hoped "Bird" or "Son" would have come out of his mouth when he addressed me—even "Ty" would have suited me, though he didn't call me that when I lived there. I was surprised that the smell of pot roast wafted in the air. As a boy, I'd only known Mom to make that at Christmas. But my reunion with Dad was no surprise at all; his attitude was no different from when I lived in Greenstone. My dread of visiting him had been justified.

"Your mother'll be out shortly; she's changing her dress. Let's have a sit in the living room."

Alex and I sat on the worn-out blue sofa, the same one I knew as a young boy; Dad sat in his old rocker; the seat he'd always preferred. He clasped his hands together with his fingers interlocked and placed them in his lap, then fixed his eyes on Alex and me. I decided I had nothing more to say to him. Alex threw me that look, the one that means do something, and I knew what she expected of me, so I complied.

"Still have old Brownie, Dad?

Should have asked about my folks, I thought.

"Brownie passed shortly after you left."

"Sorry to hear that; she was a good old gal," I said, and I meant it. I used to milk her, feed her, brush her. She was the closest thing I'd had to a pet.

"There's my boy," Mom said as she entered the living room. "How about a hug?"

I stood up, took Mom by the shoulders, and gave her a peck on the cheek. She hugged me like she used to do when I was a kid, before I told her I was too old to have her make over me like that in public. But in that moment, I wasn't too old; I welcomed her embrace. Then Mom turned to Alex and gave her a lighter version of the same. That's when I noticed how much older my mother looked. Sagging eyelids gave her a tired appearance, and though the rest of her was still slender, her stomach was a roll of loose skin that hung like a pouch, making her dress tight around the middle.

"So you're Bird's girl. Hope you had a good trip," Mom said. At least her voice was the same, warm and caring.

"Yes, I am, and the train ride was fine, Mrs. Partridge."

"Now, we'll have none of that; the name's Marta. Well, bet you're both hungry. Give me a minute, and I'll have food on the table."

"I'll help," Alex said, and she followed Mom into the kitchen.

Dad averted his eyes from me, picked up the Bible on the table next to his rocking chair, and opened it where a bookmark stuck out. His eyes moved back and forth across the page over and over, and he never turned to the next page; it appeared he was reading the same passage over and over.

"Come and get it," Mom called out.

As Dad and I made our way to the kitchen, I noticed he was limping.

"Looks like you're having trouble walking," I said.

"Been laid up a bit. Took a fall last week, and my knee gave out."

"Sorry to hear that, Dad, hope you heal up real quick."

I'd always thought his back would go first. That was the usual way it went with miners.

Mom and Alex looked like they were hitting it off. Alex was putting a big bowl of mashed potatoes on the table next to a salad, and the homemade cornbread and sliced roast beef surrounded by cooked carrots made the meal a feast. Grandma's china, used only on special occasions, was on the table too. Such meals in the Partridge family were rare. My parents sat in their usual places. I pulled out what used to be Allison's chair for Alex, then sat down in my old spot. Dad fixed his eyes on Alex.

"Start those potatoes, Alex," Mom said.

"Everything looks delicious," I said.

With our plates filled with food, we began to eat. Dad's eyes remained focused across the table on Alex, but I don't think it was her he saw. His anger and sorrow had further damaged his broken-down body; he looked ten years older than he was.

Alex stared at my grandmother's plate, stabbing the tines of her fork into the roast beef.

I shoveled in a forkful of meat, chewed and chewed, tearing and grinding it. I had words I wanted to say to my dad, but they were words I wouldn't say in front of Alex and Mom. So I swallowed the meat, bad words, and my grief over Allison's death. I swallowed the whole lump.

A trail of mascara ran down Alex's cheek. "On top of dealing with Allison's and Jacob's deaths, Ty had to deal with missing their funerals. Why would you do that to him? Because he didn't become a miner? Because he didn't write for a few weeks? Our employer's sick; we've been running her dance studio." Alex got up. "Ty, where's the bathroom?"

"Down the hall on the right."

Mom rested her elbows on the table and buried her face in her hands. Dad was staring at Allison's chair, his lined face a clutter of emotions. It occurred to me that I should get Alex and leave. But I had questions I wanted answered. *Why's he treating me like an outsider? And what gives him the right to be rude to Alex?* I thought. But one question I should have asked long ago boiled up to the surface. And it roared out of me. "Don't you want me to be *happy*, Dad?"

He got up from the kitchen table. Thinking Dad's destination might be the bathroom, I followed him and stopped in the hall, ready to step in should he start in on Alex. His back to me, Dad's shoulders slumped and his head hung; he was listening to Alex cry. Then he tapped on the bathroom door. "Alex ... come on out of there. Please."

Alex stopped crying, and I heard her turn on the faucet. "Mr. Partridge, tell Ty I'm ready to leave."

"Marta and I don't want you to leave. We want to finish our meal, visit, and get to know you and our son. I've failed Bird as a father. All I've ever known is mining, and I tried to shove it down his throat. That was wrong. Come on out; I'm begging, and I ain't ever begged for nothing in my life."

I shifted my weight. The floor creaked, and Dad turned around. "Son."

The submissive sound of Dad's voice froze me to the spot where I stood. And "son" touched me in a spot that I thought he wasn't capable of reaching out to.

Mom made her way to the hallway. "Bird, Charles and I want to make things right; ask Alex to come out of the bathroom."

The bathroom door opened with a squeak; Alex came out and stood next to me. "That's why we came here, Ty, to make things right, to be family, isn't it?"

I followed Alex and Mom into the living room; Dad did too. Mom took the overstuffed chair, and Alex sat next to me on the couch. Dad settled in his rocker and picked up his Bible from the table. He opened it where the marker stuck out and began to read silently.

When I lived in Greenstone, that Bible was always on the table next to Dad's rocking chair, but I'd never seen him open it. He'd never been much of the churchgoing type, though I thought he believed in God. I was angry, but I needed to start up a civil conversation, and I guess my curiosity about the marked place in that Bible felt as good a place to start as any. "You been reading the Bible a bit, Dad? Looks like you found a particular passage you like."

"Been trying to figure out how to be a good father. Too late where Allison's concerned. Thought maybe I could work toward it for you. Maybe after how I acted, all I've said, maybe you won't give me a chance."

While the words *sorry* or *forgive me* hadn't come out of Dad's mouth, I realized this was as close to an apology as he could get. And the fact that he had begged Alex to come out of the bathroom was as humble as I'd ever seen him. So I figured I'd meet him halfway.

"I've grown up, Dad, come to realize some things. I didn't appreciate the hard work you did as a miner, but I should have; it kept a roof over my head. I refused to follow in your steps 'cause mining wasn't right for me. After Pop taught me to swing dance, I knew I wanted to be a professional dancer. So I'm not sorry I went to New York City, but I am sorry I left on bad terms with you. Sorry I didn't tell Mom, Allison, you, good-bye. Sorry I got too busy working at The Silver Slipper to take time to write. I came back here to say something, something I've had plenty of time to think about: we've both made mistakes along the way. But we're still family. Where I live or that I'm a dancer doesn't change that."

Mom was wringing her hands and trying not to cry. "Charles, you say what we talked about, say what you told me you would."

Dad let out a deep breath. "You left Greenstone, and I didn't expect to see you again. And then Allison and my grandson died. I was losing my family. I shouldn't have spouted off to you and Alex; I'm glad you came to visit. Trying to force you into mining wasn't right; I know that now. Please, forgive me. Both of you."

Dad's hard shell had melted away. Exposed was a man that I'd never known, a man who would repent for his wrongdoings. And like when I was that boy, Bird, whose dad bought him a bike for his birthday, who painted that old bike to make it the best he could offer his son, I felt my father's love.

Later that day, I dusted off my old bike, which was still stored in my folks' barn, and visited my sister's grave. Alone. Alex had offered to go with me, but there were things I had to get off my chest, things I needed to unload, and my male ego told me to do it by myself.

The cemetery looked the same as when I'd left Greenstone, full of small, drab, concrete markers with block-style printing. Folks living there called them tombstones. I found Allison's and her stillborn baby, Jacob's, side-by-side, the hard soil dry and cracked, lifeless too.

My eyes were fixed on the miserable burial site, unsuitable for my sweet sister and nephew. A harsh March wind was blowing. My only companions, silence and sorrow, sifted into me, and all I wished for was to once again hear my sister's voice.

"Allison Jean, your big brother, Bird, is here," I cried out, as if I expected a reply.

The image of her smile, shy, but genuine, her light-brown eyes that always made me feel loved, and her petite build, so unlike mine, revisited me. My eyes flooded with tears and my whole body shook with grief. *What game am I playing? You're dead.* I thought. I dropped to my knees in front of her marker and ran my fingers across the engraved letters, feeling the rough groves of the etching on that gray slab, not fit to bear her name. *But Allison, there are things I have to say,* I thought.

"You never caused problems, never made Mom cry or Dad angry, like I did. And you *didn't snitch* about me taking Pop's dance lessons. Thank you, Allison; Dad would've stopped me from taking them, and I wouldn't have become a dancer.

"And I should have told you good-bye before I left for New York City. But Dad would have thrown a fit about me leaving Greenstone, and I didn't want that. And your funeral, I'd have been there, but I didn't know ... Drew wrote to me *after* you were buried. Forgive me, Allison, please. I wasn't a good brother."

I got up from my knees, wiped my face with my shirt, and stared at the hard ground where my younger sister and my nephew had been put to rest. "Wish I'd had the chance to know you, Jacob." I stood there a long time and then finally said,

"Good-bye, Allison Jean and Jacob Drew Proffit; I love you and always will."

When I left the cemetery that Sunday, my heart spoke to me, and I knew what my sister would want me to do. I rode my old bike to Drew's house and saw his truck parked in the driveway. No one came when I knocked on the front door, so I knocked again and waited. *He doesn't want to see me*, I thought and turned to leave. I heard the door open and turned around; a little girl with light-brown eyes and Allison's smile was standing next to my brother-in-law.

"Hannah," I said. "I finally get to see you. You look just like your mom." I squatted and hugged her, trying in vain not to shed tears.

Drew put his hand on my shoulder. "She does," he said. "Come in."

The next day, I gave Alex a tour of the town I grew up in. We walked hand-in-hand down Main Street. The display window at the Dollar Shop had fallen prey to what looked like some kid's idea of entertainment, a BB gun. A spider's web of cracks rippled out from the bull's-eye hole, distorting what I guessed to be large plastic bottles of some cleaning supply mounted on crates. And the roof of Burt's Grocery, with its missing shingles, looked like it had mange. I figured spring tornadoes were to blame.

My folks had told Alex and me that Burt Brown had died from a heart attack and that Mrs. Brown said Jack, her son, would take over the grocery business. It crossed my mind that the lard Mrs. Brown put in those bakery goods at their store might have contributed to Burt's early demise. All the shops on Main Street had deteriorated more since I'd left Greenstone, except one. The building that used to be Pop's soda-fountain shop had undergone renovation. The rickety red-and-white striped canvas awning that used to hang down on one side, leaning like it would fall if a gust of wind came along, was gone.

Mortar had been replaced between the old bricks to support a new awning that was tan-color. The red-neon "Pop's Pop" sign that used to flicker in the front picture window was gone too, and dark-blue drapes covered that window facing Main Street.

"This used to be the soda-fountain shop, Pop's Pop, Alex. It's where I learned to swing dance, but it looks different now."

I gave the new white steel door a hard rap, hoping our visit with Pop would be enjoyable. A pleasant-looking woman with short, gray hair opened the door.

"Hi, I'm Emily. Come in, Alex and Ty; Dad and I just finished lunch."

Pop had told me that his daughter, Emily, hadn't visited him after her mother died. I had painted a harsh picture of her, but the woman standing before me gave me a different vibe.

The black-and-white tiles I had danced across and thought of as a checkerboard when I lived in Greenstone were covered with dark-blue carpeting. The soda-fountain bar, the red stools with chrome legs, and the pictures—Elvis's picture—were gone too.

"Please, have a seat," Emily said and motioned to two chairs around the kitchen table. Pop was secured to his chair by a plastic strap around his waist.

I took the chair to Pop's right, and Alex sat down next to me. Emily sat down to Pop's left, and then pushed his soup bowl to the center of the table. "Friends came to visit, Dad."

"Family," I said. "We're family."

I put my hand on Pop's shoulder. His eyes remained focused on the bowl Emily had moved. "Pop, this is my girl, Alex."

All that remained of Pop's white hair was a feathery half circle on the lower back half of his head. He turned toward me, and his cloudy eyes peered at me.

"Emily, can he see me?"

"Yes. It's not his sight."

"Pop, it's Bird. You taught me to dance. You took Emma Jean and me to Wakefield, Missouri, to the dance contest, and we won.

We won, Pop." I wrapped my arms around Pop's neck and hugged him. Hugged what was left of him. Then I turned to Alex. "He doesn't remember me."

Alex scooted her chair up against mine and rested her head on my shoulder.

No glimmer of mischief was left in Pop's eyes, no smile. No recognition from the man who had treated me like his son.

"I'm sorry," Emily said. "When you called and said you were coming to visit, I should have been clearer about Dad's condition. His dementia has progressed to the point that sometimes he doesn't even know me, and I'm with him day in, day out."

I knew that Pop had had memory problems before I left Greenstone. And I'd seen his handwriting getting worse each time I received one of his letters. But I think I had blocked out the possibility that one day he wouldn't remember me.

"Thank you for taking such good care of him," I said to Emily. "Let's get going, Alex."

Alex and I got to the door. I stopped to take one last look at Pop, certain it was the last time I'd see him alive. "Good-bye, Pop," I said. To my surprise, he twisted in his chair the best that he could, strapped in like he was. He raised his hand, and I believe he tried to wave.

I'd brought a camera and had planned to ask Emily to take a picture of Pop, Alex, and me together. Thought I'd have that picture to carry with me in my wallet. But I changed my mind. Secure in my memory was a picture of Pop; it was the man Bird knew, the Pop that had taught Bird he shouldn't be afraid to go after what he wanted. And that's the picture I left with.

Alex and I spent the remainder of our time in Greenstone, visiting with my mom and dad. When they dropped us off at the Saint Louis train station, I promised them that I'd write often and that Alex and I would look forward to their letters too.

Chapter 27

I tapped on Nadia's bedroom door.

"We're home," Alex said.

"Come in," Nadia said. "Let's have a look at you two."

Margaret was sitting in a chair next to Nadia's bed. A spread of three cards, all fours, was lying on the bed in front of her. She looked to be a worthy opponent at playing rummy. "Well, you're both in one piece. No battle scars from your Dad," Margaret said.

"Now, you said you'd keep things to yourself," Nadia scolded.

"It's okay you told Margaret," I said. "Things started out rocky, but everything worked out."

"Well, good," Nadia said, a big smile on her face. "And how's Pop?"

Nadia seemed to be in good spirits, and I didn't want bad news to spoil her good mood, so I sidestepped her question. "Pop couldn't ask for a better daughter than Emily; he's in good hands."

"That's wonderful. It's good news all around, then. Margaret and I have found we have much in common. She has a two-bedroom home and would like to have a tenant. She and I have worked out agreeable terms for her to be my caretaker. She's been delightful company while you were away. Not that the two of you aren't, understand. You're both exceptional young people.

But you're young; that's my point. You shouldn't be tied down with an old arthritic, like me."

"You haven't tied us down," Alex said.

"No, not at all," I said. "You gave us a roof over our heads, a job. We're in debt to you."

"Nonsense. You're talented, smart. The two of you have surpassed what I was able to accomplish with the business. That's why I want to give you and Alex the first chance to purchase The Silver Slipper."

The dream Alex and I had talked about, owning our own dance studio, was dangling before our noses. I should have been filled with excitement, but instead, my stomach sickened with frustration.

"Nadia, that's nice of you, but we don't have enough money to consider buying the dance studio."

"I'm old, Ty, but I'm not senile. I knew as much before I offered. You have not let me specify the terms for purchase. May I finish my proposal?"

"We can at least listen," I said to Alex. She nodded in agreement.

"These are my terms. If you can not comply with what I wish, then I must advertise my property. The Silver Slipper must not be renamed, nor will you allow it to become shabby. I might visit now and then to watch dance classes, no doubt in a wheelchair. Do you have any problem with my terms so far?"

Alex and I both shook our heads no.

"Good. Now comes the part you seem to be worried about: the cost. The cost to Miss Alexandra Carbone and Mr. Ty Partridge shall be one dollar each. This is agreeable?"

Speechless, I turned to Alex. Her expression showed she was stunned too.

"You do not agree to this price?"

"We do," I said, "but—"

"Alex, do you agree to be co-owner with Ty?" Nadia said. "Help him as you have since I became ill?"

"Yes ... of course, but you can't afford to give the studio away."

"I have not been honest with the two of you. When I lived in Russia, one of the republics of the Soviet Union, my financial situation was good. But when I arrived in the United States, I had little money. I struggled to survive in New York City, like Ty did before he started working at The Silver Slipper. But after my parents passed, the large inheritance I received allowed me to quit my dreadful job and purchase my dance studio, which I built into a lucrative business. Yet, I was a woman, running a business in a foreign country with no one to lean on, no one to trust. I pretended to be a woman of meager means, then, to protect my wealth, and I continued to do the same with the two of you. But you proved to be worthy of my trust. I hope you know that I love you as if you were my children. It would please me to no end to give this studio to the two of you. Now, say you accept; I won't take no for an answer."

As soon as Alex and I got done hugging Nadia and thanking her for all she'd done for us, I gave Mom and Dad a call. "Guess what," I said to Mom when she answered the phone, "Alex and I are buying The Silver Slipper."

Chapter 28

Nadia had moved in with Margaret, and The Silver Slipper officially belonged to Alex and me. With the buckets full of rain that April brought, extra people poured into our studio wanting to learn to dance. Getting a taste of solid income suited Alex and me. The studio's business had grown, but it had the potential to grow more; the problem was, we needed another ballroom. I convinced Alex that the large ballroom we had could be divided into two teaching areas, allowing two lessons to be given at the same time. The construction of a wall with entrance to a second ballroom was completed by the end of the month, and Alex and I hired two young employees, Jennifer and James, to teach in the second ballroom. Their financial situation hadn't allowed them to finish their course work at Adelphi University of Performing Arts, but they had enough dance background that I felt confident Alex and I could teach them to be good instructors. I came to realize what I'd put Nadia through when she trained me.

It was May 19 of 1972. I was two days short of turning twenty-two. Alex was already twenty-three.

Alex and I had finished our last lesson for the day, contemporary dance. We sat down on the studio floor to take off our shoes. "Alex, know what I want for my birthday?"

"New dance shoes?"

"Not what I had in mind, but good guess; my soles *are* worn." I had looked forward to this moment for so long, yet my stomach was quivering as I reached inside my pocket and handed Alex a black velvet ring box. "What I'd like is for you to be my wife. Will you?"

"Yes. Yes, of course I will," she said, then opened it.

I slipped the small diamond engagement ring on Alex's finger, and then we kissed. And with the woman I loved in my arms, I savored the moment and thought about all the future pleasures we'd know as man and wife.

"It's beautiful, Ty," Alex said, stretching the long-*i* sound, as usual.

I always liked the way she pronounced my name, and as always, kissing her made me want *more. Just so you don't expect a long engagement,* I thought. *I'm tired of waiting.*

"We'll visit our folks right away and tell them we're getting married."

"That would be best," Alex said, then giggled. "My parents are very traditional. My father will expect you to ask for my hand in marriage. But he may not give his blessing."

"Then for their benefit, I'll ask you again; I'll get down on one knee, like I've seen in the movies. Just don't change your answer."

"Don't worry, Ty. You're locked in. But the dance studio. How can we leave?"

"We won't be gone long. I'll have James and Jennifer split up to cover both ballrooms. I trust James to open and close the studio. Something this important can't be said over the phone. Besides, I've never met your parents. And with a last name like Carbone, I might be marrying into the Mafia. I might back out."

Alex laughed. "Like I said, you're locked in."

Chapter 29

Bruno did not give his blessing when I asked for Alex's hand in marriage, 'cause I wasn't and never would be Italian. He insisted that Alex and I be engaged at least a year so we were *positive* we wanted to spend the rest of our lives together. "The Catholic Church does not sanction divorce," Bruno said. I objected. Bruno wasn't concerned about the Church. He had another motive. A long engagement would give him time to convince Alex that I wasn't right for her. But Alex pleaded with me to honor Bruno's wish. She said Bruno would never accept me as his son-in-law if I didn't. I said a few choice words under my breath, but I agreed to wait to get married.

On June 9 of 1973, Alex and I were married at Saint Michael's, the church she attended when she lived with her parents in Saint Louis, Missouri. The sunshine penetrating the stained-glass windows gave the illusion that emeralds, rubies, and sapphires were dancing on Alex's wedding gown. And I think Alex could have floated down the aisle like an angel if Bruno hadn't held onto her arm so tight. When it came time for me to take Alex's arm, Bruno's eyes hardened, and a twitch aggravated his left eye. I didn't think he was going to give her up.

Our vows completed, the priest pronounced us man and wife. I kissed Alex, and then we began our walk down the aisle. Mom and Dad, Drew, and my niece, Hannah, smiled, confirming my worth as a Partridge. And though the woman who'd taken me under her wing and mentored me, Nadia, had entered the church in a wheelchair, her new arthritis medication enabled her to sit in a pew. She and her faithful caretaker, Margaret, smiled as they dabbed at their eyes with embroidered handkerchiefs.

The bride's side of the aisle was not so congenial. Bruno's thick neck was crimson, as was his face, and that twitch in his eye had picked up its pace. A black river of mascara ran from the corner of one of Michelle's eyes to her cheekbone, and her solemn expression was more suited to a funeral. Alex's brother, Marco, waved as we walked by, and Bruno threw him a harsh look.

Two of my family members were absent, but I felt their presence. I'm certain my sister, Allison, was watching from heaven, smiling about the life I had made for myself, celebrating my renewed place as a Partridge, and delighted I got to know her daughter, Hannah. And though I knew I'd been erased from Pop's memory, I knew what the Pop from earlier years would have said: "You and Alex dance one for me."

Our wedding dinner was held at my in-laws' restaurant, Taste of Italian in Saint Louis, Missouri, on "the Hill," in the Italian section of restaurants. It was Saturday night; the place was buzzing with customers. Bruno had the hostess show us to a dining room secluded from the general public.

Two waiters wearing black slacks and vests and starched white shirts filled our water glasses, then poured each of us a glass of wine. The same two hurried back to the kitchen and returned with salads and baskets of garlic bread.

"Enjoy," Bruno said.

After we finished our salad, a platter with lasagna, cannelloni, and Italian sausage was served to each of us.

"Service is excellent. Best you find anywhere," Bruno said, directing his remarks to my folks. "Say, I hear you are a coal miner, Mr. Partridge. Is such dirty work."

"The food's delicious," Mom said. Dad forced a smile and nodded. I was grateful my folks didn't lash out at Bruno for his cutting remark.

Then Bruno turned to me. "My restaurant is very lucrative business, Mr. Ty Partridge."

Dinner conversation became sparser than fruit trees in a desert. After the wedding cake was served, Alex and I opened our gifts, which were all envelopes containing money, exactly what I had hoped for.

"We appreciate everyone attending our wedding, and thank you for the gifts," Alex said.

"Yeah, thanks," I said, then turned to Bruno and Michelle Carbone. "Thanks for providing the meal."

"You're welcome," Michelle said.

Bruno sneered and made no reply.

He's the reason Alex left Missouri and moved to New York, I thought.

We had a reservation at the Hilton Hotel by Lambert-Saint Louis International Airport. Though it was early and we weren't to fly out of Saint Louis until 1:00 p.m. the next day, I was ready to leave Bruno's lucrative restaurant, and I knew Alex was too.

"My folks offered to drive Alex and me to our hotel, so maybe we'd better get going."

Dad nodded yes.

"Sorry about the way my dad acted tonight," Alex said, "and thanks for the ride to our hotel, Mr. and Mrs. Partridge."

"No need to apologize," Mom said. "And like I said before, none of that Mr. and Mrs. business; call us Marta and Charles."

I unloaded our suitcase from the truck. Alex and I waved good-bye as Dad and Mom drove out of the hotel's parking lot.

A doorman dressed in a white shirt, black slacks, and vest held the door open for Alex and me when we entered the hotel. Hanging from the ceiling was a chandelier that lit the lobby. Alex and I walked across the polished black-marble floor to the white-marble reservation desk that had two large gold vases filled with red roses sitting on it. A gold oval mirror hung on the red-painted wall behind the desk. I was glad we'd received money as wedding gifts.

The woman standing behind the desk was wearing a red suit. The tag on her jacket read "Sarah." "Good evening; do you have a reservation?"

"Yes. Mr. and Mrs. Ty Partridge. I asked for the honeymoon suite," I said.

"Congratulations. Here's your room key, and I'll call a bellhop for your luggage."

"Thank you," I said.

Sarah hit a bell sitting on the desk. A bellhop dressed the same as the doorman showed up and took our suitcase from me.

"Take Mr. and Mrs. Partridge to room 1202, George," Sarah said.

Alex and I followed George to an elevator.

"After you," the bellhop said.

The elevator stopped on the twelfth floor. George took us to our room, opened the door, and sat our suitcase inside. He stepped back out into the hallway and hesitated.

"Oh, here," I said, and then handed him a dollar bill. He gave me an odd smile and then left.

I grabbed hold of Alex's arm to keep her from entering our honeymoon suite, then embraced her small waist and pulled her to me. She wrapped her arms around my neck; our lips met and then locked in a long, passionate kiss. With our bodies pressed together, my heart raced with anticipation, and the sensation that we were melting into each other—becoming one—struck me. I had kissed her many times before, but this one was *special*; it was the lead-up to what was yet to come. Alex gently released her arms that were wrapped around my neck and removed her lips from mine. I was eager, and my heart was still racing. And I hoped that the book I'd read on lovemaking would serve me well.

"Let's get in the room," I said. "Ready to be carried over the threshold, Mrs. Partridge?"

Chapter 30

With the excitement of our wedding behind us, Alex and I were still learning about each other, and we had a few things to get ironed out. Most were minor issues, but for me, there was one major one. I didn't like Alex's habit of staying up till eleven-thirty every night. I'd be in bed by ten-thirty, lying awake, waiting for *her* to come to bed, and when she finally did, her head hit the pillow and she conked out. Frustrated, I laid my cards on the table one night and told her my *motive* for wanting her to go to bed earlier. Once Alex understood, we were able to work out a deal. She agreed to be in bed by ten-thirty three nights a week, and I promised I wouldn't hassle her about the other four. And that suited me.

That August, we continued working Monday through Saturday, as did our two dance instructors, Jennifer and James. Though we were busy, I kept my pledge and corresponded with my family in Greenstone, Missouri, on a regular basis. I also wrote my in-laws in Saint Louis, hoping Bruno would change his opinion of me and accept me as his non-Italian son-in-law.

The ninth of December, snowflakes the size of gumdrops floated down, zigzagging like they were intoxicated. I wanted nothing more than to finish our 5:00 p.m. dance lesson and curl up in bed with Alex to snuggle. But she said it was our six-month anniversary, and she had a special evening planned.

At six o'clock, Alex hurried upstairs to the master bathroom to "get ready," as she put it, and told me to shower in the hall bathroom. I waited for our dance students to leave and then locked the studio door.

Now showered and dressed, I was splashing on cologne when I heard the doorbell. I made my way to the top of the stairs. Alex had the front door open, and food was being delivered. I figured I wasn't supposed to see what I was seeing, so I hurried back to the hall bathroom and closed the door. I heard Alex climb the steps and walk down the hall to the kitchen.

Then, again, in the hallway, Alex called out, "Ty, are you dressed yet? Everything's ready."

When I got to the kitchen, a large, red candle on the table was providing the only light. A white tablecloth I hadn't seen before and two plates, also new, were filled with lobster and scallops bathed in butter. "Very romantic," I said.

"The food's from Seven Seas. Let's sit down."

What did this cost? I thought. "They deliver?"

"No, but Marty from our advanced swing class works there. It was a favor."

"Oh. It looks great, but why didn't we eat at the restaurant?"

"Because," Alex said, "it wouldn't be the same. I have a special gift for you; I wanted us to be at home."

That the expensive meal wasn't the "special gift" gave me cause to worry I had shot low. I put the romantic card that I had hurriedly made for Alex on the table. "Hope you didn't go overboard."

"Hope not." Alex opened my card and gave me one of her special smiles.

We'd only been married six months. Why Alex was making a big deal out of it had me stumped, but I decided to play along. "You want me to guess what the gift is, right?"

"Well, you could, but dinner might get cold," Alex said. She put her arms around my neck and pulled me toward her and then whispered in my ear, "We're having a baby."

Wasn't ready for that, I thought, but I said, "Alex, that's great," and gave my wife a kiss.

After we ate our meal, Alex called Michelle and Bruno and told them the good news. Michelle said she was looking forward to becoming a grandmother, and Bruno, according to Alex, got so choked up about our little "bambino" that he had to get off the phone. That bit of news was music to my ears. I figured Bruno was unthawing.

My folks, Drew, Hannah, Nadia, and Margaret were all surprised and excited for us. When I called Pop, as I expected, his daughter, Emily, answered the phone. I asked her to tell Pop that Alex and I were having a baby.

"I will," Emily said, "but you know how he is."

"Yes, I know, but Pop's family."

The fledgling Pop had known was erased from his memory. And in truth, that young boy from Greenstone who Pop had taught to dance no longer existed. A man with a wife, a business, and a child on the way, that's who I was.

"Please let me know ... if something happens," I said to Emily. "And thank you for looking after Pop. I'll keep in touch." I hung up the phone, an empty feeling lingering inside me, as though Pop's demise was already a reality.

Chapter 31

Icicles hung from the studio's guttering like stalactites, and crystals of ice framing the windows took on hues of blue from strings of lights I had hung. A balsam fir in the foyer, complete with silver tinsel, white twinkling lights, and red ornaments announced the coming of Christmas.

By word of mouth, news had spread that our studio was the place to learn to dance, and our income had increased again. With our six-week session of dance classes finishing up, I decided that I'd only schedule Jennifer and James for Saturday classes. I didn't like it that one of the ballrooms wouldn't be utilized, but I felt it was important for my wife and me to have our Saturdays free for leisure time together before our baby was born.

We had plenty of time to prepare for the arrival of our baby, but Alex wouldn't give in to a day of lazying around that first Saturday we had off. She was like a mother bird building her nest twig by twig, shaping it for our baby's arrival. So we took the subway and went shopping, destination Schneider's Furniture off Sixth Avenue on West Twenty-Fifth Street.

A salesman showed Alex and me two floors of baby furniture. By the time we got through those mazes, we'd picked out a crib, dresser, changing table, hamper, baby chair, and one of those swings that had to be cranked up every fifteen minutes. A cash-induced headache hit me when I paid the bill. As we exited Schneider's, Alex said, "Now we need to buy sheets, a diaper bag, a little bathtub—"

"Another day," I said. "We have plenty of time."

The next day, Alex decided we'd paint what used to be her bedroom a pale yellow. That color wouldn't ever be my choice, but according to my wife, it was a neutral color for a nursery. We'd finished painting and were picking up the drop cloths. It seemed a good time for me to approach a topic that had been on my mind.

"Alex, I've been thinking, we haven't talked about what we'll call our baby. Shouldn't we have a boy's and girl's name in mind?"

"Nope. After the baby is born, we can decide."

Then Alex picked up the paint can and handed it to me. "Find a place to store that and wash the brushes, and I'll fix lunch. I want something salty; hope I didn't eat all the potato chips."

As promised, Schneider's delivered our baby furniture Monday morning at 8:00 a.m., so we'd be able to start our first dance class at 9:00. The crib, dresser, and changing table fit fine in the nursery, but the baby chair just barely fit in a nook of the small kitchen. The swing went in the living room. Our small apartment above the studio seemed to be shrinking.

Chapter 32

Christmas morning arrived, as did Alex's morning sickness. While on the phone wishing her parents and brother a Merry Christmas, the urge to vomit hit her for the third time. She handed me the phone and ran for the bathroom. I filled Michelle in and reassured her that I had things under control. That's when I heard Bruno in the background. "Ty better not have my little girl dancing."

"Michelle, tell Bruno my wife isn't dancing," I said, not qualifying the particulars, that Alex's morning sickness had just terminated it. I asked my mother-in-law if they'd received the gifts Alex and I had sent, then cordially got off the phone and made my way to the bathroom. Alex was kneeling with her head hung over the toilet, her body convulsing from dry heaves. As much as I hated to admit it, my father-in-law was right; a good husband wouldn't have had his pregnant wife dancing.

Alex had given me a play-by-play on how to decorate the ham with pineapple, maraschino cherries, and brown sugar. She'd made potato salad the night before, and under her direction, I managed to make baked beans and a lettuce salad. In went the ham at 11:00 a.m. and out it came at 2:00 p.m. I was right on schedule. Nadia walked in using a cane, Margaret alongside her with a tray of cookies. We hadn't seen Nadia for two months due to her doctor visits and physical therapy, and her marked improvement was a surprise.

Two bouts of nausea sent Alex to the bathroom during our Christmas meal. The second time she returned to us, she removed her plate from the table before sitting down. "Can't stand to smell it."

I'd imagined pregnancy as nothing more than nine months of blissful anticipation; it hadn't occurred to me that having a baby carried disagreeable consequences.

Dinner over, Alex and Nadia put on a Christmas record and settled in the living room. After Margaret and I washed the dishes, we joined them.

"Santa left a little something for our future grandchild," Nadia said and pointed to a large box I'd seen Margaret carry into the living room.

Alex unwrapped the large box. "Oh, Ty. A stroller."

"A sturdy one," Margaret said. "Those lightweight ones don't last."

"It's great," Alex said and got up to give Nadia and Margaret hugs.

"Yeah, thanks," I said.

"You kids will need a changing table," Nadia said. "Margaret and I want to make that part of our gift, but we thought it best if you picked that out."

"Thanks, but we bought one. The stroller's plenty," Alex said.

"Well, you're set then, but maybe I can give you a bit of advice," Nadia said and laughed. "If it's a boy, cover his private part when you're changing his diaper; otherwise, you may get christened."

Nadia's recommendation took me by surprise. She'd been close-lipped about her life before coming to America. Except for telling Alex and me that her Russian parents left her inheritance, enabling her to purchase The Silver Slipper, Nadia's life in the Union of Soviet Socialist Republics was a blank page. An inquisitive itch made me wonder if she had cared for a younger brother or nephew before I got to know her.

"It sounds like you've been hosed before, Nadia," I said.

Her face took on an odd expression.

She hesitated and then said, "No, I just think that a cold draft could prompt such an incident."

"And if the baby draws up its legs and cries, like my Theodore used to, it has gas," Margaret chimed in.

So the afternoon went, with this tidbit and that from Grandmas Nadia and Margaret. With Mom and Michelle in Missouri, it was good to know our former employer and her caretaker would be quick to fill their shoes. And at least Margaret had experience caring for an infant. Around 5:00 p.m., Nadia announced it was time for her and Margaret to go home. Nadia needed her arthritis medication, and their cat, Matilda, needed to be fed.

"Wait," I said, and handed each one an envelope. "We got you guys something too."

Nadia opened hers first. "Tickets to the ballet; you know how I love the dance. Thank you."

"You kids are so good to us," Margaret said when she opened hers.

While my wife rested, I called to wish my folks in Greenstone Merry Christmas. Mom told me that Hannah had come down with the flu the day before, so chicken noodle soup was their Christmas dinner.

"Sorry to hear that," I said. "Alex didn't enjoy Christmas dinner either; she started in with morning sickness today."

"Have her suck on peppermint candy. Helped me," Mom said.

"We'll try that. If it doesn't work, I'll call the doctor."

"Such a good husband."

I wasn't so sure about that; all I was sure of was that I was feeling my way through foreign territory.

"Appreciated the card. But the money, that was too much," Mom said.

"No, not enough. Alex thought those embroidered pillowcases you sent were the prettiest she's ever seen. Thank you. There's someone else I want to call and wish Merry Christmas, so I'd better go. I love you and Dad. Have a Merry Christmas."

"I love you too, Son. Dad wants to say something before you hang up."

"Bird, wanna wish you and Alex a Merry Christmas. Tell Alex to take care; Marta and I are praying for her and the baby."

"I'll tell her, Dad. How are you doing?"

"Just the regular aches and pains. Old age, that's all."

Coal mining, I thought. "Naw, you're still in your prime."

"That's stretching it a bit, Son."

"Well, I better get going. Merry Christmas, Dad." I hung up the phone. I was a long way from Greenstone, but closer to Dad than when I lived there.

My final call that day put a damper on the season with a blanket of sadness.

"Hello," Pop's daughter said.

"Hi, Emily; it's Ty. Called to wish Pop a Merry Christmas."

"Ty, I appreciate that you think so much of Dad, but he won't know who's speaking to him."

"I know, but I want to tell him anyway."

"All right. Hold on a minute," Emily said. Then, "Okay, I've got the phone to Dad's ear."

"Merry Christmas, Pop. This is Ty. You mostly called me Bird, though. Remember? Wish I could be there, visit with you, but I'm too far away." But I knew had I been right beside him, he'd still have been out of reach. "I think about our good times together, about all you did for me. Remembering those times makes me smile."

A deep sigh came through the receiver. I wanted to say more, wanted something I said to put Pop back in touch with me, to bring back the man Bird knew, but I knew my effort was futile. "You sound tired; I'll call back another time. Bye, Pop."

Emily got back on the phone. "The doctor told me Dad can't hang on much longer."

"I hate to hear that. You'll call, won't you?"

"I will," Emily said.

I hung up the phone, hoping that when God took Pop to heaven, He'd make his trip easy; Pop had suffered enough.

Chapter 33

Class size for the new six-week session of dance lessons at The Silver Slipper had dropped drastically. Many of our former students' New Year's resolutions must have been to tighten their belts after emptying their pockets for Christmas gifts. Enrollment for all levels of swing dance was down, as was beginning and intermediate ballet. Just three students were taking the contemporary-dance class. And though ballroom classes had the largest enrollment numbers, they were still 25 percent less than that of the previous session.

Alex had again sat on a chair in the ballroom and given verbal directions to our dance students while I taught. She approached me after the last class of the day. Her strained facial expression spoke to me.

"Ty, we have a baby on the way, bills to pay. What are we going to do?"

"All businesses experience slumps; we'll bounce back."

But I was worried. I had to get into our savings to pay some of the bills. If the next six-week dance session had low enrollment, I figured I might have to cancel some classes and lay off our dance instructors, James and Jennifer. Both lived in rundown apartment buildings and barely scraped by as it was. I knew what that was like. As if that wasn't enough, what worried me most was how I'd pay the hospital bill when it came time for Alex to deliver our baby. But I was head of the household; it was my responsibility to figure things out.

"Everything will be okay," I said, thinking it might not.

By March, Alex's morning sickness was gone, but as her belly got larger, the responsibility of becoming a father grew in my mind. Our small apartment above the dance studio wasn't an ideal place to raise a child; we needed more living space. But a larger apartment was out of the question. Another low enrollment for dance classes that February had made our financial situation worse. Still dipping into the little savings Alex and I had left, I kept our instructors, hoping that enrollment for the April session would be better, knowing that if it wasn't, the savings Alex and I had left would be gone. And The Silver Slipper would be closed.

While I thought it was too early, my wife signed us up for two weeks of Lamaze classes at Coler Memorial Hospital. We spent our evenings with couples much further along in their pregnancies, practicing the prescribed breathing technique on a mat. I wanted to be a good breathing coach for Alex, but I was distracted. Paying the ob-gyn and hospital bill when Alex delivered was a concern. Alex's doctor visits and expenses for running The Silver Slipper got paid, but we were chipping away at our savings. Our once-lucrative business seemed like a figment of my imagination. I was worried about holding onto The Silver Slipper that was both our business and our home.

Chapter 34

April erased nature's dormant state and left its mark of spring, a thriving lush green. As if former students had been released from hibernation, they returned to The Silver Slipper, and new dance students flooded in. Our classes filled to capacity for the next six-week session, and Alex and I again had financial security. That we were able to keep our instructors, James and Jennifer, was a relief too.

At Alex's appointment in May, I spoke up and asked the obstetrician, Dr. Stromberg, a question.

"Doctor, my mom said when she was pregnant, she carried me low and in front and craved salty foods. And that's how she knew she'd have a boy. Alex is carrying that way too, and she sure likes potato chips. You think *we'll* have a boy?"

"Just a minute," Alex said. "I'm the one who's put on fourteen pounds, and I don't want to know the sex of our baby until it's born. That's supposed to be a surprise."

Dr. Stromberg laughed. "Ty, your mother had a 50 percent chance of guessing right that she was carrying a boy, but her assumption was based on old wives' tales, not facts."

Well, Dr. Stromberg sure set me straight, I thought. Any number of girls' names would've suited me just fine, but if we had a boy,

I had a particular name in mind. And I thought this would be my opportunity to make a pitch for it. But, even if Dr. Stromberg would've said we were for sure having a boy, my stubborn wife would've held her ground.

Chapter 35

With lack of money no longer being a problem, I contacted a Realtor and asked him to find us a suitable apartment or house. With a child on the way, Alex and I needed a larger place to live. The thought occurred to me to call my father-in-law, Bruno, and gloat about how financially sound we were. But I didn't. I'm not sure why I was reluctant to brag; maybe it was instinct, a premonition of what was to come.

"I'd better get downstairs; students are arriving," I said to Alex.

"Be down in a little."

Since Bruno's remark at Christmas, *"Ty better not have my little girl dancing,"* my pregnant wife had been grounded from being my dance partner. Alex didn't like not being able to teach with me, and I didn't like it either. I had to draft lady dance students to help me demonstrate; I missed having my wife by my side.

Ten minutes into the lesson, Alex walked into the studio and approached me with tears streaming down her face. "Ty, I'm bleeding."

"Sit down," I said.

I dismissed class, explained my urgency to leave, and then ran to the office and called 911. "I need an ambulance; my pregnant wife's bleeding," I said to the dispatcher.

"Location's at Lexington Avenue off Fifty-First Street, correct?"

"Yeah; our apartment's above The Silver Slipper. Please hurry."

I called Dr. Stromberg's office to let him know we were headed to the emergency room at Coler Memorial Hospital. Then I told James and Jennifer, who were teaching in the second ballroom, that I was taking Alex to the hospital. I asked Jennifer to post a sign on the front door of The Silver Slipper stating that my classes were canceled due to a family emergency. In a few minutes, the ambulance came down our street with its siren blaring and stopped. The medics put Alex on a stretcher and loaded her into the ambulance. I squatted down next to my wife. She took hold of my hand with a firm grip, and tears filled her eyes. The ambulance sped away.

Dr. Stromberg was waiting for us and promptly examined Alex. "The amount of blood I see is of concern. This is the kind of bleeding I see more often in the first trimester, and it's usually a sign that the woman will have a miscarriage. But you're well past that, so I'm not sure what's going on."

"Alex, did you lift something heavy or strain yourself somehow?"

"No."

"I'm going to let you rest and have the nurse give you something to slow the bleeding. I'll be back to check on you."

At 11:45, Dr. Stromberg came back and examined Alex one more time. "The bleeding seems to have stopped. I'm going to release you, but if you experience any cramping or heavy bleeding, give me a call and get to the emergency room right away. Don't lift a bag of groceries or anything heavy, and stay off of your feet as much as possible."

I called for a cab. The cabbie dropped Alex and me off at The Silver Slipper. I helped my wife to the front door and we entered the studio.

"The Blue Danube Waltz" was playing in the second ballroom, where James and Jennifer were teaching. Alex and I reached the steps leading to our apartment; the light, airy music quickened in pace, and the melody grew louder. Each of the fourteen steps was a labor. I helped Alex get in bed, and then I got in too.

Before the bleeding incident, all Alex's checkups had been good. My sunny excitement of that morning as I digested the fact that I'd soon be a dad transformed to fear—fear for Alex's life, for the baby's. One minute, I'd been at the top of Mount Everest; the next, I was at the bottom of the Grand Canyon.

Chapter 36

July 7, Alex woke me at 3:00 a.m. "It's time; get me to the hospital."

I rolled over, my hand searching for the lamp on the nightstand. "You're not due till August."

"Ty, I'm having strong contractions; I'm going to deliver here!" It was early, by the doctor's due date, but Alex's urgency said it was a certainty. I was praying the delivery would go well and wondering how life would be if it didn't. I called for an ambulance and helped Alex put her robe and house shoes on, and then I got dressed. The ambulance arrived, and we were out the door and on our way to Coler Memorial Hospital.

We arrived at the hospital at 3:14. Dr. Stromberg was scrubbed and in the delivery room waiting for us. Alex was laid flat on her back in the bed, and her feet were put in stirrups. Then Dr. Stromberg examined her. "Hm. I was hoping this was a false alarm, Mrs. Partridge, but it isn't. You're not fully dilated, but labor's in progress.

"Pull up that chair, Mr. Partridge," Dr. Stromberg said, as he pointed. "I'm going to check another patient down the hall, then I'll be back."

I did my best to divert Alex's attention from her contractions, to divert my attention from the fact that our baby was coming too soon. "He, he, who," I chanted, like I'd done in Lamaze class. "Come on, Alex, keep your focus; control your breathing."

After two rounds of "he, he, whos," Alex said, "Stop. It's not helping."

I'd spent two weeks in Lamaze class for nothing.

Back and forth Dr. Stromberg went between delivery rooms. I didn't know how the other pregnant woman was doing, but by 6:00 a.m., Alex was grouchy. With every check of Alex's cervix for full dilation, Dr. Stromberg's answer of, "Not yet," didn't set well with her—or me, either. My wife had said she was ready to deliver when we left the apartment, and the pained expression on her face reinforced that.

"Why's it taking so long?" Alex shouted, after the doctor exited the delivery room once again. "Something's wrong with the baby."

Dr. Stromberg had to have heard Alex answer her own question. He came back into the delivery room and gave her an epidural block to ease her discomfort. "The monitor shows your contractions are coming closer together, Mrs. Partridge. It won't be long now."

The nurse came bustling in. "Dr. Stromberg, Mrs. Markowski down the hall is ready."

Twenty minutes later, Dr. Stromberg returned with his nurse. Alex wasn't complaining like before, but she looked tired. "Let's have a look, Mrs. Partridge."

Then Dr. Stromberg turned to his nurse. "She's ready; I'm going to break her water."

"Mrs. Partridge; you'll feel some pressure."

The warm flow of water lit up Alex's face, and the monitor showed Alex's contractions were coming rapid-fire and strong.

"Here we go, Mrs. Partridge. Push when I tell you to."

Then the doctor turned to me. "Stand alongside me; you'll see the head crown."

Dr. Stromberg's eyes were on the monitor. "Push now, Mrs. Partridge. Again, hard as you can."

"Alex, I see our baby's head!"

"One more long push," Dr. Stromberg coached. "You're almost there."

Out came our baby, with a face as red as Alex's.

Dr. Stromberg held our baby up for us to see. "It's a boy," he said, then gave our son a tap on the bottom. Our son protested with an ear-piercing revolt.

"What a set of lungs," I said. Alex was crying and laughing at the same time. I could tell she was tired but otherwise okay. My wife looked beautiful, my son too. Dr. Stromberg said our son weighed plenty; he wasn't premature. That seventh day of July, 1974, I was back on top of the world and happier than I'd ever imagined I could be.

The nurse took our son to the nursery to get him cleaned up. Alex was all smiles and glowing in motherhood, so I decided to pitch in my two cents about naming our baby boy. "You did good, Alex. Great, in fact. Been thinking a long time about names, especially boys'."

"I already know his name."

I readied myself. Didn't want to name him Ty. And Bruno wasn't acceptable.

"When I realized I was pregnant, I knew there was only one suitable name if we had a boy. His name will be Robert."

"Robert. Yeah, I like that."

"I knew you would. But I had my own reason for picking Robert. Had it not been for Pop, you wouldn't have made it to New York City; we'd never have met."

"Bradford okay for his middle name, Alex?"

"Robert Bradford. Sounds good."

Things were back to normal—well, not quite, but having Alex and Robert at home made my world seem whole again. Robert woke three times a night. Each morning, I got out of bed as quiet as I could, hoping Alex could catch a few more winks. I taught my first dance class half asleep. This routine went on for three and a half weeks, before Robert settled into a new pattern, waking Alex and me once through the night. At eleven weeks, our little angel slept through till 6:30 a.m.

Chapter 37

I had felt my way through more than nine months of changing diapers, giving Robert his bottle, and in general making a fool of myself entertaining my young son. That April twenty-third of 1975, President Gerald Ford had given a televised speech declaring that Saigon, South Vietnam's capital, had been captured by the North Vietnamese. The Vietnam War was over. Though I didn't like the outcome, a feeling of relief washed over me. My night blindness had ceased to be a problem for me thanks to a vitamin-A supplement, but now my being inducted for military service was no longer a concern. I had obligations, not only as a husband; I was a father too, with a family to support and a dance studio to run. In my cocoon of happiness, I continued to savor Robert's infancy, which seemed to melt away like a delicious ice-cream cone on a hot summer day.

Afternoon dance lessons were canceled to celebrate Robert's first birthday that following July 7. We turned one of The Silver Slipper's ballrooms into a kids' heaven. Our dance instructor, Jennifer, wore a Big Bird costume and flaunted yellow feathers and a large beak, and her coworker, James, dressed as Oscar the Grouch, was furry and green. Robert pointed and laughed, recognizing his favorite characters from *Sesame Street.*

Robert's cooing stage had advanced to "Da Da," which he chanted as Big Bird and Oscar the Grouch were dancing and singing "Happy Birthday." How my head swelled. We were applauding our special guests' performances when my folks and Alex's showed up in the ballroom.

Nadia whispered in my ear, "Thought his other grandmas should be here. Grandpas too."

"You paid for their flights?"

"I'm an old woman, Ty, and circumstances in my life have deprived me in some ways. I must snatch up every thrill I can. Robert is the grandchild I get to spoil. It is my pleasure to do this small thing. Just play along."

Nadia wishes she'd married, I thought.

Now able to navigate well with her cane, she joined Margaret, who was cutting Robert's Big Bird cake.

Mom, Dad, Michelle, and Bruno were thrilled to see their grandson and celebrate his first birthday with us. Leery as I was that I'd get a jab from Bruno, since his name wasn't passed on to my son, the topic never came up. And in fact, Bruno went out of his way to be pleasant. To this day, I believe Nadia had a hand in Bruno's ultimate acceptance of me as his son-in-law. Our folks' stay with us went without a hitch.

Chapter 38

Alex and I had been working on a final addition to our family. Early in January of 1977, my wife whispered in my ear once again, "I'm pregnant." With Robert starting three-year-old preschool at Saint Boniface in August, the timing felt right, and with fathering experience under my belt, I felt ready. Though I didn't express my wish, I secretly hoped Robert would get a little sister.

Our small apartment above The Silver Slipper in midtown Manhattan was already insufficient living space for the three of us. When our baby was born, we'd need more room. Our studio was thriving, and money wasn't the obstacle, but while the apartments and houses the Realtor had shown us were suitable in size, they weren't in a neighborhood I wanted our children to grow up in. Alex agreed to wait until the Realtor found us what we wanted.

On October 8, I got my wish for a little girl times two. Alex gave birth to identical twins, Angela Michelle and Andrea Marta.

My wife seemed exhausted when she and the twins came home from the hospital. I figured the birthing process had worn her out. With Alex taking time off from teaching at The Silver Slipper to recuperate, women in my classes were my dance partners. Like before, when Alex was pregnant and grounded from dancing, teaching without her was more difficult.

Every day, after I finished working, I noticed how tired and stressed-out Alex was from taking care of Robert and the girls. It was routine for her to nap while Robert entertained the twins and I did my best to prepare dinner. After dinner, my wife either lounged on the couch or went back to bed, and I did the dishes.

It was a Friday; I'd finished teaching for the day and made my way up the steps to our apartment. When I unlatched the child-safety gate at the top, I heard Robert's voice coming from our children's shared bedroom.

"Look. I built a house."

When I entered the bedroom, Robert was on the floor with his Legos. A paper plate with what remained of a peanut butter and jelly sandwich was next to him. Two empty baby bottles were on the dresser, and Angela and Andrea were in their cribs.

"Hi, Daddy," Robert said.

"Hi, Son, where's Mommy?"

Robert's blank expression told me he didn't know.

I changed the girls' diapers, then went to find Alex. She was in our bedroom asleep. I wondered how long our three children had been left unattended.

I re-entered the kids' bedroom and fastened the girls in their pumpkin seats. With a seat in each hand, I said, "Come on, Robert; let's go start dinner." He trailed behind, and we made our way to the kitchen.

I placed the twins, nestled in their seats, on the table. "Be my helper, Son; entertain your sisters while I fix the food."

"Okay, Daddy."

I got out a pan and began frying burgers. Robert started dancing around the table, singing the "Alphabet Song" to the girls.

Alex stormed into the kitchen. "Can you make any more noise, Robert?"

Robert stopped singing and looked to me for help.

"He was singing, and it wasn't that loud."

Alex glared at me. "This apartment's too small. How am I supposed to sleep?"

"Sorry, Mommy."

"It's okay, Robert," I said. "Alex, the burgers are ready."

"Don't want any. Going back to bed."

"Mommy's just tired, Robert; let's eat."

Day after day, my domestic duties kept increasing. Changing diapers, running errands, cooking, laundry, and whatever else Alex chose to dump on me was her idea of interacting with me. Running The Silver Slipper solo, serving as both mother and father, and dealing with my wife's moodiness was a juggling act. I was unhappy.

The following Monday, I got finished teaching classes and made my way upstairs to our apartment. The TV was playing, and Andrea was bawling when I walked in the living room. Alex was lying on the couch with a throw pillow covering her face. The twins were on the floor in their pumpkin seats facing the TV, and a stockpile of toys were scattered on the floor. Robert was leaning over Andrea. "What's wrong?" he asked.

I squatted down and checked Andrea's diaper; she was soaking wet, as was the pad in her pumpkin seat. "Alex, Andrea needs her diaper changed."

My wife uncovered her face and stared at me. "Then take care of it."

Alex got up from the couch and retreated to our bedroom. I changed Andrea and threw the urine-soaked pad in the washer.

That my wife was tired and needed me to help with our three small children was a certainty, but I was growing resentful and feeling misplaced in her world. Alex conveyed no interest in me or our studio, and that she deposited the twins in their pumpkin seats or cribs all the time, leaving Robert to entertain himself, concerned me.

Owning my own dance studio meant a lot to me. But I had traded off the idea of dancing on stage years before, afraid to leave Alex's side at The Silver Slipper, fearing another guy would snatch her away from me. And after we married and had Robert, I was a family man, devoted to being a husband and father. Robert, Angela and Andrea added joy to my life, but being both father and mother to them was taxing. I thought I'd never regret not dancing on stage, but I did. I loved Alex even more than when we got married; she'd given me three beautiful children, but my love for her came at a high price: I was unhappy.

Chapter 39

The reality of two cribs end-to-end against one wall of the so-called nursery and Robert's bed against the opposite wall wasn't going to cut it anymore. As sluggish as Alex was, she continued to nag me about getting a larger place to live. Hopeful that the added space might alleviate the pressure cooker I was living in, we bought a house in upper Manhattan in the Washington Heights neighborhood. On October 29, we moved in and called it home.

The moving guys had deposited the furniture in the rooms we designated and left. Nadia and Margaret were watching the kids downstairs while Alex started cleaning the kitchen. I began installing drapery rods in the four bedrooms upstairs, then hung curtains in the three we'd be using. Finished, I went downstairs and asked Alex to show me how she wanted our bedroom furniture situated. An extra set of hands would have been helpful, but Alex went back to her work in the kitchen. I managed to put our bed back together and moved our dresser and nightstands by myself.

I went to find Alex, who was moving like a snail, still working in the kitchen. "Our bedroom's done. Come show me where you want the furniture in Robert's room."

"I'm busy. Can't you do anything by yourself?"

"I can, Alex, but you'd say it wasn't right, and I'm not moving that furniture twice."

Alex threw down her wet rag and stormed up the stairs. I followed.

She put one hand on her hip and pointed with her free hand. "Put Robert's bed there. Obviously, the dresser has to go there."

Alex's facial expression transformed from irritation to an antagonistic sneer. "What've you been doing? Robert's cabinet is still in the box; get it assembled and put these toys away. But first, come with me."

I followed my wife to the bedroom our twins, Angela and Andrea, would share. Her hand again on her hip, she pointed. "One crib there, the other there. Put the dressers side by side against that wall. The changing table goes there. Got it?"

Alex left the twin's bedroom and went downstairs to the kitchen.

I went back to my son's room and assembled his toy cabinet, placed it on the wall opposite his dresser, and then filled it with his toys.

Finished with Robert's room, I started on the girls' bedroom. I assembled the cribs and put them on the inside wall where Alex wanted them. After removing the drawers from their dressers, I dragged each chest across the carpet to the back wall. My stomach rumbled from wanting food, and I was ready for a break.

Alex walked into the girls' bedroom. "Ty, come downstairs. I want you to put up that towel rack I bought for the kitchen."

"How's their room look?"

"Fine. Come on," Alex said, "I want to get done sometime today."

"Ok, but take a look at Robert's room first."

Alex sighed, followed me to his room, and then pointed. "What's that toy cabinet doing there? It goes on that wall. Why don't you listen to me?"

"You didn't say where you wanted it."

"Yes, I did. Move it over there," Alex said and pointed again. "That's where I want it."

"It's filled with toys; I'm not unloading it. It's staying where it is."

"I'm still cleaning the kitchen, Ty. And nothing's been put away in the cabinets. I won't be cooking until that gets done."

"That's a joke; I can't remember the last time *you* cooked."

Though the moving men had left the front door open and the cool autumn air had filled our house, my shirt stuck to me with sweat. My doughnut and cup of coffee from that morning were used up, and my stomach growled in revolt. I was bushed from packing and unpacking, from lifting and moving things to suit Alex, and the thought of a sandwich and rest were top priorities.

Nadia had managed the steps with her cane and entered Andrea and Angela's bedroom.

"Stop working and rest. And above all, stop shouting at each other. You're both crabbier than two old women needing a midmorning nap. And by the way, it's past noon. I've ordered food; it'll be here in a few minutes. I'm going back downstairs to help Margaret with the children, and I don't want them hearing any more of your nonsense."

Alex followed Nadia. I sat down on the floor in Robert's bedroom, rested my head against the wall, and closed my eyes. When Margaret announced that the food had arrived, I joined everyone in the kitchen.

Except for Robert's request from Grandma Nadia for more fried chicken, there wasn't much conversation. After the food was eaten, Nadia and Margaret said they needed to get home. Both women had to be at least sixty-five, though I never dared ask their ages. I felt ashamed of myself. There I was, a strapping young man, worn to a thread. I'd bet Nadia and Margaret passed out in their beds and didn't see the five o'clock news that night.

After our adopted grandmothers had gone, Alex made an announcement. "I'm taking a nap."

"Fine," I said. Alex's indifferent stare registered; she didn't want to be around me any more than she had to be.

Chapter 40

After two weeks, Alex had our new home in order—as well as it could be with three small children—but the ordeal of moving seemed to have taken its toll on her. She wore the same pair of jeans day after day, and her hair, often in need of a shampoo, was always in a ponytail. I'd never seen her appearance slide like that before. But that November, something shook me up more than Alex's untidiness: her silent hostility. Day after day passed the same; my wife spoke to me only when it was necessary.

By the tenth of December, I was certain aliens had abducted my wife and replaced her with some look-alike extraterrestrial. I was living with a stranger.

"Alex, I thought we might put up the Christmas tree today." It was Saturday, and our employees were handling dance lessons. "Should I bring it up from the basement?"

My wife didn't reply. She was standing two feet from me in our living room, but the hollowed-out look in her eyes said she was somewhere else. Andrea awoke from her nap and began to cry; Angela chimed in, and Alex flopped down on the couch. I started to go upstairs to attend to Andrea, when the phone rang.

"Hello."

"It's Bruno, Ty. Called to see how Alexandra, my grandchildren ... you are doing."

Huh, didn't ask for Alex.

Alex's parents had no inkling about our strained marriage or my wife's odd behavior. My folks didn't, either, for that matter. "Not sure how to answer that, Bruno."

"Not sure? What does that mean?" Bruno's voice reeked of annoyance. Revisiting was the old Bruno, the one who wished he'd gotten an Italian son-in-law.

"Alex doesn't want anything to do with me. She's gone from screaming at me to not speaking to me at all. She's disconnected from the kids too. I don't know what to do."

There was a long pause. "My little girl sounds unhappy," Bruno said. "Overwhelmed."

I knew what I wanted to say to my father-in-law, but if I said it, I knew I could never repair the damage. So instead, I said, "I think you're right."

Bruno's heavy cigar-induced breathing was transmitted through the phone, and his voice was uncharacteristically soft. "Michelle had a hard time after Alexandra was born. Went into what the doctor called postpartum depression. Maybe Alexandra should see her doctor."

I had braced myself for the blame I thought Bruno would dump on me. His admittance that Michelle had experienced postpartum depression shocked me. My father-in-law wasn't the kind of man to air his dirty laundry. "I'll get her an appointment right away. And ... thanks."

"Let us know what the doctor says, Ty."

"I will."

"If you need Michelle and me, say the word; we'd be glad to help with the kids."

"Thanks," I said. Bruno hung up without saying good-bye.

I called Dr. Stromberg's office. He had delivered our children, and I figured he was who I should reach out to for help. My description of Alex's unusual behavior, my suspicion of postpartum depression, must have made an impression on the doctor's receptionist; I got Alex an appointment for Monday at 1:00 p.m. The next day being Sunday, I decided to wait until Monday morning to tell Alex about her doctor's appointment. My wife was curled up on the couch, oblivious to either of my phone calls.

There was another war cry from Andrea, which was Angela's lead to join in, so I made my way upstairs. With a girl in each arm and Robert in front of me, hugging the banister with each step, we made it to the living room.

"I need a drink," Robert said. Alex opened her eyes and shuffled into the kitchen to get him a cup of water. I put the girls in their swings and turned the cranks, hoping the movement would put Andrea and Angela to sleep. Then I went to get the Christmas tree and decorations from the basement. Without further coaxing to get Alex to help decorate, I put the tree up with my little helper, Robert, cranking up the twins' swings every time they stopped. Alex didn't move from the couch. The more I thought about Bruno's sympathetic attitude toward me, the more suspicious I became of Alex's behavior. My father-in-law understood my situation 'cause he'd been there. I was sure my wife had been sucked down into a deep, dark hole.

Chapter 41

I had arranged for my dance instructors, James and Jennifer, to split up and cover dance lessons in both ballrooms Monday. I told them Alex wasn't feeling well and that I was taking her to the doctor. I told them I'd try to make it back to The Silver Slipper for my 3:00 p.m. class.

It was 9:00 a.m., and Alex hadn't made it out of bed. I had showered, changed the twins' diapers and given them a bottle of formula, fixed Robert a bowl of Cheerios, and a second load of laundry was drying. Nadia and Margaret were due later to watch the kids. Both grandmas had commented about how tired and quiet Alex seemed. I told them Alex's appointment with Dr. Stromberg was for a checkup. Everything was set—everything except that I hadn't told Alex about her appointment.

At 10:00, I went upstairs. Alex was in bed with the covers over her head. "Time to get up," I said. No answer, no movement. I pulled the covers down.

"What do you want?" Alex snapped, then threw the covers back over her head.

I sat down on the bed next to her. "You haven't been yourself since the girls were born. I made you an appointment with Dr. Stromberg for one o'clock today."

Alex threw the covers off and gave me that deadpan stare. "Not going."

"I need my wife; the kids need their mother. Get up and get dressed."

The thought of losing Alex, that girl who took my breath away the first time I saw her, losing the mother of my children, swallowed me. I yanked the cover off the bed. "You're going. If I have to carry you, I will!"

Alex sat up. A moment of clarity burned in her eyes. She caressed my shoulder and rested her head against my chest. I took her in my arms and savored this moment of recognition.

Nadia and Margaret arrived. At 12:30, Alex and I were getting in a taxicab and on our way to Dr. Stromberg's office located in the Coler Memorial Hospital complex.

Alex and I sat in the same seats we'd occupied many times before. Pregnant women accompanied by a husband, boyfriend, or mother filled the waiting room that had held my anticipation of happy events, the births of our children. Now the same seats held me a prisoner of dread. My wife studied the wallpaper, her eyes following the border of yellow ducklings lined up one after the other in a row. I wondered what it would take to fix my wife, and then I wondered if I was being unrealistic.

After a fifty-minute wait, the nurse, wearing a smock of pastel pink-and-blue bears, called out, "Alexandra Partridge." I took hold of Alex's arm and helped her stand. We followed the nurse to an exam room.

Alex slouched in the chair, her eyes cast down toward the speckled tile.

Dr. Stromberg entered the room. "Mr. and Mrs. Partridge, what brings you here?"

"Alex is having difficulty since she delivered the twins," I said. "She sleeps a lot and doesn't want much to do with the kids and me."

Alex righted her head and stared at Dr. Stromberg. With her oily bangs plastered to her forehead and her makeup-less face, I hardly recognized the woman I married.

"Huh. What's going on, Alex?" Dr. Stromberg said, taking in her untidy appearance.

Alex held her stare and shrugged her shoulders.

"She's been like this since she got home from the hospital, Ty?"

"Not appearance-wise; that came later. At first, we fought. Didn't matter how much I helped with the house and kids; it was never enough. But now she ignores the kids and me. And those clothes she has on ... I can't tell you how many days she's worn them. Dr. Stromberg, Alex's mother had postpartum depression."

"That's what I suspect is wrong with Alex," Dr. Stromberg said.

The doctor stepped out of the room and came back with his nurse. "Susan will give you a script for Valium and will set up an appointment with a psychologist in this building. Dr. Franz's office is down the hall in suite thirty-one. I'll have Alex's file delivered to his office.

"Follow Susan to the front desk. And Ty, get the prescription filled right away."

Chapter 42

The fifteenth of December, Nadia and Margaret, adopted grandmothers to my kids, came to babysit while I took Alex to see Dr. Franz.

"Mr. and Mrs. Partridge, please have a seat," the psychologist said. His voice had a soothing quality, but his camel-colored cardigan and plaid house shoes seemed like unusual attire for a professional in New York City. He pointed to two of the overstuffed chairs that were situated side by side and then sat across from us in the other. Dr. Franz's receptionist placed three glasses of ice water on the coffee table that was positioned between our chairs and his.

"Thank you, Claudia," Dr. Franz said.

Claudia closed the door behind her.

"I've read Dr. Stromberg's notes and reviewed your file, Mrs. Partridge. I see he's prescribed Valium. His notes also state that you wouldn't talk with him. Getting people to talk about their problems is my job. You understand?"

Alex's deadpan stare was her answer.

"I'd like an answer," Dr. Franz said and then looked down at the chart on his lap. "Alexandra, is that a yes?"

"She goes by Alex," I said.

"Then that's how I should address her. Thank you, and may I call you Ty?"

"Of course."

"Do you understand that as your psychologist, I want to help you work through the emotional problem you're having?"

Alex stared at Dr. Franz. "Don't have a problem."

"You don't? You look sad; are you?"

Alex looked at her hands folded in her lap. "Nothing's wrong with me. Ty shouldn't have made me come."

I made eye contact with Dr. Franz and shook my head.

"Alex, you don't interact with your husband and children. You sleep long periods of time, and you don't have the energy to run your household. Is that a fair description of what's going on with you?"

Getting no reply, Dr. Franz turned to me. "Have I given an accurate description of your wife?"

I nodded to affirm.

"Alex, do you realize you're depressed?" Dr. Franz said.

No reply.

"Do you understand that since the twins were born, you've acted differently?"

Alex shrugged her shoulders.

"Let's try it this way. Do you feel different now than you did after delivering your son, Robert?" Dr. Franz said.

Alex shrugged her shoulders again.

Dr. Franz continued asking Alex questions. Each of her responses was a nod or shrug.

Then the psychologist asked, "Alex, is Ty a good husband?"

My wife closed her eyes and became frozen in an unresponsive slump.

"We're done for today, Alex. My goal with the first appointment is to evaluate the patient. Our next session will be longer and will require that you give all verbal responses."

Dr. Franz turned toward me. "Ty, it's imperative that I see your wife Monday through Friday."

The psychologist patted Alex's arm. "You don't trust me, but you will. And I promise that you will be emotionally healthy again."

"Ty, wait here; I'll get Claudia to help Alex to the waiting room."

Dr. Franz closed the door after Claudia and Alex. "Ty, get someone to stay with Alex and the children while you're at work. And when you administer the Valium, make sure she swallows it. Be patient with her; recovering from postpartum depression takes time."

After setting up Alex's appointments, we went home.

My wife shuffled upstairs to the bedroom. I thought about asking Mom and Dad to come to New York City to help with the kids. But I didn't know how they'd handle the flight, or for that matter, the Big Apple. My father-in-law had lent me a sympathetic ear concerning Alex's depression, but Bruno's past rude remarks were reason enough to not ask him and Michelle. The fact remained that while I taught at The Silver Slipper, someone had to keep watch over my family at our home in Washington Heights. I decided to explain the raw truth to Nadia and Margaret; I needed their help.

Chapter 43

Alex remained in bed, sleeping. I threw in laundry, gave Robert a bowl of Cheerios, and after giving Andrea and Angela their bottles, I went upstairs with a glass of water to give Alex her Valium. She was lying in a fetal position with the covers over her.

"Sit up, Alex; it's time for your medicine." Her curled-up form didn't move.

"Nadia and Margaret are coming to watch the kids; I have to get to The Silver Slipper."

Alex didn't stir, so I threw the covers off of her and helped her sit up.

Sitting next to her, I held out my hand, the Valium resting in my palm. "Take it." I handed Alex the glass of water and her medicine. My wife put the Valium in her mouth, got a drink, then spit everything out, drenching my face. I took the glass from Alex and sat it on the nightstand.

Robert had climbed the stairs and stood at the end of the bed. With it being Wednesday, he didn't have preschool, and he was trying to be my helper. "Dad, it smells like Angela dropped a load."

"I'll be down in a minute."

"Why's your face wet?" Robert said.

"Mom's glass of water spilled on me. Go keep your sisters company till I get there to change Angela."

Robert, eager to be my helper, went downstairs.

The tranquilizer pill had rebounded from my face and was lying on the sheet. I picked it up and put it in Alex's palm, then handed her the glass of water.

"Swallow the Valium," I said, "or I swear I'll call Dr. Franz and have you put in the hospital."

Alex gave me a defiant look, put the pill in her mouth, took a drink, and swallowed.

"Open your mouth and stick out your tongue," I said. My wife smirked, but when I looked in her mouth and searched with my index finger, the pill was gone.

"And if you want that sheet changed, do it yourself," I said.

Alex threw the sheet over her face, and I went downstairs to change Angela's dirty diaper. When Nadia and Margaret arrived, I left to give lessons at The Silver Slipper.

One of my better swing-dance students, Kathleen Hendricks, had taken the advanced swing class from Alex and me. After I announced that Alex was taking time off from our dance studio to care for our infant girls and son, Kathleen offered to fill in for my wife during swing lessons. She and I were teaching the intermediate East Coast class.

"Ladies, choose a gentleman for your partner," I said.

Two women grabbed Fred Wright by the arm, but one yielded and partnered with Jim Bard, a lonely widower, who gave dancing his best effort but had a habit of stepping on the ladies' feet.

"You already know one of the swing moves in the sequence Kathleen and I are teaching today. Watch while we demonstrate the sequence, then we'll break it down into parts."

"Ready, Kathleen?"

She smiled and replied, "Of course."

Starting in closed position, I led Kathleen into a basic step, then guided her into an inside underarm turn. I brought her back, across slot, with an outside underarm turn so we faced each other. Taking her in a two-hand hold, I led her into a tunnel. As Kathleen came out of the tunnel, I made a hand change, holding her right hand with my left. I brought her back into closed position and led two tuck-and-returns, and we finished the sequence with the Imperial Walk.

"Kathleen and I will teach the tunnel first. Watch while we demonstrate."

Thirty-five minutes later and with special attention given to Jim Bard, everyone knew how to do the tunnel.

Then I told my students to watch while Kathleen and I reviewed the Imperial Walk. "Now I'll watch while you do it," I said.

"Looks good. Now onto the last new move of the dance sequence, the tuck-and-return. Watch while Kathleen and I demonstrate it."

I walked my students through the last move, then had them practice it.

I put all parts of the sequence together and had my students practice it first without music. By the end of the hour lesson, everyone in the class—except Jim Bard—could do the complete sequence to music. Then it was lunchtime.

Kathleen approached me after the students cleared the ballroom, smiled, and stood close enough that I caught her mint-laced breath. "Ty, want to grab a sandwich at the deli down the street?"

"Can't. Got paperwork. But thanks."

"Well, you're so *welcome*," Kathleen said, then left.

I got my sandwich from the kitchen upstairs and ate while I paid bills.

After lunch, I taught three sections of waltz lessons: a beginner, an intermediate, and an advanced. I partnered up with the best lady student in each class, but teaching wasn't the same without Alex.

CHAPTER 44

Though our decorated tree was lit Christmas Day of 1977, a dark mood dimmed the holiday. Grandmas Nadia and Margaret were there to watch Robert open his presents and help the twins open theirs, but Alex refused to get out of bed.

Day after day, Nadia and Margaret had shown up to babysit and keep an eye on Alex while I worked at The Silver Slipper. They picked up Robert from preschool and watched the kids when I took Alex to her psychotherapy sessions with Dr. Franz. Even though Alex was taking her medicine and getting therapy, I doubted family life would ever be normal again. The few Christmas gifts I'd bought were quick stops made on workdays during lunch break. I hadn't had the nerve to ask our adopted grandmas to stay with the kids and Alex while I shopped for presents. Nadia's and Margaret's gifts, ballet tickets, weren't enough to show my appreciation for all they'd done. And while Angela and Andrea, a little over two months old, had no expectations about Christmas, Robert was disappointed. His warm, brown eyes, so much like his mother's, reached out to me.

"Santa didn't bring me much. Was I a bad boy?"

Dealing with Alex's depression was the reason my son didn't get many gifts. But how could I explain that to a child Robert's age? So, I told a white lie. "Guess Santa's elves couldn't get enough toys made this year, 'cause Mom and I know you've been a very good boy."

Chapter 45

The thought of me doing more cooking wasn't appealing New Year's Day. I fed Angela and Andrea, then put them in their swings and made ham sandwiches for Alex, Robert, and me.

After lunch, we settled in the living room. Alex stretched out on the couch for a nap. I removed the twins from their swings and placed them on their backs on the carpet. Robert and I sat next to them and began playing with his new Etch-A-Sketch.

"Watch, Son," I said, and turned one of the dials. "This one draws a straight line; if I turn the other one too, I can make the line curve, see?" I shook the Etch-A-Sketch and cleared the screen. "Now you draw."

Robert turned the dials, then held up the Etch-A-Sketch. "Look, Mommy, a candy cane."

Alex turned her head, and her blank eyes gravitated to Robert's drawing.

"I see the hook at the end; that's a great candy cane," I said. "Show your sisters too."

Robert held the Etch-A-Sketch close to Andrea's and Angela's faces. Angela kicked her feet.

"Look at that, Robert; she likes your picture," I said.

Alex showed no expression.

With no indication that Alex's postpartum depression was releasing its hold on her, I didn't think it was fair to expect Nadia and Margaret to keep sitting with my wife and kids every weekday while I worked. I hired two graduates of Adelphi University of Performing Arts, Peggy and Jonathan, as dance instructors to teach my classes every Monday, Wednesday, and Friday. Tuesdays and Thursdays, Nadia and Margaret stayed with my family while I taught at The Silver Slipper, and Margaret took the bus and got Robert home from preschool. As much as I felt that I was imposing, I continued asking them to watch Andrea, Angela, and Robert when I took Alex to see Dr. Franz for psychotherapy.

I couldn't see that Alex was shaking her depression. But that January of 1978, Dr. Franz continued to praise Alex for completing what he called her "homework assignment." Getting up at 7:30 in the morning, showering, and dressing didn't seem like a big achievement to me, but it made the psychologist smile. "Alex is getting better," he would say. But I didn't see it. What I saw was Dr. Franz's different-colored cardigan at each session and his same plaid house shoes.

CHAPTER 46

It was pouring down rain when Nadia and Margaret arrived, and the cold temperature had Nadia's arthritis acting up. Alex had been throwing a fit about her appointment with Dr. Franz, using the weather as an excuse to not keep it. I opted to call a taxi instead of taking the subway to Coler Memorial Hospital.

A few minutes into the ride, the rain turned to nickel-size hail, and the car in front of our taxi slowed to fifteen miles per hour. Our cabbie had the windshield wipers on, but visibility was bad, and I couldn't tell how many cars were ahead of us. We had twenty minutes to get to Dr. Franz's office. Mr. Motivator in the car behind us laid on his horn and provided incentive for our cabbie to join in. Traffic came to a stop. "Great, we're going to be late, Alex."

My wife stared at the windshield, focused on the hail as it hit the glass, seeming oblivious to the blaring horns or the fact that I'd spoken to her.

I hit the back of the seat in front of me with my open hand. It made a loud pop. Then I said a few choice words.

The cabbie turned his head and said what I guessed to be some choice words too, but in a foreign language. Then he turned around and gave the horn a rest.

Alex turned to face me and yelled, "That's enough, Ty!"

Her clear-headed response sent a rush of excitement through me. *Making progress*, I thought.

The hail stopped and traffic started moving. We arrived at Dr. Franz's office ten minutes past our scheduled time; his receptionist showed us to the same room we'd met in before. A vase of red roses was on the coffee table.

"Good afternoon, Alex and Ty," Dr. Franz said. "Please take a seat."

The three of us sat in the overstuffed chairs arranged in a triangle. Dr. Franz had on the same plaid house shoes and another cardigan, this one navy.

"Alex, tell me how you accomplished the homework I assigned you," he said.

She sighed. "Set the alarm for 7:30, like you told me to, got up as soon as it went off, showered, and dressed."

Dr. Franz turned to me to verify.

"Yes," I said. "But—"

"Alex completed her homework, Ty. Did you praise her?"

I was raising our children, keeping house, and running the studio, while my wife ignored me; I didn't want to hear about Alex completing "homework" anymore. Dr. Franz's strategy of talking to Alex like she was a child had gotten old. He acted like a retired schoolteacher, instead of a psychologist. But he was the professional, so I played along. "You did good, Alex."

"Yes, excellent," Dr. Franz said. "Tell me about other positive things that happened since our last session."

Alex shrugged her shoulders.

With Dr. Franz's fees costing a pretty penny, the stretch of silence got on my nerves.

"She yelled at me. That's something positive, isn't it?"

Alex turned and sneered at me.

"Tell me why you yelled at Ty," Dr. Franz said.

"Traffic came to a stop because it was hailing. That idiot in the car behind us and our cabbie started honking. Then Ty hit the front seat of the taxi with his hand and was cursing."

"Ty annoyed you, so you said ... what to him?"

"'That's enough, Ty,' that's what."

"I was just acting like a New Yorker, Dr. Franz."

"Alex was conveying that she didn't appreciate your attitude. Don't you agree that communication is important, Ty?"

Any response out of Alex was better than being ignored, so I said yes.

"Good." The psychologist scratched the bald spot on top of his head. "Ty was correct; the yelling episode was a step forward for you, Alex. But even when situations arise that anger you, I want you to speak, not yell, to express yourself. Unpleasant words and screaming aren't productive communications, understand?"

"Yes."

"You will continue setting your alarm and get up when it goes off, shower, and get dressed. Keeping a neat appearance boosts self-esteem. And I have additional homework for you: once a day, you will have a talk session with Ty that must last fifteen minutes. For five of these minutes, discuss a show on TV, the news, or whatever you want, but the remaining ten, you must talk with Ty about Robert, Angela, and Andrea. Begin this new homework tonight."

Alex's face tensed, she wrinkled her forehead and puckered her mouth. Her eyes filled with wetness, and I was sure she was going to cry. But she didn't.

"By the way, Alex," Dr. Franz said, "those roses on the coffee table are for you. See you at our next session."

Alex grabbed the vase of roses and was out the door.

CHAPTER 47

My days were nothing but unwavering routine. Mondays, Wednesdays, and Fridays, I stayed at home being Mr. Mom to my kids and Alex. Tuesdays and Thursdays, Robert and I took the bus to Saint Boniface School. After I dropped him off at three-year-old preschool, I took the subway to midtown and taught at The Silver Slipper. Nadia picked Robert up from Saint Boniface after he finished his half day and took him back home to stay with Margaret and her. Our grandmas had their hands full caring for Robert, Angela, Andrea, and Alex too.

It was the fourth Thursday in January; I'd finished at the studio and taken Alex to her therapy session. Grandmas Nadia and Margaret had the kids fed when Alex and I got home. They put the twins in their swings and left. My wife and I ate a bowl of the chili Nadia and Margaret had made for us, while Robert sat at the kitchen table, finishing his assignment for preschool, printing the alphabet.

"Look, Alex; didn't Robert do a great job?"

Alex got up and went to the living room. I washed the dishes, and Robert joined Alex and the girls.

When I got to the living room, the twins were in their swings, Robert was looking at a pop-up book, and Alex was lying on the couch watching *Three's Company*. I played with the kids and then read a story to them before tucking them into bed.

I heard water running in our bathroom and went to remind Alex that she hadn't done her homework assignment. She had changed into her pajamas and was brushing her teeth.

"After you finish, we need to have that talk session Dr. Franz assigned you."

Alex rinsed and put her toothbrush in its holder. "Too tired," she said.

"Fifteen minutes is all I'm asking for."

"I'm going to bed, Ty," Alex said and walked out of the bathroom.

"No, you're not."

Alex began to turn down the bedspread. I grabbed her hand.

"Sit down. I've had it."

"Fine. Talk," Alex said and plopped down on the bed. Her eyes filled with tears.

I sat next to her. "What am I supposed to think? You're on Valium, getting therapy, and I do everything I can to help you. If you won't talk about our kids, talk about that TV show, *Three's Company*, you had on tonight. You're interested in *that*."

Alex covered her face with her hands.

"Just say something!" I pulled her hands away from her face; tears streamed down her cheeks.

"I'm ashamed."

I drew my wife next to me and held her until she stopped sobbing. Then Alex talked.

"Robert's caring way with his sisters is something so special, and our infant girls show such independence by entertaining themselves. Our kids remind me of you. I've been in some kind of maze that I couldn't find my way out of. But even as lost as I was, I never stopped loving you and the kids. Never."

Dr. Franz's fifteen-minute talk requirement lasted over an hour, and Alex did most of the talking. She assured me that she was well, but I had my own way of knowing that was true. That special way my wife used to look at me was back. And that was the bottom line.

Chapter 48

Dr. Franz released Alex from his care January 31. My wife had to be weaned off Valium, but she was free of that demon, depression. Family life was good again, and I couldn't have been more grateful.

By the second week in February, I was putting in a full week, working Monday through Friday at The Silver Slipper, and Alex was back helping me teach dance lessons. James and Jennifer were still covering ballroom two on weekdays, and I decided to keep our part-time instructors, Peggy and Jonathan, on board to cover Saturday classes. Now that my wife was well, I wanted Robert, Angela, and Andrea to have some quality time with their parents.

To relieve Grandmas Nadia and Margaret, I hired a sitter, a former dance student, to come to our house and watch Andrea and Angela while my wife and I were at work. Alex took Robert on the bus to Saint Boniface's preschool in the morning, then took the subway to midtown to help me with dance lessons. She commuted back to get Robert after his half day of school and returned to our studio with him. Robert loved spending the remainder of the afternoon with us at The Silver Slipper.

Alex and I were between classes, eating a sandwich in the office before starting the next lesson, and the phone rang. "Hello, Ty Partridge."

"Ty, it's Emily Bradford."

I swallowed a large bite of sandwich whole.

"Dad passed this morning," Emily said.

"Oh," I said, sure that I sounded surprised, but I wasn't. Emily had told me that Pop was declining fast. "I'd have called to check on Pop, but my wife wasn't well."

"I understand. I hope Alex is feeling better. Dad's wake will be Thursday at Riner's Funeral Home, four till eight. Friday's the funeral. You have your family; don't feel obligated to come."

"Oh, I'll be there, Emily; Pop was like a father to me."

I hung up the phone and told Alex about Pop. I was a husband, father, and dance studio owner in New York City; my life was so different from the one I had led in Greenstone. But from the core of that young boy, Bird, whom Pop had taken under his wing, came sadness. And like when my sister, Allison, died, guilt surrounded my regret. I had let Pop down too.

I caught James and Jennifer in ballroom two before the next dance lessons began and told them that Alex and I would be gone Wednesday, Thursday, and Friday due to Pop's wake and funeral in Greenstone, Missouri. Then I called Peggy and Jonathan and asked them to cover lessons in ballroom one while Alex and I were gone.

With our last lesson finished, I turned to Alex and said, "I'll be back in a few minutes." I went upstairs to our old living quarters and sat down on the floor of what used to be our bedroom. I closed my eyes and summoned Pop, the Pop I knew when he knew me as Bird. I told him I was sorry. Then I returned to ballroom one, and Alex and I finished our workday at The Silver Slipper.

After my wife and I got home, I called Grandmas Nadia and Margaret. They said they'd be happy to come early Wednesday morning to stay with Angela, Andrea, and Robert. Then I phoned Alex's parents and mine to let them know we'd be arriving in Greenstone to attend Pop's wake and funeral. Mom and Dad offered to pick Alex and me up at Wakefield Airport.

Chapter 49

Thursday evening at Pop's wake, Emily asked me to stand by Pop's casket with her while the townsfolk paid their respects. Besides the once-young teenagers, like me, whose lives Pop had touched, mere acquaintances showed up, as was customary in a small town like Greenstone. I was looking for Mrs. Brown, Burt's widow; Pop used to send me across the street to Burt's Grocery to buy cookies she baked. Emily told me Mrs. Brown had passed too. Drew and Hannah stopped by to pay their respects. How my brother-in-law had aged from mining, and how my niece had grown. And as Alex's folks and mine sat on those well-used folding chairs in that small parlor of Riner's Funeral Home, I saw in them too, that time was leaving its footprint.

Friday at 10:00 a.m., Pop's service was held at Riner's. Though I'd never known Pop to speak of going to church, a minister gave a brief sermon, one that seemed run-of-the-mill. And while many Greenstone folks had attended Pop's wake, it seemed they believed their obligation was completed Thursday evening. The funeral procession included the hearse and two cars: Alex, me, and Emily with Alex's parents, and Mom and Dad with Drew and Hannah. And when we drove away from Pop's gravesite, the thought struck me that he was much more than the fifteen-minute sermon had expressed, more than the small tombstone bearing his name as proof that he once existed. My folks drove Drew and Hannah home. Alex's parents said they'd drop Emily off at Pop's house before they took Alex and me to the airport.

Bruno parked parallel to the picture window, where the fluorescent sign, "Pop's Pop," used to hang. "Sorry for your loss, Emily," I said. "Pop was a good man."

Emily opened the backseat door and got out. "Almost forgot something. Before Dad's dementia got too bad, he told me to give you something after he died. I'll go get it."

I rolled down the window in the backseat; the cold air numbed my cheeks. In a few minutes, Emily returned to the car and handed me an old, leather photo album. A musty smell accompanied it through the window.

"Dance photos?"

"Yes. Dad thought you'd enjoy seeing what he looked like when he and Mom competed at the Wakefield Dance Contest. The other pictures were taken after he and Mom were married, when they went to dances at Eddie's Place. He thought the album should be yours."

I ran my hand over the fine hairline splits in the leather that meandered on an uncertain course, and then I opened the album. In the first picture, a young guy and girl dressed in red-sequined dance outfits were posed, holding a trophy. I recognized the outfits, but the young man with a full head of dark, wavy hair and good posture, I did not.

"Thank you, Emily. You don't know what this album means to me."

Since I'd arrived in Greenstone for Pop's funeral, a question had been on my mind. Pop had told me that his daughter had bitter feelings about Greenstone, so I figured I knew the answer to my question, but I needed to ask it anyway. "Emily, will you stay in Greenstone?"

Emily leaned into the open car window. "I own a house in Wakefield and work as a secretary at a law firm there. I want to sell Dad's home as fast as I can. Jack Brown approached me after Dad died; he told me that he'd like to buy it. Jack said Burt's Grocery doesn't have enough storage space. He wants to use Dad's place as a warehouse."

I was trying to think what I wanted to say. No, that's not true; I knew, but the words were stuck in my throat 'cause I didn't know how Alex might react to them. The place I once called Pop's Pop was going to be used as a warehouse. I figured Pop was turning over in his grave. Alex, sitting next to me in the backseat, touched my arm. I turned and made eye contact with her.

"Emily, perhaps you'll give Ty and me a call when you decide on the asking price for your dad's property," Alex said.

I knew Alex loved New York City; there was no logical reason for my wife to imply an interest in Pop's place, but just the same, I wanted to buy it.

"Really?" Emily's eyebrows arched. "Well, I'll do that. You'll have first chance at buying it."

With little time to spare to get Alex and me to Wakefield Airport, Bruno drove with a heavy foot. Striations of gray ran through the cloudy winter sky as Alex and I boarded the plane to take off for New York City, the place I had come to call home. That restless feeling about flying rose up in me when I got seated. I closed my eyes and pretended to sleep. Nothing more was said about buying Pop's place that gloomy day.

Chapter 50

It was the second week of April; the sky was dark, bruised with gray clouds, and a spring thundershower seemed likely. Andrea crawled after Angela, chasing her around the living room; Robert was watching a cartoon, and Alex had left to get groceries. Having seen the mailman, I made a dash for the mailbox. Just as I stepped inside the front door, I heard Robert talking on the phone in the kitchen.

"Dad's outside."

I made my way to the kitchen. "Robert, give me the phone." I put the receiver to my ear. "Hello."

"This is Emily Bradford. Is this Ty?"

"Yeah, hi, Emily."

When I lived with Pop, I didn't see that he had that much stuff to sort through. And knowing that Pop's daughter wanted to get rid of his house as quick as possible, I wondered why it had taken her so long to call.

"Hi, Ty. I wanted to let you know I'm ready to sell Dad's house. After he died, I took my two weeks of vacation from the law firm I work for to clear out his belongings. I fell off a chair reaching for a box on the shelf in his closet and broke my tibia. My leg required surgery, and I'm still in a cast. Whoever buys

Dad's house will have to remove the rest of his things. I'm not up to doing it."

"Sorry to hear about your broken leg, Emily."

"Thanks. I was wondering if you're still interested in buying Dad's house."

"I am. Do you have an amount in mind?"

"Jack offered me $5,500," Emily said. "When you and Alex visited Dad, you saw that I had remodeled his soda-fountain shop to make it more suitable as living quarters. Jack wants Dad's place 'cause it's located on Main Street across from Burt's Grocery, and he plans to use it as a warehouse. I know Dad would rather you have it; that's why I'm giving you first chance to buy. But something puzzles me. You live in New York and have a dance studio there; why do you want Dad's old, run-down place?"

I'd left a piece of me in Greenstone. While the single-minded, backward ways of the town I grew up in still rubbed a sore spot in my backbone, the boy known as Bird was fighting to keep his place with me.

"Oh, I guess 'cause it's where I learned to dance, Emily. Had some good times with Pop there. Can you give me until next Saturday to let you know? I want to discuss the price with Alex."

"Of course, Ty."

We said our good-byes and hung up. I had my beloved Alex and children. And in my youth, owning a dance studio had seemed like an impossible possibility. I'd been blessed. I couldn't uproot my family or sell The Silver Slipper. But I didn't want Pop's place to slip through my fingers. After Pop's funeral, Alex had asked Emily to call when she had a price in mind for his house, and I had wondered why ever since.

I heard the taxi's horn; Alex was back. I made my way out to the street to help carry in groceries.

With the three bags now on the kitchen counter, Alex and I started putting the groceries away.

"Emily called," I said.

Alex's hand let go of the refrigerator handle, and she laid a bag of green grapes on the counter. "What did she want?"

My wife's eyes told me that she knew what Emily wanted, but that I was obliged to spell it out anyway. "Emily quoted me a price and asked if we wanted to buy Pop's place."

"*We*? Don't you mean *you*?"

"What about the day Pop was buried, what you said to Emily?"

"What was I supposed to do, Ty? You looked like you were in a trance; your silence was so awkward. I was bailing you out when I told Emily to call and give us her asking price. You had to know I didn't want to buy Pop's house, or soda-fountain shop, if that's how you think of it. We have a house and a studio here. And what about our kids? You'd drag them to that God-awful place? That day in Greenstone, how you acted scared me. It wasn't just the funeral, was it? You miss the place. You miss your family."

Alex's brown eyes were glazed with a coat of tears.

"Why are you upset? I didn't say we're going back there to live. But Mom and Dad are there, and yes, I do miss them. I moved to New York City to become a dancer, but I was also running away from a bad relationship with my dad. Running away from mining, a job I couldn't stomach. I was naïve about what it takes to be head of the household and to raise children. A lot was on my dad's shoulders; I realize that now."

"So the kids and I are a burden, Ty?"

"No, I love you and the kids. I'm saying that when I was young, I didn't understand the pressure Dad felt to be a good husband, a provider for his family. That's why he was stern. Don't ever think you and the kids are a burden. You're not. That's where I went wrong when I was a teenager. I thought I was a burden to my dad."

"Greenstone isn't some place I could get use to. I was raised in Missouri too; but Saint Louis is nothing like that place. You used to think Greenstone was Hicksville. How could you even consider asking the kids and me to adapt to that way of life?" Alex sat down on a kitchen chair and cradled her face in her hands.

An important statement: "I didn't say we're going back there to live," hadn't penetrated my wife's anger, hadn't reached my wife's brain.

While owning The Silver Slipper was a dream come true, I hadn't adapted to living in New York City as well as my wife thought I had. The traffic, noise, the hustle-bustle of people in a hurry all the time, the idea that I'd never be comfortable letting our children play in their own yard unsupervised, were concerns that intensified after Robert was born. I should have done more than hint about those concerns, but I hadn't. Alex liked the Big Apple, and it was *home*. I still wanted to buy Pop's place, but there was only one right thing to say.

"Alex, I'll call Emily and tell her we aren't interested in buying."

"I understand," Emily said. "You have a family and a business in New York City, Ty."

If Emily would have chosen to make Pop's place her home, that would have been fine by me. But Jack Brown using it as a warehouse for Burt's Grocery seemed cold. Knowing that boxes of canned goods, flour, and sugar would be stacked one on top of the other on the floor I once danced on stung worse than a nest of hornets.

Chapter 51

My son and I made our way inside the house, Robert carrying the boxes of sparklers we'd bought at the store.

"How many more days till the Fourth, Dad?"

"Two."

"Bet there's a lot of sparklers in these two boxes. Can I light some *tonight*?"

"No, Robert. And I told you when we bought them, I'll be the one lighting them on the Fourth. If you promise to be careful, you can hold them after they're lit."

"Okay."

I was looking forward to the Fourth of July, hoping a family barbecue would lighten the mood between Alex and me. The topic of buying Pop's place in April had caused a rift between us. The quarrel itself was short-lived, but Alex's attitude toward me was proof that resentment remained with her. And to be truthful, I hadn't rid myself of bitterness, thinking about those canned goods stacked in Pop's former soda-fountain shop.

"Give me the sparklers, Robert," I said as we entered the kitchen.

Alex was waiting for us. Her strained expression spoke to me.

"What's up?" I said, putting the sparklers in a cabinet.

"Son, the girls are in the living room. Be Mom's helper; keep an eye on them for me."

Robert, always glad to play the big brother part, was off.

Between the look on my wife's face and her standard way of getting Robert out of earshot, I knew something was wrong.

"Marta called. Your dad had a stroke."

"How bad is he?"

"Your mom said it's not good. The right side of his face is paralyzed, and his speech is slurred; she can't understand anything he says. They took him by ambulance to Wakefield about 1:00 p.m."

Once a week, I phoned my folks. Last call, Dad hadn't let on about not feeling well; he sounded the same as usual, worn-out, but happy to hear from me. I looked at my wristwatch; it was 2:30. By myself, I could be out the door in a hurry and get the first available flight, but then Alex would be left behind, and her insecurity about me abandoning her would flare up again.

"Did you get the phone number for the hospital?" I said.

Alex picked up a paper from the counter and handed it to me, and I dialed.

"Wakefield Memorial Hospital. This is Pamela. How may I help you?"

"I'd like to be connected to Charles Partridge's room."

"Hold on, please," Pamela said.

Second after second passed. The marked pulsing in my temples quickened.

"Mr. Partridge is in intensive care," Pamela said. "Are you family?"

"Yes, I'm his son."

"I'll connect you to the nurses' station," Pamela said.

"Intensive care, Marjorie speaking."

"My father, Charles Partridge, is being treated for a stroke. My mother's there with him; I'd like to speak to her, please."

"Of course. Hold on; I'll get her."

An exhausted breath came through the receiver. "Ty, it's Mom. Dad's had a second stroke; get here as quick as you can."

I hung up the phone. I didn't want to rock my marriage; things between Alex and me weren't as solid as they should have been. Knowing that going to Wakefield, Missouri, without my wife could resurrect her notion that I might not return to her was trouble I didn't want to deal with.

"Alex, Dad's had a second stroke. Mom's scared, and I need to leave on the first flight I can get. I'll call Nadia and Margaret and ask if they can stay with the kids. I hope they can, but if not, you understand I have to go, don't you?"

That suspect look I'd seen on Alex's face before was there again.

"Why are you looking at me like that?"

"Some men leave and never come back," Alex said.

"I'm tired of this. Why do you think I'd abandon you?"

My wife's eyes filled with tears. "Bruno isn't my biological father, but he married Mom before I was born. Supporting a wife and kid wasn't my birthfather's thing."

That's why she freaked out before; she thought if I went to Greenstone alone, I wouldn't return to her, I thought.

I drew Alex to me and felt her heart beat against my chest. "Well that's not me. I love you and the kids. I swear I'll never leave you. Believe me?"

Alex nodded to affirm.

That Bruno wasn't her biological father came as a shock, but that he had raised her as his own exposed a redeeming quality in him.

I called our adopted grandmas, and Nadia answered.

"Dad's had a stroke, and Alex and I need to get to Wakefield Memorial Hospital in Missouri as soon as possible. Can you and Margaret watch the kids?"

"Yes, of course," Nadia said. "We can come whenever you say."

"Come now; I'm hoping we'll catch a break when I call the airport." I hung up feeling thankful we had two willing grandmas living in New York City and grateful that Alex would be going with me.

"They'll come," I said to Alex. She hurried upstairs to pack that Tuesday afternoon, while I called LaGuardia Airport. There was no flight available for Wakefield, but a plane was departing for Saint Louis, Missouri, at 4:20 p.m. Eastern Time. I called my brother-in-law, Drew, and asked him to pick us up at Lambert Airport. Then I called our dance instructor, James, and told him my dad had a stroke and that Alex and I would be gone a few days. James said he'd get Peggy and Jonathan, our part-time instructors, to cover our dance classes at The Silver Slipper.

Chapter 52

Our plane landed at 5:30 p.m. Central Time. Alex and I deplaned with our carry-on bags, and Drew was waiting for us. He dropped us off at Wakefield Memorial Hospital a little after 7:00 p.m. Minutes later, we were standing next to my dad.

"Glad you're both here," Mom said. Dad's face had an ashen hue to it; his eyes were glazed, and the lid of the right one drooped as he fixed his eyes on me.

"Whatcha trying to pull here, Dad?" I said. When he moved his lips to speak, his mouth on the right side drooped, and I couldn't understand a word he said.

I wanted to find out what the doctor thought, if there was a chance Dad could get back to normal, or if the chance I should be worried about was whether he would live. Dad's eyes reached out to me, and he kept trying to tell me something.

My opportunity to get some answers about Dad's condition came sooner than I thought. A tall man with the build of a lumberjack walked through the door, smiled, and said, "I'm Dr. Pickford."

The doctor spoke like common folks do and explained the damage Dad's stroke had done.

"The first stroke Charles had caused his right eyelid to sag and the right side of his mouth to droop. That damage will be with him the rest of his life."

Dad's face was disfigured and that would never change. I knew I'd have to prepare Robert, Angela, and Andrea for Dad's appearance before Alex and I decided to take them to visit their grandpa.

"The first stroke also affected Charles's speech," Dr. Pickford said. "Speech therapy should return his speaking ability to near normal. The second stroke affected his right arm and leg. When we get him to a regular room, he'll start physical therapy, and like speech therapy, that will continue when he gets home. Charles will eventually be able to move his arm at will again, but fine motor skills, like holding a pen or picking up coins, may continue to give him a problem. As far as the damage to his right leg, we'll have to see what progress he makes in physical therapy. He may always need to use a walker, and he'll be taking the blood thinner Coumadin the rest of his life. Do any of you have questions? Charles?"

Dad had tears running down his cheeks as he shook his head no. Then the doctor did something I'll never forget. He took a tissue and wiped Dad's eyes.

"Your brain's fine, Charles. And your wife told me you've been a miner a long time. So you're used to hard work. I expect you'll give therapy your best."

Dr. Pickford handed Mom a business card. "My office is on-site. Suite 301 in the Physician's Building. If any of you think of questions later, call."

That night, Mom slept in a chair alongside Dad's hospital bed in the intensive care unit; Alex and I slept in the waiting room.

At 6:30 a.m., I left Alex asleep on the couch and tiptoed into Dad's room to check on him. Dad was sleeping, but Mom was awake, leaning forward in her chair, her eyes steady on him. Minutes ticked away, and no words passed between Mom and me, and then in walked Dr. Pickford. His eyes were bloodshot, and he leaned against the wall as he spoke.

"Charles's blood has thinned to where I want it to be," he said, keeping the volume of his voice low. "That'll help prevent further clots from forming. He's stable; as soon as a room opens up, we'll move him."

"Doctor, my husband won't have another stroke, will he?"

"He's out of the woods for now, Mrs. Partridge, but there's no guarantee for down the road. The Coumadin will help prevent another one, though. I've left orders at the nurses' station to check on your husband every half hour, at least today."

The doctor left, his stride long and quick. He had somewhere else to be.

Mom collapsed back into the chair, and I continued to stand. Dad's eyelids quivered. That cleft in his chin, his high cheekbones, and the way his thick, once all-black eyebrows stretched above his deep-set eyes in a straight line were so familiar to me. And I realized for the first time how much I looked like him.

I went back to the waiting room, woke Alex, and filled her in on Dr. Pickford's report. Then my wife and I found a payphone down the hall; we needed to call home.

"Hello." Margaret's tone had an edge to it.

"Hi. It's Ty. Called to check on how you and Nadia are doing with the kids."

"Fine. Everybody's fine." The quality of Margaret's voice was smoother. "How's your dad?"

I could hear music in the background and Andrea putting up a stink about eating breakfast; I imagined Robert dancing, trying to soothe her objection. "Well, we're waiting for a bed to become available, and then they'll move him to a regular room. He's had two strokes that caused paralysis and speech problems, but the doctor seems to think therapy will help. Alex and I would like to stay tomorrow yet, see how Dad's making out, if that's okay with you guys."

"Stay as long as you need to," Margaret said. "We're—"

Nadia's voice broke in. "By all means. The kids are fine."

"Thanks a bunch," I said. "Uh ... Robert might be a problem tomorrow night. I promised I'd light a few sparklers on the Fourth and let him hold them. Put him on the phone; I'll explain that he'll have to wait till I get home to do that."

"Nonsense," Nadia said. "I'll keep that promise for you, and don't worry, Robert won't get hurt. Now put Alex on the phone so we can say hi to her."

Alex went through the whole "mother" routine, everything from making sure Robert's bowels were moving, to clueing Nadia and Margaret in on the fact that Angela was fond of Robert's crayons, which if left on the floor, she would try to eat. After Alex exhausted her checklist of possible problems, she hung up, and we went back to Dad in the ICU.

Dad couldn't speak his mind, but his defeated sighs and angry grunts were as clear a message as any roadside billboard. At 6:25 p.m., Dad was taken from the ICU to Room 204, and we hit it lucky; there was no patient in bed two. We used one of the chairs from the other side of the curtain, and all three of us could sit. A nurse came in every half hour, as Dr. Pickford had said they would, and at 9:00 p.m., Dad was given a sleeping pill. He went out like a light. We washed our faces and brushed our teeth in the bathroom down the hall, and then Alex and I retired to the waiting room. Mom slept in the chair next to Dad's bed.

My wife and I went downstairs to get coffee and breakfast food from the cafeteria. Alex had been a good sport to this point, but not getting to shower again wasn't setting well with her. If Dad's condition warranted that we stay longer, I knew I'd have to get us a hotel.

With our trays of food in hand, we waited for the elevator. The door opened, and Dr. Pickford bustled out.

"Doctor," I called out as he passed Alex and me. He turned around, and his expression revealed he didn't recognize us. "Charles Partridge's son and daughter-in-law," I said.

"Ah, yes." He pushed his wire-rim glasses back up to the bridge of his ski-sloped nose.

"Glad we caught you, Doctor. Can you tell us how long my dad will be here? We have small children."

"If all goes well, two more days. But after Charles gets home, that'll be the long haul. Even after months of therapy, he'll never work as a miner again, and he may experience depression. If I were you, I'd go home to your children. Your mother might need your help more when Charles gets home."

The elevator chimed and opened; Alex and I got on.

I put Mom's coffee, pancakes, and sausage on the nightstand and told her Alex and I would be taking the first flight home the next morning. Dad was asleep again, something he was doing a lot of. What Dr. Pickford had said worried me. If Dad couldn't work, he'd feel useless. If it came down to Mom needing my help, Alex would have to manage The Silver Slipper alone. And my wife wouldn't like me being in Greenstone and leaving her and the kids in New York City.

Depression, I thought. Dealing with another family member's depression, depressed me.

Chapter 53

Four days after Dad was released from Wakefield Memorial Hospital, the phone rang. Startled, I rolled over to reach the phone on the nightstand and saw the alarm clock. It was 6:15 a.m. My wife pressed her body next to mine and put her ear near the receiver.

A rigid tension settled in the back of my neck that tenth day of July in 1978. *What's happened?* "Hello."

"Bird, it's Mom. I don't know what to do with Charles. He's acted up so, I had to stop sitting for Hannah."

I could tell Mom was sobbing when she spoke. "Calm down, and tell me what's wrong."

"Charles won't eat, and I can't get him out of bed. He won't mind the therapists, either. Bird, he's so down in the dumps; I don't know what he might do. Please come home; bring Alex and the children. Seeing all of you might help Charles. I need you."

"Mom, I'll call LaGuardia Airport and get the first direct flight to Wakefield. And I'll call you back when I know my arrival time."

That Alex would want to go with me to my parents' home in Greenstone, Missouri, was a certainty. My mother's description of Dad's behavior gave me reason to believe that Dr. Pickford's warning had become a reality. I didn't think Robert, Angela, and

Andrea should see their grandpa with his distorted face and in the throes of depression. But to impose on Nadia and Margaret again didn't seem right.

Alex shot out of bed and left our bedroom.

"Mom, put Dad on the phone."

Minutes passed.

"Okay, he's listening," Mom said.

"Dad, I'm coming back to Greenstone, but you do what Mom says till I get there. Understand?"

A throaty noise was the best Dad could produce.

While I was calling LaGuardia Airport, Alex tossed two suitcases on the bed.

"The kids and I are going," she said.

The fact that there was a flight into Wakefield Airport that same day, to my notion, was divine intervention. I booked the flight for my family and me, then called Mom back to tell her our arrival time. She told me Drew was down in the back, but her waitress friend, Annie, would pick us up at the airport.

Then I called our dance instructor, James.

"Hello."

"James, this is Ty. Sorry to call so early, but a situation has come up in Greenstone; my Dad isn't doing well. My family and I are flying out today to check on him. We'll be gone five days, and I need both ballrooms covered."

"Hope your dad feels better, and don't worry about the studio," James said. "Peggy and Jonathan are always glad to get extra teaching time; they'll cover your dance classes."

"Thanks. I appreciate your help."

At 4:05 p.m. CST, we landed at Wakefield Airport. Annie was waiting at the baggage carousel and took Angela from me so I could get our luggage and the twins' car seats from the conveyor belt. I loaded our belongings onto a cart, then pushed it out to

Annie's car. I installed the car seats, and Alex and Annie fastened the girls in the backseat while I put our luggage in the trunk.

Alex sat in front with Annie. Robert was in the backseat on my lap, secured with my seat belt, and the girls, snuggling their favorite stuffed toys, were next to each other. I didn't think the twins would be alarmed by Dad's sagging eyelid and drooping mouth, but I was concerned about how my four-year-old son would react. The drive to Greenstone was to be my opportunity to prepare Robert for his grandpa's distorted face. Ten minutes into our drive, I had mentally rehearsed what I wanted to say to my son, but all three kids had fallen asleep.

Annie's car bumped over my parents' graveled driveway. We parked behind Dad's old Chevy truck, and all three kids woke up.

"Robert, girls, we're going to see Grandma and Grandpa Partridge," I said.

The dilapidated screen door swung open; a corner of the mesh was hanging loose from the frame. Mom, in one of her print housedresses, made her way to the car. She thanked Annie for her help, then carried Angela into the house. Alex carried Andrea, who was crying in a high-pitched tone that usually meant a protest of hunger, and Robert followed behind them. I brought up the rear with the suitcases.

Dad was in his wheelchair, I'm sure only because of my conversation with him on the phone. He reached out his arms to Robert.

"Hi, Grandpa," my son said and climbed up onto Dad's lap.

Mom went into the kitchen with Angela and brought out sugar cookies for the kids. Alex broke off a small piece of the soft cookie and put it in Andrea's mouth. Her crying ceased. At least as far as the kids were concerned, all was good.

A pot of potato soup awaited us for supper. Dad ate little, then clamped his mouth shut when Mom put the spoon to his lips. My mother hadn't exaggerated the circumstances. I didn't want my three children to hear the conversation I was going to have with their grandpa, so I bided my time to have a talk with Dad.

At 8:30 p.m., Alex and I had the kids bedded down. I asked Alex to sit with Mom in the kitchen, then I pushed Dad into the living room. He looked at me, the strokes' handiwork imprinted on him physically, emotionally—and I saw what Mom had seen. He didn't want to live.

I positioned Dad's wheelchair to face where I would sit in the rocking chair.

"After I hung up yesterday, I thought about what I'd say to you when I got here. I remembered something you said to me the first time I brought Alex here to meet you. You said you wanted to figure out how to be a better father. Remember?"

Dad shook his head yes.

"Well, somewhere along the way, I figured out I should be a better son. I've always been a disappointment to you."

Dad squirmed in his wheelchair, trying to work his lopsided mouth. The paralysis brought tears to his eyes. After several attempts to voice his thoughts, he shook his head and croaked out, "Not."

I leaned forward and placed my hand on his shoulder. "I was fed up with your stubborn mind-set when I left Greenstone. Then I paid my first-month's rent in Queens, and I realized something; the remainder of my money wasn't going to last long there. That's when I understood why you said the things you did to me when I lived here. You knew in Greenstone I'd have a steady paycheck as a miner, and you were worried that I wouldn't find a job dancing in New York City. Things were rough for a while. I had to work at a crummy bar so I didn't become homeless. But I didn't stop pursuing a career dancing, 'cause I was *meant* to be a dancer. Eventually, I got a job as an instructor at the dance studio Alex and I now own. Dad, don't give up; don't let those strokes keep you from being the man you're meant to be."

"I won't," he said and gave me his best possible smile.

Dad's broken language, both coarse and sparse, was music to my ears. "I won't," was all I needed to hear.

Alex, the kids, and I spent our five days with my folks, and then we flew back home to New York City. I knew Dad would cooperate with Mom and his therapists. And I knew my dad was one tough old miner that no stroke could hold hostage.

Chapter 54

Scarce remains of orange, red, and yellow leaves in November proclaimed that Christmas was approaching. Big brother Robert had the Sears catalog and a red marker out that Saturday afternoon. He was helping Angela and Andrea draw circles around pictures of toys Santa should bring them.

Dad had been released from speech therapy, and I decided to call and get an update on how his physical therapy was going. If his motor skills were better, I wanted to make him and Mom a proposition.

"Hello," Dad responded after the second ring. His voice was strong and clear.

"Dad, it's Ty. You sound great. Running any foot races yet?"

"Too old for that, Son. But I'm good. My speech only slips up now and then, and I'm moving around with this here walker. The physical therapist says soon, I'll just need a cane. May need it the rest of my life, but I'd like to think I'll be able to toss it someday too. How're Alex and the kids?"

"Everybody's great. Alex and I wondered if you and Mom would be up to coming here for Christmas. The flight would be our present to you."

"I don't know; neither of us has flown, Ty. Better let you speak to Marta. Hold on."

"You won't feel like you're up in the air," I said, and then I told one other lie: "I'd rather fly than drive," which won Mom over. I hung up the phone and told Alex that my folks said they'd come. Then it occurred to me that it wouldn't be right if Michelle and Bruno weren't invited too.

"What about your folks, Alex?"

"Are you crazy? The way my dad's thrown his restaurant success in your dad's face. Hard telling what else he might say to Charles. I don't want things stirred up, especially at Christmas. Besides, we don't have enough bedrooms."

"We'll buy an extra bed and I'll hang drapes in the spare bedroom for my folks. Your folks can have our room, and we'll get a rollaway bed set up for us in the basement. You know Nadia and Margaret can't stay out of the kitchen; you'll have plenty of help with Christmas dinner. We can afford it now. If we wait, we might not get the chance to have them visit; my dad could have another stroke, or one of your folks could have health problems."

"Yeah, I get it. And you're right. But promise you'll be the designated referee if there's a problem," Alex said.

"Promise."

Chapter 55

My folks had insisted on delivering their gifts to Drew and Hannah on Christmas Eve Day before leaving Greenstone, and my father-in-law had a large party booked at his restaurant in Saint Louis for lunch on the twenty-fourth. Of course he had to be there to supervise. Alex's folks were flying out of Lambert Airport in Saint Louis and mine were flying out of Wakefield on Christmas Eve.

At 7:00 p.m., I called for a taxi. The cabbie arrived at our home in Washington Heights at 7:15. In twenty minutes, Alex and I were being dropped off at Terminal A at LaGuardia Airport. No one except Alex's dad looked frazzled from the flight when we met our folks at their baggage carousels. After their luggage was all collected, I hailed a taxi.

Nadia and Margaret had the kids in bed when we got home with our folks, and sandwiches and homemade cookies awaited us. A little after ten, our adopted grandmothers left, and the rest of us turned in for the night. With a sense of satisfaction at having my parents and Alex's in for Christmas, I fell asleep. I had no inkling what Christmas Day would bring.

I heard a loud thump and sat up in bed. Disoriented from my broken sleep, I wasn't certain that the noise was real. I looked at the other half of the bed where Alex should have been, but wasn't. My gut told me that one of the girls climbing out of their crib, which happened on occasion, couldn't have made such a loud sound. But I ran down the hall to the twins' room just the same, 'cause the thump sounded like it came from that direction. Sprawled out facedown on the wood hall floor, just past the twins' room, was my dad. His cane lay alongside him. "Dad," I yelled and squatted down beside him.

"Ty, I heard it from our bathroom," Alex said as she came running down the hall. "How bad's he hurt?"

"I'm not sure."

"Dad, I'm going to turn you over," I said.

Dad looked up at me; blood trickled down his nose—but worse than the blood was the shame in his eyes.

Mom made her way to us and knelt next to Dad. "Charles."

"Don't worry yourselves none; I'm okay, just got to get my wind back."

Bruno had refused the spare bedroom we'd offered him and Michelle. The two of them made their way upstairs from their rollaway in the basement. Seeing the obvious, my father-in-law said, "Took a fall myself at the restaurant carrying a box of chicken breasts out of the freezer. Slipped on a freshly mopped floor and bit my tongue so hard, I bled all over the place. Things happen."

I knew Bruno would continue to boast about his lucrative business, but his attempt to ease my dad's embarrassment that Christmas morning meant he was at least capable of showing empathy. That made me optimistic that Bruno might soften up his attitude toward me, his non-Italian son-in-law. I only hoped I didn't have to bloody my nose to find some common ground with him.

We got Dad to his feet and helped him to the hall bathroom, where he'd been headed when he fell. Mom washed his face, and we concluded that nothing was broken. Somehow, the kids slept through all that commotion. We went on our way to get showered and dressed, so when the kids got up, we could see what Santa had brought them.

Nadia and Margaret had arrived, and we were all sitting in the living room, waiting for the kids to get up. At 8:30, Robert came downstairs; then Alex and I got the girls up and brought them downstairs too. Robert took the silver bell off the tree and rang it, as was customary, meaning the kids were going to open their gifts.

The wrapping paper made a collage of red, green, gold, and blue on the living room floor as Angela, Andrea, and Robert made quick work of their stash. It felt good to be able to buy those nice toys for the kids. I got a kick out of watching Mom and Michelle entertain the twins with Kermit the Frog and Miss Piggy. Angela and Andrea giggled as their grandmas brought the stuffed characters from *The Muppet Show* to life. I picked up the crumpled paper, and then Robert and I had a car race with his new Hot Wheels.

The smell of fried potatoes, bacon and eggs, blueberry pancakes, and especially the coffee, which I needed, grabbed my attention. I went to get a cup. That's when I remembered. Nadia had asked if it would be okay for her to invite a guest, a guest she sidestepped giving a name to. I quietly took Nadia aside and asked when her guest was arriving.

"Probably not for breakfast. Maybe for dinner. We'll see."

Nadia went to the refrigerator and took out a carton of half-and-half to fill the creamer. I knew her well enough to know that she was dodging further discussion about the topic. I got a cup of coffee and went back to the living room for another car race with Robert.

With our stomachs full, we grown-ups talked, drank more coffee, and watched the kids play with their new toys in the living room. The bay window framed a picturesque scene. Large snowflakes were falling, first floating down lazily, then falling faster, sticking to the glass, giving off hues of blue as the sun's rays worked its magic. The morning passed with easy conversation and yes, some midday catnapping. In my cocoon of happiness, with a feeling of family unity, I had no idea what would happen later that afternoon.

Nadia, Margaret, and Alex were in the kitchen again preparing a meal. Nadia's mystery guest hadn't shown. I quietly took her aside and asked, "Should I ask Alex to hold things up, till your guest arrives?"

"No. I guess he isn't coming. Oh, those onions I chopped are burning my eyes."

Nadia wiped at her cheek, then continued helping Alex and Margaret. She had never spoken of a man friend. But whomever *he* was, the probability that he wasn't going to show was breaking her heart, 'cause I'd never seen her cry before.

A little after 4:00 p.m., we sat down and I said grace. Out loud, I thanked God for our food, but in the quiet of my mind, I also thanked him for healing injuries of the heart, for my family gathered together under my roof. The brown-sugar-and-pineapple-glazed ham decorated with maraschino cherries, potato salad, baked beans, slaw, and homemade apple custard pie were heavenly. Even my Italian father-in-law praised the cooks.

We men headed for the living room. Dad and Bruno flopped on the couch. I sat on the floor and watched Robert, Angela, and Andrea, while the women did the dishes. The TV volume was turned up, so Bruno, who was in need of a hearing aid but wouldn't admit it, could hear over Angela and Andrea's racket as they played. Somehow, I managed to hear the doorbell.

Looking through the glass pane in the door was a dark-haired man, graying at his temples, in a tweed overcoat. I opened the door. He was holding a huge bouquet of red and white roses.

"This is the Partridge home?" The man said, his accent different, yet so familiar.

"Yes." The imposing size of the man was mismatched with his mellow voice.

"Ah, good. I am Gavril Slovinski."

"Slovinski?"

"Nadia Slovinskia's son."

Son? I thought.

"Mother told you I was coming. Yes?"

"Of course. Come in. Nadia's in the kitchen. Follow me."

Nadia was at the sink washing dishes. Gavril put his finger to his lips, snuck up behind her, and put his massive arms over her head, displaying the roses.

She turned, her hands dripping with soapy water, and took the bouquet. "Son, you came." Tears ran down Nadia's cheeks, but this time she offered no false excuse for their existence.

Gavril leaned down and kissed his mother's forehead. "I'm sorry."

"You need not apologize. Come, I will introduce you."

I put a movie in the VCR, one of Robert's favorites, *Pete's Dragon.* He knew the songs in it by heart. The twins would be entertained by their brother, if not by Elliott the dragon. I asked Alex's folks and mine to keep an eye on Robert, Angela, and Andrea. Nadia fixed Gavril a plate of food and asked Alex, Margaret, and me to sit back down at the kitchen table while he ate.

Why'd Nadia never mentioned Gavril? Why's he here now? I thought.

"Gavril, I never told my family here that I was married and had a son. Believing I would never be reunited with you, that part of my life was too painful to share. And fearing that you might change your mind and not come today, I did not tell them who I was expecting. It is time to tell Alex, Ty, and Margaret about my life before I came to the United States."

"As you wish, Mother."

I had known Nadia as an accomplished dancer, successful business owner, generous mother figure to Alex and me, and an angel of a grandma to my children. But that Christmas Day in 1978, I found out that she and I had another special connection. We'd both been severed from family.

"I married Gavril Slovinski, and as was customary, an *a* was added to the end of my new surname. I became Mrs. Nadia Slovinskia. Gavril, like my parents, owned a vodka distillery in Russia, in the Union of Soviet Socialist Republics. He had been a long-time friend of the family, had good business sense, and was twelve years older than me, and I felt very secure at first. But then Gavril insisted I become pregnant and give up my ballet performances. I had studied ballet for years, even as a child, and pleaded that I could be both mother and performer. But Gavril said *no*. I obeyed my husband. At age twenty-two, I gave birth to my son, and my husband denied me any say in naming him. 'He will be named Gavril, and do not question me about this,' he said.

"My husband's domination of me grew worse, and he beat me if dinner wasn't to his liking. I hid ten years of abuse from my parents and Gavril Jr., but one day, my husband held a knife to my throat. I decided I must take my son and escape. I wrote to the American Ballet Theatre in New York City, stating my qualifications to become part of their ballet company, and they were interested in hiring me. I applied and received a professional visa for employment in the United States, and my plan to escape from Gavril Sr. was in motion.

"I was caught in the process, and my husband took Gavril Jr. from me, put me on the steamship to America, and lied to my son and parents, saying I had deserted my family to pursue a ballet career in the United States. When the ship docked at Ellis

Island in Upper New York Bay, I was heartbroken not having my son, Gavril Jr., with me and also terrified at being alone in a foreign country."

I left Greenstone to escape Dad's control. I left family behind too, I thought.

"I wrote to my parents every day for a month, trying to convince them of what really happened. But my husband had always acted charming around them, and they believed his lies about me. Only after Gavril sold his vodka business and he and Gavril Jr. were nowhere to be found, did my parents believe me. And then they tried in vain to assist me in finding my son. It was as if my husband and son had vanished.

"My work for the American Ballet Theatre was minimal; I mostly filled in for injured dancers. My working as a waitress in New York City was necessary for me to pay my rent. I had no money to return to the USSR until my parents, Edik Petrov and Agafia Petrova, died, and my paternal uncle sold their distillery and sent me my inheritance. But even though I now had money, the diplomatic consular post would not allow me to return to the USSR. My husband, Gavril, had told yet another lie about me. He had reported me as a traitor, disloyal to the socialist system.

"Years passed. I grew older, sure I'd never be reunited with my son. But then two months ago, my friend, Askana Volkova, whom I've kept correspondence with, wrote that she'd seen an advertisement for the Saint Petersburg Imperial Orchestra, and Gavril Slovinski Jr. was listed as a featured cellist. I sent a letter to Gavril in care of Saint Petersburg Imperial Symphony Hall and explained what happened when he was ten. Five days later, I received a letter from him. He said that he'd secured a seat with the orchestra shortly after his father died from liver failure. I found out that my son had a family and that they lived in the town of Zelenogorsk in Saint Petersburg. And my heart jumped with joy as I read the last line of Gavril's letter: 'I will come to Manhattan and meet with you Christmas Day.'

"Margaret, Alex, Ty, I apologize for being secretive about my past. I thought I could bury my hurt by throwing myself into my work. But that never happened. Even as much as I loved running The Silver Slipper, the thought of not seeing my son again wouldn't allow that."

Gavril took a photo of his wife and two grown boys from his wallet and handed it to Nadia. "Mother, come home. My wife Alena and sons Alek and Arman want to know you. Come live with us."

How could I resent Nadia's reunion with Gavril? I knew what it meant to me when I was reunited with my folks and my dad again accepted me as his son. But if Nadia chose to live in Russia, I'd lose a member of my family. I smiled, trying to hide my wish that she would refuse Gavril's offer.

Nadia seemed taken aback that such an offer was on the table. Her eyes reached out to Margaret. To me. To Alex. I held my breath in that split second, not sure how she'd respond.

"Gavril, such a wonderful son. Such a generous offer to a mother you haven't seen since you were a child. How blessed I am. As much as it pains me, I must decline."

"Mother. Why?"

"Gavril, this is my home. But to visit you would be wonderful."

"As you wish, then, Mother."

Relief washed through me, and my selfish interest in preserving my connection with Nadia gave way to the bittersweet pain I knew she felt when she reached across the table and placed her hand on Gavril's forearm.

"You will go back with me tomorrow morning for that visit," Gavril said.

"I can't return to the USSR."

Gavril handed Nadia an envelope. "You can. My father's lie about you being a traitor is no longer an issue. A political friend helped me resolve that."

Early the next morning, I called a cab for Nadia and Gavril that took them to LaGuardia Airport. How glad I was that Nadia had decided not to live with Gavril and his family. Her son in America loved her too.

Chapter 56

One year had passed. It was a frigid Monday morning that January in 1979. Alex, not yet dressed for work, was at the kitchen table in her gingham robe, drinking a cup of coffee. The doorbell rang, and I got up to see who it was. The mailman handed me a clipboard and asked me to sign for a registered letter. I looked at the return address, then made my way back to the kitchen and sat down in the chair next to my wife.

"Who was that?" Alex said.

"The mailman. Had me sign for this. Look at the return address."

Alex took the letter from me. "Schuester and Schuester Law Firm?" She opened the envelope and began scanning a handwritten letter. "It's from Emily, Ty."

"Emily?"

"Yeah; Jack Brown kept trying but couldn't get a loan to buy Pop's place. Emily is leaving it to you, if you'll take it. The letter says she married her former boss; they've retired, and her husband's sold his half of Schuester and Schuester Law Firm to his brother. Emily and her husband are moving to Saint Charles, Missouri, and they want to be rid of Pop's house. Must be well-off to give the place away."

Alex removed the staple securing Emily's note to some typed pages.

"That may be, but Pop told me Emily couldn't stand Greenstone," I said. "Thought her mother died 'cause she didn't get out of there. I believe Emily just wants to be rid of anything connecting her to Greenstone."

"But why didn't Emily offer to give Pop's house to Jack Brown? She knows he wants it for extra storage for his grocery store."

"Jack wasn't close to Pop like I was, Alex. Besides, Emily knows Pop wouldn't want canned goods stored there."

"All you have to do is sign your name on this document, and Emily's going to give you the deed to Pop's house. Are you going to do it?"

Electrifying excitement shot through me, but Alex's tensed face was reason enough to not show how pleased I was about Emily's offer. I was trying to come up with a way to convince my wife to let me sign my name, and Alex didn't appreciate my silence.

"I love you, and I understand what Pop's place means to you, but if you think you're moving the kids and me to Greenstone, think again."

"Just hear me out. I love you too; I'd never force anything you didn't agree to."

Alex's face relaxed; her eyes softened.

"Dad's strokes took away his ability to work as a miner, but he's made a better recovery than we thought possible. He's tossed his cane and Mom can't find enough for him to do around the house. It wouldn't cost much to turn Pop's place back into a soda-fountain shop, and Dad could run it; he'd be happy to have a job. Swing-dance lessons wouldn't be offered like when Pop ran the shop, but at least the kids in Greenstone would have a place to hang out. I'd put a red neon sign in the window with 'Pop's Pop' on it, like Pop used to have. The place would be a memorial to Pop and a new beginning for Dad. It'd mean so much to me."

A big smile spread across Alex's face, and that special way she looked at me made me lose my train of thought. She leaned over, wrapped her arms around my neck, and kissed me. "Call your dad; make sure he's on board before you sign."

Chapter 57

My goal was to turn Pop's house back into Pop's Pop, the soda-fountain shop I'd known as a teen in the sixties. I took the third and fourth weeks of January off from The Silver Slipper to work with Dad on the restoration.

It was apparent that Dad had more know-how than me when it came to remodeling. He told me how to take up that glued-down carpet in Pop's house. By the time I had scraped the remnants of backing off the floor with a putty knife, Dad had the pieces of carpet rolled up and tied. And his carpentry skills building the soda fountain bar surprised me too. I did the heavy work, but Dad did the brain work. After we got done buffing those black-and-white tiles on the floor, the place looked like Pop's Pop again, except for some finishing touches. Dad had reinforced what I'd already known: those strokes he'd had couldn't keep a guy like him down.

By Wednesday of our second week, chrome-leg stools were lined up at the soda-fountain bar, and tables and chairs almost like Pop used to have were in place. I had a picture from Pop's photo album enlarged of him and Mary when they were teens, holding their first-place trophy at the Wakefield Dance Contest. I hung that picture, giving it center stage on the wall behind the soda-fountain bar. Pop's recording artists' pictures that Emily had left in a closet were put on that wall too. Propped against the crate I once used as a nightstand, Emily had left the red-neon "Pop's Pop" sign that I knew as a kid. I couldn't help but think that Pop was laughing when his sign flickered in that picture window once again.

It was 6:00 p.m. when we finished Wednesday night.

Dad pulled a chair out from one of the tables. "Have a seat, Son, got a surprise for you."

A few minutes later, my old dance partner, Emma Jean Johnston, formerly Wilmyer, showed up with her husband, John.

"Emma Jean's got the other gals coming who took lessons at Pop's Pop. They'll be here soon," Dad said.

"What's going on, Emma Jean?"

"Bird, none of us girls have danced since we got married, and our husbands have *never* danced. But your dad said, 'Teaching dance is how my son makes a living; he'll make darn good instructors out of you and your spouses.' He wouldn't take no for an answer."

"That's your surprise, Son; we're gonna offer swing lessons at Pop's Pop."

Sally Jo Forne, formerly Merkel, and Patti Mumper, formerly Baker, showed up, dragging their husbands with them. I spent Wednesday, Thursday, and Friday evenings teaching men who were tired from working all day in the mine how to do basic swing-dance steps. Luckily, Emma Jean had retained more than she'd thought she had. She was good help refreshing the other former dance girls' minds. When I left Greenstone, the team of dancers knew enough to teach a beginners' swing-dance class.

That February first, Dad called me. "Your soda-fountain shop, Pop's Pop, opened for business today, Son."

The Silver Slipper, Robert, Angela, and Andrea kept Alex and me busy, but once a week, I called to check in with Dad to see how things were going at Pop's Pop. Dad would give me a complete rundown of how business was and how the dance instructors were doing with their students. I felt closer to my dad than I'd ever felt in my life. By April, twenty-two kids in Greenstone were taking swing-dance lessons at Pop's Pop.

"Darnedest thing," Dad said one day when I called him, "Charlie's what those youngsters call me."

Back in the day, that wouldn't have gone over. But I could tell that Dad liked it.

Chapter 58

Another year passed. It was May of 1980. Alex, the two cute Wiggle Sisters, and I were seated in Saint Boniface's gymnasium at 4:00 p.m., attending Robert's kindergarten graduation. Robert's two adopted grandmas in New York City couldn't attend. Gavril had sent two airplane tickets for his mother and Margaret to visit him and his family in the Soviet Union.

"Robert Bradford Partridge," Sister Mary Alice announced.

Robert made his way to the lectern where Sister handed him his diploma. As he was walking back to his seat, his shoe got caught in his long, black robe, and he took a not-too-graceful tumble.

After the ceremony was over, we further celebrated Robert's climb up the scholastic ladder by going to the Rock 'n' Rollin Restaurant, touted as having great burgers. The hostess seated us at a booth and brought booster seats for Andrea and Angela. I placed Robert's graduation gift on the table, then we ordered, burgers and French fries all around.

"Want to open your graduation gift before we get our food, Robert?" Alex said.

"Sure." He ripped off the wrapping paper, opened the box, and removed the black spandex pants and shirt trimmed in red.

"Now you'll have a dance costume to wear when you're at The Silver Slipper with Mom and me," I said.

"Can I wear it now?"

"Yeah, come on. I'll take you to the men's room to change."

Robert and I made our way back to Alex and the girls. He was flaunting his new dance outfit, snapping his fingers to the Beatles' "I Wanna Hold Your Hand," which was playing on the jukebox.

Pictures of recording artists were on all the walls. Opposite our booth were photos displaying Elvis's stardom from his youth to seasoned adulthood, when he was nearing timeless celebrity status. One was the same picture Pop had hanging in his soda-fountain shop when I was a teenager living in Greenstone. And it was among the recording artists' pictures Dad and I had hung when completing the renovation to reopen Pop's Pop.

A group of young boys and girls who must have been dropped off by their parents were sitting in a booth near ours. Two of the girls who looked to be no older than twelve had on miniskirts, tight T-shirts, and their faces were caked with makeup. They got up, walked to the display of Elvis's pictures, and stood in front of it.

"Hope that guy sang better than he dressed," one of the girls said.

"Yeah, what's up with that fringe on his jumpsuit?" the other said.

Look how you're dressed, I thought, but I wanted to say that and more out loud. Elvis had started out as a poor boy, and those girls had no appreciation of his achievements.

"Quite a few teens here," Alex said.

"Must be the burgers," I said.

Sitting through Robert's kindergarten graduation and Sister Mary Alice's long speech had been trying for Angela and Andrea. Being confined again in booster seats at the restaurant had made the twins downright cranky. We finished our meal at the Rock 'n' Rollin Restaurant and went home. Alex and I put the kids to bed early and collapsed on the couch to watch TV.

Ring ... ring.

Startled, I withdrew my arm that had been wrapped around Alex and maneuvered to get to the kitchen. In my semi-awake state and with the only illumination the TV screen, I thought it was much later than it was. An agonizing thought struck my muddled brain. *Another stroke.* I took the receiver off the wall, placed it against my ear, and listened.

"Hello ... Bird? Ty? Somebody there?"

"Yeah, Dad, I'm here. Sorry, phone woke me up."

"Didn't figure you'd be in bed yet. Thought only us folks in Greenstone hit the hay by nine. Should I call back tomorrow?"

"No. No need for that. Alex and I fell asleep on the couch. Must have gotten bored with TV. It's good to hear from you, Dad. Really good."

"You don't sound quite right. Everything okay there?"

"Everything's great," I said, now realizing my anxiety had been conveyed through the phone.

"Good. Glad to hear that. I called to tell you some good news. I convinced two of our students at Pop's Pop to enter the dance contest at Wakefield like you and Emma Jean did. It's the fifteenth of June."

"That's great, Dad. Emma Jean's a talented dancer. Knew she'd do a good job heading up a dance program for you."

"Yeah, she's worked real hard with all the kids. And I'm so proud of how Jessica and Chris have come along. I thought ... well, maybe you ought to take a look at them and give them some pointers, seeing how you made a career out of teaching dance. I ran the idea past Emma Jean, 'cause I didn't want to step on her toes. She's okay with it. Thought maybe you and the family could get here on Sunday, the ninth; that'd give you six days to work with Jessica and Chris. And I was hoping you'd go to the competition on Saturday too. What'd you think, Son?"

Back when Emma Jean and I won the dance competition in Wakefield, Dad thought dancing was a waste of time. His enthusiasm about Jessica and Chris competing at the Wakefield Dance Contest proved he now respected me and my chosen career.

"We'll be there."

Chapter 59

Sunday morning, June 9, my family and I boarded a plane at LaGuardia Airport. One hour and forty minutes into the flight, the wind began tapping its fingers against the plane, and then the seat-belt sign came on. Claps of thunder followed flashes of lightning, and the wind's soft drumming changed to a fist knock. Rain hit the window so hard, it sounded like broken bits of glass.

"This is Captain Morgan." His deep voice coming over the intercom was clear and confident. "We're passing over Indiana and a thunderstorm is in progress. The seat-belt sign will remain on until we get through the storm; I expect that'll be a matter of minutes."

I looked at my watch; it was 10:42 a.m. I had an aisle seat on the 737 plane, and Robert was seated next to me with his eyes glued to a Dr. Seuss book, *The Cat in the Hat*, which he had memorized from Alex reading it to him so many times. I reached across my son to the vacant window seat and pulled the shade down. Alex and the twins, across the aisle from us, had headsets on and were watching a movie, and like Robert, they didn't seem the least bit bothered, either.

Eight minutes had passed since the captain's announcement, but we were still in the throes of the storm, and the seat-belt sign was still on. Two stewardesses walked the aisle, checking that the overhead compartments were secured and that all seat belts were fastened.

A gush of wind pushed against the right side of the plane where Robert and I were seated. The stewardesses hurried down the aisle to the front of the plane to get fastened into their seats. The thunderstorm was now bombarding us with what sounded like a truckload of rocks. My palms were sweaty, my stomach was queasy, and pressure in my lower abdomen had grabbed my attention.

Captain Morgan's voice came through the intercom again. "The wind has picked up, and we're still experiencing heavy rain. The seat-belt sign will remain on until we get clear. Radar indicates we'll be out of the storm soon."

Robert wiggled in his seat, got a candy bar out of his snack bag, and continued looking at his book. The wind continued to push against the right side of the plane, strong-arming it. My urge to use the bathroom grew more intense.

Whoosh! A blast of wind hit the right side of the plane, but this time, the plane tilted. I put my right arm across Robert's chest and grabbed hold of his right armrest. Robert stopped eating his candy bar and dropped his book in his lap. "Dad, what's happening?"

"Everything's okay, Son, just some bad weather."

I wanted to embrace my family, hold onto each one of them. Alex and the girls, seated across the aisle from Robert and me, were sloped down. Andrea's left hand was braced against the window, and Angela had a grip on Alex's arm. Alex mouthed to me, "Love you."

"I don't want to die," the woman seated behind me cried out.

A chorus of low sobs, hysterical cries, and frantic praying for survival rang out from some, and others, silent clingers, held onto the person next to them, searching for comfort.

"Robert, I've got you," I said, my arm still anchored across his chest. Then I turned my head, my eyes reaching out to hold Alex and the girls. I reached out to God too, and silently prayed. Before my plea was completed, the plane was righted, but we were descending.

Static came over the intercom and then Captain Morgan spoke. His voice had a metallic edge to it. "We're out of that side-wind, but the storm's not giving up. Traffic control gave the okay to fly at a lower altitude. Stay buckled up."

The woman seated behind me, the one that had yelled, "We're going to die," screamed, "I can't breathe!" And fresh panic spread.

The young, slender stewardess in her tailored suit walked down the aisle and stood next to the distressed passenger. "Ma'am, you're hyperventilating," she said and handed the woman a brown bag. "Breathe into this."

The inflating and collapsing paper bag crumpled noisily between the woman's whimpers. Robert squirmed in his seat. "Dad, what's that?"

"Just a paper bag."

In a soothing tone, the stewardess said, "Ma'am, breathe slower." In what seemed to be less than a minute, the sound from the bag inflating and deflating stopped, and the stewardess said, "You're okay now."

The woman's sobbing stopped, but other passengers were overwrought, some in full-blown fits of laughter.

The plane had stopped descending, and the stewardess, with her hair pulled up in a gray snowball, walked down the aisle, stopped midway and clapped her hands. "I need your attention," she said.

I made the "*sh*" sound; a few of the other passengers joined in, and it got quiet. I released my right arm from across Robert's chest, wrapped it around his shoulder, and pulled my son close to me.

"We're about twenty-two minutes from Wakefield Airport," the older stewardess said. "Captain Morgan has more than thirty years of flying experience. I've clocked more than ten thousand flight hours with him. We're through the worst of the storm, and our new altitude has decreased turbulence. We're in the home stretch. Everything is fine."

It occurred to me that the captain should have been the one reassuring us, that the seasoned stewardess was damage control. But a short while after "the taming of the passengers," the captain's deep, calm voice came through the intercom. "This is Captain Morgan; we'll be on the ground in fifteen minutes. Stewardesses, prepare for landing."

The composure in Captain Morgan's voice and his message brought me relief. I lifted the shade on the window and saw the hazy terrain of Wakefield. Then I heard the landing gear being lowered. I hugged Robert, though I knew he didn't appreciate that in public. Then I hugged Alex, Angela, and Andrea with my eyes, holding sight of them without a blink. They hugged me back. I rested my head against the seat and closed my eyes. And in appreciation for the way He answered my prayer, I said, "Thank you."

My folks were parked outside Wakefield Airport terminal waiting for us. Alex, the kids, and I made a pact: Grandma Marta and Grandpa Charlie (as Dad liked to be called now) wouldn't be any wiser about our harrowing experience. Like me, they weren't big on flying. Had they found out what happened, I knew they'd never board an airplane again to visit my family and me in New York City.

Chapter 60

After I got Alex and the kids settled in with Grandma Marta Sunday afternoon, Emma Jean and I began rehearsals with the dance couple who was going to compete at Wakefield. Dad tended to the soda fountain at Pop's Pop and was our DJ, playing swing music from the jukebox. I danced Jessica's and Chris's legs off, and I'm sure they went home with blisters, like Emma Jean and I had when Pop coached us. Emma Jean and I held a three-hour morning practice and a two-hour one in the evening at Pop's Pop Monday through Friday.

Emma Jean had offered to drive her old station wagon that Saturday morning the five of us left for the Wakefield Dance Contest. Robert was disappointed I wouldn't take him along, but I thought it best that he stay in Greenstone. I promised I'd call my son after the competition and let him know how Jessica and Chris did.

Except for a new pane of glass in the door, the outside of Eddie's Place looked the same that June 15 in 1980 as it had when I competed there. A cloud of cigarette smoke hung inside the bar, just as it had when I was a kid. The noise from the jukebox, clanging billiard balls, and drunks at the bar were all-familiar to me too.

We made our way past the commotion and opened the door that led to the ballroom. Hopeful kids in colorful dance costumes were practicing their routines, trying to calm their nerves before they performed.

Jessica and Chris drew performance slot four out of the eleven couples in the competition. The sixteen-year-olds from Pop's Pop had been well schooled in swing dance, but I knew the first time I saw them dance in Greenstone that they wouldn't win the Wakefield Dance Contest. Their technical skills were accurate, but Jessica and Chris lacked something important: a love of dance.

While Dad got everyone else in the car, I used the pay phone in Eddie's Place to call Robert and tell him how the competition had gone, as I had said I would.

"Sorry, Dad."

"Nothing to be sorry about, Son; the best dancers won."

We left Eddie's Place and began driving back to Greenstone. Emma Jean and Dad seemed disappointed that Jessica and Chris didn't win the dance contest, but the young dancers didn't appear to be upset at all.

Emma Jean's old station wagon started making unusual sounds. I didn't—and still don't—have a mechanical bone in my body. As I listened to Chris and Jessica chatter in the backseat, I hoped the station wagon wouldn't break down.

"Can't wait to get home, work on the Chevy I bought from the neighbor," Chris said. "Needs new brake lining and spark plugs. And after I do some body work, I'm gonna give it a new coat of paint. She's gonna be beautiful."

"Sounds like you know what you're doing," Jessica said.

"Guess I should. Dad's taken me to his garage since I was twelve. During the summer, I work every weekday, and when school starts, I work Saturdays."

"Is that what you want to do after you graduate?" Jessica said.

"You bet. Can't think of anything else I'd rather be than a car mechanic. What about you?"

"Well, I worked weekends at Harriett's Beauty Shop washing hair for a while, thinking I might become a hairdresser. But I crossed that off as a possibility; I didn't like listening to all the customers' troubles. I've read about court reporters; that job sounds exciting. I'd have to go away to college. Have to get a job in a big city. Actually, I might do that, if I can get the money together. That's a big *if*."

Chris took notice of the racket from Emma Jean's station wagon. "Say, Emma Jean, hear that noise your car's making?"

"Oh, it's been doing that for a while."

"Well, I know what's wrong with it. Bring it to the garage Monday, and I'll fix her. Won't charge you for the labor, just the parts."

"It's good when a young man sets his sights on what he wants and goes after it," Dad said. "Bet you'll make a darn good mechanic, Chris."

"Yeah, Charlie, a much better mechanic than dancer."

That Saturday night after we got home from the Wakefield Dance Contest, Dad asked if my family and I would attend a church service with him and Mom the next morning. I was taken aback, not ever knowing Dad to set foot in a church, except when he married Mom, but I said we'd go.

CHAPTER 61

Sunday morning, we got in Dad's old Chevy truck and drove a mile and a half down the road from my folks' house. Dad pulled into a graveled lot, parked, and we got out. I remembered that as a kid, I had ridden my bike past the little wooden church there many times.

"You remember that little stream that winds around the backside of the church?" Dad said.

I had to stop and think, dig to recall it. "Yeah, I do. Little more than a trickle, no wider than the length of my foot."

"Well, that trickle winds for miles and miles and eventually ends up part of the Mississippi River," Dad said.

He never told me that when I lived in Greenstone; why tell me now? I thought. But I smiled and said, "Imagine that."

Inside, the church was as plain as the outside. On the walls were exposed bulbs that gave off a faint yellow light, and as I walked, my shoes caught on the rough, unstained wooden floor. The pianist, a woman of some years, had long hair combed back from her face. She was playing a preservice hymn with such enthusiasm that I couldn't fault her for her lack of skill. We filed into a pew with Mom leading and Dad falling in behind her. I sat next to Dad and held Angela on my lap, and Robert sat between Alex and me. My wife wanted the aisle seat in case Andrea, sitting on her lap, got rambunctious. Besides us, five other people were in attendance. The pianist's fingers silenced, and a rawboned minister stood in front of the small congregation in a starched white shirt and dark trousers.

"Morning," the minister said, not warming his stern face. "I'm Reverend Maynard. God's blessing to all. Our opening hymn is number 238. Miss McGillin, please."

I opened a hymnal to the correct page and gave Robert a plastic sandwich bag filled with Cheerios to share with his sisters.

Miss McGillin's slender fingers pounded out the first note of the hymn, and though I didn't know the melody, I mouthed the words. Alex seemed absorbed by the church's simplicity. Mom had her hands folded in her lap, her eyes closed. Dad was looking off to the left of the altar, like he was in a trance.

The hymn finished. Reverend Maynard climbed the steps of the pulpit that was unadorned, except for the wooden cross nailed onto the front of it.

"Brothers and sisters," Reverend Maynard said. Then his sky-blue eyes zeroed in on Robert, Angela, and Andrea. "And beloved children. Today's sermon is a special one about accountability of parents." The reverend leaned forward, his eyes narrowed, his tone serious. "Of course parents must clothe and feed their children, but that isn't my focus this morning. I trust that you parents already attend to that. My emphasis today is this: parents, raise your offspring according to God's book, the Bible, and they will honor you. 'Well, the reverend's referring to God's commandment: honor thy father and mother,' you're thinking. And you're right. But parents, do you understand God expects you to *earn* that honor, that respect, from your children?"

Reverend Maynard relaxed his posture. "Had a man come to me, oh ... some years back, don't remember how many. I'm too old to be that particular with numbers anymore. His daughter had just passed; he was in mourning, and his broken relationship with his only child left, a son, doubled his grief. He was a father with no children. And by the way, before this man came to me with his heavy heart, I'd only seen him in this church, let's see, when he married, and when I baptized his two children right over there." The reverend pointed to the baptismal font.

I knew what Dad had been looking at, knew why he'd asked my family and me to attend church.

"Not what I'd call a regular in the congregation. Nonetheless, I listened to the man's story, how he and his son had always been at odds. How at this time in his life, he longed for a good relationship with his son."

A knot formed in the middle of my throat. The reverend's words painted hurtful memories, and an old wound I had thought was forever closed was oozing.

Reverend Maynard's knotty finger scratched at his white handlebar mustache. "This unhappy father said, 'My boy wouldn't listen to me. He ran off to chase a rainbow.'"

"'Well, what's the matter with that? *I* chased a rainbow,' I told the man.

"'You became a preacher,' the father shot back.

"I told the troubled man, 'Yes, I did. Praise be to God, I didn't give up on my dream. My pa wanted me to be what he wanted me to be. Pa said I didn't have the mouthpiece to be a preacher. So I stood up to him. Didn't do it to disrespect him; did it to find my place on this earth.

"The distressed man said, 'I don't know how to be a good father.' I put my arms around the man, who I believe to this day only meant good for his son. Just like I know my pa meant good for me.

"I told the man, 'It wasn't until my pa heard one of my sermons that he knew I'd gone after the right rainbow. Then he understood; it had been my right to go after what I wanted. That's when things got straightened out between Pa and me.'

"After I told the distressed father my story, he recognized he'd been like my pa, stubborn and unwavering in his demand that his son obey him, though that would have put his son on a path of misery. In order to be a good parent, in order to have our children's respect, a father must respect his children. I gave this father a Bible verse to read, Ephesians six, verse four: 'Fathers, do not provoke your children to anger, but bring them up in the discipline and instruction of the Lord.'"

The image of my dad sitting in his chair with the Bible open revisited me. I knew what he'd been reading over and over again.

"My final words," the reverend cleared his throat, "to this troubled father were: 'Listen to your son's dreams, accept them, and cheer him on to achieve them. That's being a good father.'

"I didn't see this man for many years. Then two Sundays ago, he showed up in this church with his wife. He approached me after the service and told me how hard he had tried to make amends with his son. He said his son had been home for a visit, and he thought the hard feelings between them had healed. He said his son and family were coming home again soon for a special event. I listened to the particulars of this man's attempts to right his wrongs, to prove his love for his son. 'Am I now a good father?' the man asked, doubt in his eyes. I told him to come to church and bring his son and his family."

Dad shifted in the pew and turned toward me. Our eyes met. His face was flushed, and he was fidgeting with a hymnal. That Reverend Maynard's sermon was about the bad feelings there'd been between Dad and me was a surprise to Dad too.

Then something happened I never would have expected; Dad embraced me. "Sorry, Son," he whispered, "didn't know what the reverend had planned. So sorry too for all the hollering I did at you when you were younger. You chose right, Ty; teaching dance is what you were meant to do, not mining. I'm proud as I can be of you."

"The man did as I asked him to, so today I will answer his question," Reverend Maynard said. "In my eyes—and more importantly, in the all-knowing eyes of our heavenly Father—this man has amended his ways. Truly, this man is a good father. Let this story inspire all of us. Whether we are young or aged fathers, we are to honor our children. For then it follows that they will honor us in return. Amen."

When my family and I got back home to New York City, I had a neon sign made that read "Pop's and Charlie's." Before I mailed the sign to Dad in Greenstone, Missouri, I enclosed a note:

> *Dad, retire the Pop's Pop sign and hang this one in the soda-fountain shop's window. Thanks for all you've done for me.*
>
> *Love, Ty*

Chapter 62

We were celebrating Robert's thirteenth birthday that hot July 7 in 1987. Our twins, Angela and Andrea, who would turn ten that October, had helped Alex make Robert's cake.

"I made the yellow roses," Angela said.

Robert made a sour face. "Guys don't want flowers on their cake."

"Yeah, what a dumb thing to do," Andrea chimed in.

"Stop it, you two. Your sister's very artistic," Nadia said.

Nadia and Margaret arranged the candles on the cake and lit them, and then we sang "Happy Birthday." Alex began to cut the cake. Something my mother had said when I was younger revisited me: "The older you get, the quicker time flies."

Robert's a teenager. How can that be? And my sister, Allison, and nephew, Jacob, dead more than fourteen years. Pop's been gone more than eight.

I excused myself from the table. "Need to use the bathroom," I said, though I didn't.

I threw some water on my face and then flushed the toilet for effect.

There was a knock on the door. "Ty, I have cake cut for you, and Robert's ready to open presents. Hurry up. Can't wait to give Robert his Fratelli dance shoes."

The sound of Alex's footsteps faded as she walked down the hall.

I went back to the kitchen table and sat next to Alex to celebrate Robert's birth, his youth, and the man he would become one day. In the quiet of my mind, I celebrated the lives of my deceased family members: Allison, Jacob, and Pop.

Chapter 63

After graduating from Fiorello H. LaGuardia High School of Music & Art and Performing Arts in May, Robert started taking classes at Adelphi University of Performing Arts that fall of 1991. That he decided to major in dance was no surprise to his mother or me. His interest in dancing had been apparent even at age three when he'd spent afternoons with Alex and me at The Silver Slipper.

Midway through August, our two part-time dance instructors, Peggy and Jonathan, quit. They had secured full-time work elsewhere. Robert jumped at the opportunity to earn some money teaching Saturday dance classes at The Silver Slipper. He brought on board a fellow dance student from Adelphi University, Ashley, to team teach with him.

That October of his freshman year, Robert sprung a surprise on his mother and me one evening when his girlfriend Elizabeth (Lizzie) Mathews was at our house eating dinner with us.

Andrea, observant and outspoken as usual, turned to her sister and said, "Look, Lizzie has a promise ring."

The diamond was nothing more than a small chip, but its implication seemed huge to me. My son had serious feelings for Lizzie. I swallowed my mouthful of pizza in one gulp.

"Andrea!" Robert said.

"I just gave it to Lizzie last night," Robert said, making eye contact with me. "I was going to tell you and Mom at the dinner table tonight. Thanks a lot, Andrea."

Lizzie was doing well in her business classes at Manhattan University and was well liked by our family. But she and Robert were young. Though it wasn't an engagement ring that Robert had given Lizzie, I was concerned that they'd want to get married before they finished college. With Robert's only income from teaching dance classes Saturdays at The Silver Slipper and Lizzie working part-time at Chase Bank as a teller, their combined salaries wouldn't support them. I knew what it was like living from day-to-day, wondering if the rent would get paid. I didn't want Robert and Lizzie in that position.

"Mom and I know you've been seeing a lot of each other. I hope you'll get your degrees and find steady jobs before you get married."

"Don't worry, Mr. Partridge," Lizzie said. "We will."

Chapter 64

A little more than two years passed. We had our customary Christmas dinner at home. Mom and Dad, as well as Michelle, Bruno, and Alex's brother, Marco, were present. Robert and his girlfriend, Lizzie, as well as Angela's boyfriend, Danny, and Andrea's occasional date, Jake, made for a full house. But Grandmas Nadia and Margaret were absent from our table. Nadia had received two airline tickets in the mail from her son, Gavril. Though I missed them, I was glad that Nadia would have time with her family in Russia, which had become part of the Commonwealth of Independent States.

The tree in the entrance of The Silver Slipper was still lit that December 27 of 1993, and the glow of Christmas was still with me. Alex and I had finished a dance lesson, and I was going over my usual pep talk, reminding our students to practice at home. My last word of encouragement given, I turned around toward the studio doorway. There stood Gavril, his face gray, his shoulders slouching.

"Gavril's here," I said and motioned to Alex.

Alex stayed to deal with stragglers who had questions about the lesson, but her face showed she too was alarmed. I went to

Gavril, and without questioning his presence at the studio, I led him into the office.

"Ty, Mother passed Christmas Day. There was much to take care of. Arrangements. Consoling poor Margaret. And I wanted to tell you in person."

I hadn't yet wrapped my head around the fact that Nadia was dead when Alex walked in the office. The expression on my face must have spoken to my wife.

"Ty, what's wrong?"

"Nadia's dead."

"No," Alex cried out. "Gavril, how?"

"After dinner, Mother said she didn't feel well and suspected that she had indigestion. While she was sitting on the couch, her hand went to her chest and she fell into Margaret, seated next to her. It was very quick."

"Where's Margaret?" I said.

"She stayed in Saint Petersburg. My wife, Alena, is looking after her, preparing her for Mother's funeral. Mother loved you and your children. You were her family, as much—no, more so than me. Thank you for all you did for her."

The next morning Alex, our children, Gavril, and I boarded a plane at LaGuardia Airport in Queens. We left at 10:00 a.m. and had a direct flight to Saint Petersburg.

Our plane landed at 4:21 a.m. Moscow Standard Time the morning of the twenty-ninth. Gavril's two sons, Arman and Alek, met us at Pulkovo International Airport to transport us to the Slovinskis' home in the town of Zelenogorsk in Saint Petersburg, Russia. Because Gavril was a cellist in the Saint Petersburg Philharmonic Orchestra, the old, two-story house, a faded shade of red, wasn't what I was expecting.

We carried our luggage in the front door that led into the living room. The dingy-gray, stone fireplace blended into the light-gray walls, and the wooden floor needed to be refinished. Gavril introduced us to his wife, Alena, and then we were shown to our designated bedrooms. We needed to rest and be prepared physically and mentally for Nadia's wake that evening.

I heard a light tap on the bedroom door and looked at the clock on the nightstand. It was 1:00 p.m. I got up and opened the door. It was Gavril.

"Ty, Alena has prepared sandwiches and soup for lunch. We'll need to leave by 2:30 to be at the funeral home by 3:00."

"Okay; we'll be down shortly."

I had tried to sleep sitting up in an overstuffed chair, but I couldn't. Robert was sound asleep on the floor, and the girls and Alex, sharing the king-size bed, hadn't been disturbed by Gavril's knock, either. The eight-hour difference in time zones had my circadian clock confused, and I had a serious headache.

"Alex," I said, touching my wife's arm, "Alena has prepared lunch for us. Get up."

She opened her eyes but looked dazed. "What time is it?"

"It's one p.m. here."

Alex got out of bed as quietly as she could.

The two of us washed our faces and got dressed in clothes appropriate for Nadia's wake. We slipped out of the bedroom, allowing Robert, Angela, and Andrea to sleep a little longer.

Margaret looked worn-out when she sat down at the kitchen table. "Where are Robert and the girls?"

"Still asleep," Alex replied.

A large platter of sandwiches sat in the middle of the table, and bowls of soup were waiting for us. We finished eating and helped Alena clear the table.

"Could we take three sandwiches upstairs to our children, Alena?" Alex said.

"Certainly, and I will get you three glasses of tea."

We had our quiet time in the small chapel of Hogenkamp Funeral Home before public visitation for Nadia's wake began. Except for Askana Volkova, Nadia's friend who had informed her that Gavril was a cellist for the Saint Petersburg Philharmonic Orchestra, only family members attended the wake.

Nadia's funeral the next day was more difficult than her wake. With the closing of her casket, the finality hit; my family and I wouldn't see her again until we were reunited in heaven.

Odd as it seemed, Gavril buried Nadia next to his father, the abusive husband Nadia had fled from, the man who lied to his son. I didn't protest Gavril's decision, though I thought Nadia's resting place inappropriate on another count as well. But I had no blood rights to object; if I had, she would have been buried in New York City close to my family and me.

Nadia's will provided Margaret with all the comforts she could have hoped for. Also, all Nadia's grandchildren received an inheritance. Robert's, Angela's, and Andrea's college tuition would no longer be a concern for Alex and me, and Gavril's two grown sons would each have their own nest egg.

The day after Nadia's burial, Alex, our children, Grandma Margaret, and I flew home. My heart was heavy with sadness but filled with fond memories of a woman I loved as a mentor, mother, and grandmother to my children.

Chapter 65

Little did I know that two events during the spring of 1995 would leave their mark on me, one giving me reason to rejoice, the other, concern about what lay ahead.

Robert's graduation ceremony that May at Adelphi University of Performing Arts started the ball rolling. I was so proud of my son's accomplishment. My family from Greenstone, including my brother-in-law's new wife, Jenny, who I tried in vain not to like for filling my deceased sister's shoes, attended, as well as Alex's family from Saint Louis, Missouri. Our New York City grandma, Margaret, was there, though now she walked with a cane. And Lizzie's parents from New York attended also.

After the ceremony, we ate at a little Italian restaurant that I'd made reservations at. "Good service," Bruno said as the waiter made one more pass with the water pitcher. I figured I had scored a few points with my father-in-law.

With the meal over, congratulatory cards and gifts were placed on the table for Robert to open. There were two wrapped gifts; the rest were envelopes. Robert opened the larger gift first, a frame for his graduation picture from his Uncle Drew, Aunt Jenny, and Cousin Hannah. Then he opened cards from Lizzie's parents, Karen and Richard, Alex, the girls and I, and Margaret's envelope was opened last. One small gift remained on the table.

I thought it odd that Lizzie used floral paper and a white bow to wrap Robert's gift. My son picked up the last gift, scooted his chair away from the table, and stood.

"What a great day. I've completed my course work and earned my degree. And all of you celebrating with me makes that even more special. But there's another reason this day is special to me. To Lizzie."

My Robert took hold of Lizzie's hand, and I realized what was happening.

"Lizzie, ever since we started dating, I've thought about when I'd be able to ask for your hand in marriage. I love you, and I can't imagine going through life without you."

My future daughter-in-law didn't look the least bit surprised.

Robert turned and gave his mother and me a big smile. I nodded my approval.

Then Robert turned to Lizzie's parents. "Adelphi University of Performing Arts has hired me as a part-time dance instructor, and I teach every Saturday at The Silver Slipper. I'm also going to be dancing in a performance at New Amsterdam Theatre in Manhattan. Lizzie will continue working part-time at Chase Bank and finish college. I promise I'll take good care of her. So ... Karen and Richard, may I have your permission to marry your daughter?"

After their formal affirmation, my son knelt next to Lizzie's chair. "Will you marry me?" He asked, handing her what I had thought was his remaining graduation gift.

"Yes!" She tore off the bow and floral wrapping paper and opened up the small black-velvet ring case.

Robert removed the solitaire diamond engagement ring that sparkled like the North Star and placed it on Lizzie's finger. Then he stood. Holding Lizzie's hand, he said, "Lizzie and I have decided we don't want a lengthy engagement; we want a simple ceremony, and we're getting married this August. That way, we'll get a short honeymoon before I start teaching at Adelphi University."

Alex's eyes got big as saucers, and I understood her concern. How could a wedding be planned that fast? And I was ill-at-ease about something else, too. Was being able to have a honeymoon the *only* reason my son and Lizzie wanted such a short engagement? But I wasn't going to insist on a long engagement like Bruno had when Alex and I wanted to get married; I was happy for my son and future daughter-in-law. To see Robert graduate from college and announce his engagement on the same day was great. And hearing that Robert would dance on stage sent me back in time to when I told Pop I wanted to do the same.

Chapter 66

Classes were filled to capacity, and though I needed Alex at the studio, she took time off to help with Robert and Lizzie's wedding. My wife yakked on the phone with Lizzie's mother, Karen, so much that I thought the receiver would become permanently attached to her ear. I'd have thought my wife would have been talked out about the wedding details, but at every meal, Alex went on and on about bridesmaids' dresses, flowers, food, and music selections. I'd get up from the table with indigestion. Robert and Lizzie appeared to be relaxed about their upcoming wedding, but Alex was hyper, wanting everything to be perfect for the August seventeenth wedding. Antacids became my best friend. Between running The Silver Slipper solo and Alex demanding my undivided attention about the wedding, I felt wrung out, like some decrepit man had overtaken my body. Some nights, I'd wake up in bed with my forehead and T-shirt moist with sweat.

One evening, Alex insisted that I help Robert's best man plan the bachelor party, and that was the final straw. I knew I shouldn't leave, but my wife's stress was stressing me, and I needed a break, so I told her a lie. I said Dad had called and asked for my help with repairs at Pop's & Charlie's. I made arrangements for

James and Jennifer to split up and cover both ballrooms at the dance studio. And though Alex wasn't happy about me leaving, on the nineteenth, I flew out of LaGuardia Airport.

My folks were waiting for me at Wakefield Airport. During the one-hour drive to Greenstone, they asked one question after the other about Robert and Lizzie's upcoming wedding. Once that was out of the way, I was glad to see them, glad to get back to Greenstone, Missouri, the place I couldn't wait to get away from when I was younger.

To get that little voice inside me, my conscience, to stop hammering me about lying to Alex, I initiated work projects at Pop's & Charlie's, things that, if left unattended, would be future problems dumped in Dad's lap. Some shingles on the roof had worked their way loose, and the gutters, full of leaves from the previous fall, needed to be flushed out with a hose. Dad and I working together on the soda-fountain shop felt good, and Mom's biscuits and gravy, fried chicken, and homemade apple pie were welcomed comfort foods that relaxed my nerves stirred up by all the wedding talk at home.

Refreshed from my stay with Mom and Dad, I returned to giving dance lessons at The Silver Slipper, a labor of love, so much a part of my life.

CHAPTER 67

It was 5:00 p.m. on May 28, and I was done teaching dance classes at The Silver Slipper. Alex had told me she and the girls would be shopping for prom shoes when I got home. I was looking forward to a ham sandwich and the evening news, with my feet propped up on the coffee table. I locked up and started my walk to board the subway at the Lexington/Fifty-First Street Station. All at once, a dull pain crept across my left shoulder and then hung like an anchor on my chest. Beads of sweat formed on my forehead, and I couldn't take a deep breath. Heading home wasn't an option; I stepped off the curb into the street and hailed a cab.

"Get me to a hospital," I said, trying to catch my breath.

"Mount Sinai on One-Hundredth Street and Fifth Avenue?"

"Yeah; hurry up."

Traffic was congested with taxis, bike commuters, and bike couriers. Drivers were shaking their fists and their moving mouths were no doubt expressing profanities.

The cabbie took me to the emergency entrance drop-off area. I walked into Mount Sinai, my right hand pressed against my chest marking the pain. The woman at the registration desk saw me coming. "Get a wheelchair," she said to someone not in my line of sight.

There was no paperwork or wait for me. Two nurses had me seated and wheeled into an exam room faster than I could have said "Jiminy Cricket." Then a young ER doctor came in. I'm sure he told me his name, but it didn't soak in. "The nurse said you were clutching your chest. Open your mouth; I want to place a tablet under your tongue. It will dissolve quickly."

I did as the ER doctor said. Then two nurses attended to me: one took my vitals; the other drew blood. "Mr. Partridge," the nurse who seemed to be in charge said, "is there a wife or family member we can call?"

"No. My wife can't be reached; she's shopping."

The nurse nodded and wrote on a clipboard, then handed it to the doctor.

His eyes narrowed. "Does your chest feel better now, Mr. Partridge?"

"Yes, the heaviness and pain are gone."

"Good. Do you have a history of heart problems?"

"No."

"I suspect you had a heart attack," the ER doctor said.

Heart attack?

"I'm ordering an electrocardiogram. You might have heard it called an EKG. After I look at the results, we'll talk, Mr. Partridge."

I nodded and hoped the pain I'd felt was nothing more than severe indigestion.

Electrodes were placed on my chest, and the EKG was quick and painless. After the electrodes were removed, a nurse inserted a needle into a vein on the top of my hand, and I received an intravenous drip.

The ER doctor returned. "The EKG confirms that you had a heart attack, Mr. Partridge. The good news is that little damage was done to your heart, but the bad news is that without proper monitoring, you could have another one. I'm referring you to a cardiologist."

"I understand, doctor."

"That has blood thinner in it," he said, pointing to the bag feeding my IV. "You can leave when the bag is empty, but you'll need a ride home. My nurse'll give you contact information for the cardiologist and instructions before you're released."

The ER doctor left, and the nurse who seemed to be in charge handed me a business card. "I'll schedule an appointment with Dr. Brugger's office, located in this complex. Call after ten tomorrow morning to find out when he'll see you." Then the nurse handed me a pill enclosed in a small, transparent envelope and said, "Take that before bed. Now who are we calling to get you home?"

I had no intention of calling my wife; in fact, I was hoping she and the girls hadn't gotten home from shopping. I gave the nurse James's phone number. I insisted I could walk out to the cab with my dance instructor's assistance, but the nurse insisted I had to leave the emergency room in a wheelchair. James was sworn to secrecy. I didn't want my family to know I'd had a heart attack.

A light was on in the kitchen; the rest of the house was dark. Robert had left a note on the kitchen table; he and Lizzie had gone out to eat and see a movie. Alex and the girls weren't home from shopping. All was good; I had sidestepped an explanation for my whereabouts. Big plans were being made for a prom and bigger plans for a wedding. It wasn't a good time to throw bad news at my family. I got a glass of water and took my pill, then went to bed.

Chapter 68

Tuesday morning, Alex was back helping with dance lessons at The Silver Slipper. Though I didn't think the heart specialist would approve of me dancing, I knew I was dancing anyway. I needed the reality of my heart attack curtained for a while, and I knew dancing would do that. We'd finished our morning lessons and were on lunch break. I was feeling good, like nothing was wrong with me. Alex had gone upstairs to the kitchen to make sandwiches. I closed the door to the office and called the cardiologist's office.

"Dr. Brugger's office, Nancy speaking."

"Hi, my name's Ty Partridge. The ER nurse at Mount Sinai Hospital was supposed to set up an appointment for me with Dr. Brugger. I'm calling to get the date and time."

"You're scheduled for this Thursday at three, but a patient canceled for today. I have a one o'clock available if you'd like to come in."

"I'll take it. Thanks."

"We're in building one, suite three in the Mount Sinai Complex," the receptionist said.

Fabricating an excuse to get away from Alex for my doctor's appointment hadn't crossed my mind, and now the urgency to invent one was upon me.

I had just turned forty-six. It seemed surreal that I'd had a heart attack, but it was crystal clear what I'd miss and what baggage I'd leave behind, should an early demise be my fate. Robert's wedding was on the brink, and Andrea's and Angela's nuptials were future realities. And the love of my life would have hard years ahead managing the studio alone. Being short-changed of years with my family was worse to think about than death itself. I had to get to that appointment with the cardiologist.

Alex called out to me, "Ty, lunch is ready."

My call completed, I hurried upstairs to the kitchen with the deposit bag in my hand.

"What were you doing?" Alex said.

"Counting our cash," I said, holding my tool of deception. "There's too much money lying around; I'm going to the bank."

"Now? Why are you acting so strange? Last night, you were asleep when the girls and I got home; you don't go to bed that early. And you didn't have much to say this morning before lessons."

"Last night, I was bushed. This morning, well, you know me; I was thinking about what I wanted to teach. Sorry, Honey. Everything's good." I smiled and gave Alex a kiss, hoping she believed me, hating the fact I had told her another lie. I picked my sandwich up off the plate; time was ticking away; I had to get going. "If I'm not back to start the next class, review the last lesson. We'll start something new when I return."

I hurried down the steps, not giving Alex time to protest. I caught the number-six train at the Fifty-First Street Subway Station; that took me to the eastern border of Central Park. Dr. Brugger's office was at One-Hundredth Street and Fifth Avenue. I made my way to building one and found suite three.

The waiting room was wall-to-wall people. All of them were senior citizens, with drooping jowls and brown-spotted skin hanging from their arms. I approached the check-in window.

The receptionist slid the glass partition open. She was a bright-eyed young lady whose wrinkle-free face was a drastic contrast to that of the seniors', or mine, for that matter.

"Ty Partridge. I have a one o'clock."

"I'll need to make a copy of your insurance card, Mr. Partridge."

"Sure." I handed her the card, wishing she'd have called me Ty. "I'm really pinched for time; I have to get back to work."

"Don't worry, Mr. Partridge." The receptionist smiled, then copied my insurance card and handed it back to me.

I looked for a spot to stand, since sitting wasn't an option. A man with coal-black hair, obviously dyed, was seated at the end of a row of chairs along the back wall. I went and stood next to him.

"Jammed in here like sardines in a can," the man said. "Haven't seen many your age here; most are old farts, like me. Just dang bad luck, I guess. The name's Earl." He stuck out his hand.

"Ty," I said, hoping he'd leave things at that.

"When'd you have yours?"

The look on my face must have told Earl that what he said hadn't registered.

"Your heart attack. When'd it happen?"

"Yes ... yesterday." I'd had enough of Earl. And I was sure he was going to inquire more about my heart attack. "Something's caught in my throat; I need to find a water fountain." Not waiting for Earl to throw in his two cents on where I could find one, I left the waiting room.

When I returned, a seat on the other side of the room was vacant. I sat down, closed my eyes, and pretended to be asleep till my name was called.

"How are we doing today, Mr. Partridge?" The nurse asked, her voice sounding robotic.

"Fine," I replied, to be polite.

The exam room was a putrid color of yellow, like vomit, and smelled of disinfectant.

"Have a seat on the exam table and unbutton your shirt, Mr. Partridge. Doctor will be right in." The nurse closed the door behind her.

The room was drafty; goose bumps popped up on my exposed chest. With each gust of cold air, a hissing sound snaked through the vent directly above the exam table. I stood on the table and closed the vent. I had no sooner sat down when there was a tap on the door.

A strapping man in a polo shirt with a golf club embroidered on the pocket entered and stuck out his hand. "Hi, I'm Dr. Brugger. Sounds like yesterday was rough, Mr. Partridge."

The deep wrinkles in his forehead and around his eyes made me think Dr. Brugger was eight or ten years older than me. And for some reason the way he said "Mr. Partridge" didn't offend me. "Scared the hell out of me."

"Yes, I know what you mean, felt the same when I had my heart attack. Doctors get blocked arteries too. But I changed my lifestyle, and my pipes are in good shape now."

After examining me, Dr. Brugger discussed guidelines for healthy eating. Gone were my days of eating chocolate cake. Fried foods were out too. The cardiologist told me that losing weight, eating a low-fat diet, and exercising was the ticket to improve my health. I left his office with scripts for cholesterol medicine and Coumadin, a blood thinner. Dr. Brugger also wrote an order for me to get a blood test in a week. He told me to call his office two days after my blood was drawn to get the results.

I was running late but went to the bank anyway; I needed a deposit slip to give to Alex. When I walked in the ballroom, she was finishing the foxtrot lesson. I gave her a peck on the mouth and said, "Sorry you had to teach by yourself." I didn't like keeping secrets from my wife, and the fact that she had no time for herself made me feel guiltier yet. With prom preparations for the girls, Robert and Lizzie's upcoming wedding, and helping me with the studio, Alex's to-do list was never done. I wasn't going to burden her with my health problem. I'd tell Alex about my heart attack when her schedule lightened up.

Our next class was advanced swing. I decided we'd give a dance exhibition before we started instruction. I put a CD in the player that had a fast song, one that the younger me, Bird, could have danced to. The class applauded our performance, but I'd gotten a wake-up call. I was winded, and my legs felt rubbery.

My wife and I finished teaching for the day, and it occurred to me that in my effort to conceal my doctor's appointment from Alex, go to the bank, and get back to the studio for lessons, I hadn't gotten my prescriptions filled. As luck had it, Alex was helping decorate the gym that night for the girls' upcoming high school prom. That would be my opportunity to get to the pharmacy.

CHAPTER 69

It was Saturday night, the twins' prom night. Angela and Andrea looked beautiful in their gowns. Alex, having volunteered to serve as a chaperone at the event, was a ten—no, an eleven—in her black evening dress, her long, black hair in an updo, like my daughters.' I looked through the camera at my not-so-little girls and my beautiful wife. *Click, click, click*, my finger went, each picture my attempt to preserve the moment.

Two young men dressed in tuxes arrived. They were clean-cut, polite, and in my daughters' opinions, both cream-of-the-crop smart. In my opinion, they were three rungs up the ladder from the previous guys I'd seen my daughters date.

"Dad, this is Tom Barton," Angela said. "We're working on a graphic art project together."

"And this is Blake ... Blake Shore," Andrea said. "He works at his dad's law firm. He gave a lecture at one of my classes."

"How about a few pictures with your dates, girls." I looked through the camera window. "Ready? Smile." My daughters had blossomed and become women.

Alex left with our daughters and their dates in a taxi, and I turned on the television and relaxed.

Chapter 70

With Robert and Lizzie's wedding date set for that August seventeenth, Lizzie's mother, Karen, and Alex were frantic, attempting to get everything arranged in two and a half months. Booking a hall for the reception on short notice was a problem. But Robert's membership in the Performing Arts Guild proved to be an asset. A fellow member had an uncle who owned a hotel with a large banquet room that Karen and Richard were able to rent. That Lizzie and Robert had opted for a short engagement caused Alex and Karen considerable grief. But for me, it brought to mind a question. Robert had said that he and Lizzie wanted to squeeze in a honeymoon before he started working at Adelphi University, but I wondered if there was a more pressing reason my son and Lizzie chose to get married so quickly.

Alex being occupied with the wedding gave me the perfect excuse to volunteer for grocery shopping and meal preparations. It afforded me a way to work harder on improving my diet and still keep my "secret" from Alex. She didn't question my motive for practicing dance routines that we then demonstrated at our classes, and my three-mile walks were done on the sly three times a week. Salads that I had become an expert at preparing were passed off as quick, easy meals. But one day, I was washing broccoli at the kitchen sink, and Alex became inquisitive. "I've never seen you eat this way before. When did you start liking broccoli?"

"I don't, but its low-cal. I want to lose weight and look good for the wedding." That wasn't a total lie, just a half-truth. If Alex hadn't been distracted with Robert and Lizzie's wedding, she'd have pressed me more about the change in my eating habits. My girls' prom was past, but Robert and Lizzie hadn't had their big day; Alex wasn't finding out about my heart attack yet.

Chapter 71

It was Saturday morning, August seventeenth, 1995, the day of the big event: Robert and Lizzie's wedding. My wife had made an appointment for me with my barber, Phil, for a trim—*trim* being a noteworthy word, since all he could do with the top of my head was buff it.

"Ask Phil to trim your eyebrows and take care of those nose hairs too," Alex said. I wondered why the hair in my nose thrived, when the hair on my head wouldn't.

I removed my tux, hanging in the bedroom closet. Alex said it was time for me to get dressed for the wedding. After I put it on, I looked in the mirror. My belly bulge was gone. But those tails on the black jacket and that white shirt made me look like a penguin. *My gray suit would have been fine*, I thought.

Twenty till three in the afternoon. Almost showtime. The organist was playing prelude music, while guests were being seated by the ushers. I was standing in the back of Trinity Lutheran Church, Lizzie's church, and the church that my son was considering committing his membership to. Everyone in the church was chatting, oblivious to the musical arrangements. I was uncomfortable in my penguin suit, the wetness under my arms adhering to my shirt like Super Glue, and that bow tie might as well have been a boa constrictor; it was crushing my Adam's apple. I should have remained downstairs with the rest of the wedding party and been with Alex to help ease her stress. But the women in the wedding party were franticly combing hairdos that had been professionally styled, and the men, except for Robert, were pacing and adjusting their bow ties. I didn't want any part of that.

The altar, adorned with beautiful wood, framed a life-size picture of Jesus, his gown flowing, his arms raised as he ascended into a blue and billowy whiteness, heaven. And the sun shining through stained-glass windows onto the picture gave a mystical quality to Jesus's face. Soon, my son was to walk down the aisle and stand before friends and family and God and proclaim his lifetime partnership with Lizzie, as I had done with Alex so many years before.

I looked at my watch. Ten till three. My folks, my sister-in-law, and niece, Hannah, had already been seated. My in-laws, Bruno and Michelle, as well as Marco, Alex's brother, had been ushered to a pew also. I knew Alex had to be missing my presence in the church basement, knew her tunnel vision on details of the wedding had gotten around to her and me having an usher escort us to our designated pew. I hurried downstairs to get my wife. We made our way to the back of the church, and my brother-in-law, Drew, ushered Alex to her seat. I trailed behind, then sat next to my wife in our designated pew.

Alex began fidgeting with her burgundy gown, and her color-matched shoes did a silent tap dance on the church's wooden floor. I took my wife's hand and held it in mine. She smiled, as if to say she'd make it through. Karen, Lizzie's mother, who was seated across the aisle, wiped her eyes; her husband, Richard, was not by her side to calm her jitters. The soothing music stopped. Conversation ceased. The church was filled with silence. Then, the pipes of the organ danced with Handel's "La Rejouissance," and I swiveled in my seat. At the back of the church, three young women in flowing gowns the color of pink wine stood with their escorts, the bride and groom not yet within sight. The organ sounded a long chord, then the organist continued with the musical selection.

Angela, escorted by Robert's friend, Todd, a fellow member of the Performing Arts Guild, strolled down the white runner. Next, Andrea was arm-in-arm with Lizzie's maternal cousin, Mark. When I saw my two raven-haired daughters, the thought came to me that I might be seated in the parents' pew again in the near future. That then I'd be handing over to another man the job of protecting one of my daughters. The maid of honor, Lizzie's paternal cousin Lisa, was escorted by Robert's best man and best friend, Ron. The bridesmaids and groomsmen, their bodies angled toward the white aisle runner, watched the ring bearer and flower girl approach. And finally, everyone except the bride and groom stood one step down from the platform where the picture of Jesus took center stage.

The organist played louder, holding yet another long chord, and then began playing Johann Sebastian Bach's "Wedding March." Everyone stood, and the bride began her walk. A sheer veil trimmed with white lace covered Lizzie's copper-colored hair and hazel eyes. Richard, his steps mindful of his daughter's gown, had a smile on his face, but I'd have bet that his heart ached. The organ music stopped, and all of us in the pews sat down.

The minister asked Richard, "Who gives this woman to be married to this man?"

"Her mother and I," he said and then sat down.

Robert's broad shoulders were the perfect mold for his black tux jacket, and Lizzie, the young girl who Robert first introduced to us, now was at his side as a grown woman. How perfect that moment seemed, yet I knew how imperfect life could be. And I prayed that whatever hardships life threw their way, their bond would steady them and see them through, as it had Alex and me.

Chapter 72

Mr. and Mrs. Robert Partridge were on their honeymoon, and I was still digesting the fact that Robert's notes explaining where he'd gone for the evening were a thing of the past. The big event was done. There was nothing left to do but accept this change, nothing but to love Robert and Lizzie and wish them a wonderful life together.

I went to find my lovely wife, Alex.

Monday morning was and still is laundry day at our house; Alex was in the basement folding a load of underwear. It was almost time for us to leave the house; dance lessons started at nine. It was time to tell Alex about my heart attack; the girls' prom and Robert's wedding were out of the way. And besides, she wasn't preoccupied with a to-do list anymore; it was only a matter of time before my wife would put two and two together and extract my secret from me. So, I told her the way most men tell their wives things they'd rather not have to say at all. I got right to the point. As Alex folded the last of my T-shirts, I said, "Honey, I had a heart attack."

A wave of shock, that kind of breath-holding panic that makes a guy wish he'd have eased into things, morphed my wife's face. I drew Alex to me and embraced her, and she rested her head against my shoulder. At least a minute must have passed. Then she took a step back and eyed me up and down. Finally, her expression relaxed.

"I knew something was wrong," Alex said. "When did it happen?"

"May 28."

"Were you giving dance lessons?"

"No, I had finished my last class at The Silver Slipper and had started walking to the subway to go home. It felt like I had a weight on my chest, and I was sweating. I hailed a cab and went to Mount Sinai Hospital. The ER doctor ordered an electrocardiogram, and it showed I'd had a heart attack. That Friday, when I left the studio at lunch and you had to start the lesson without me, I had an appointment with Dr. Brugger, a cardiologist. He has me on medication, and my blood test results have been good. I'm okay now, Alex. Really."

"You were eating different, losing weight; I should have realized something happened to make you change like that. But I was so preoccupied with shoes, dresses, flowers. I'm an awful wife."

I kissed my wife's wet cheek. "No, you aren't."

A peek at my watch told me more time had passed than I realized. "Well, Mrs. Partridge, we need to get to the studio."

"Should you be dancing?"

"Honey, the heart specialist told me dancing was great exercise. Good thing, cause I couldn't give it up if I had to. Let's go; we have students to teach."

Chapter 73

By October, I had convinced my wife that I'd be around to share my life with her and our family for a long time. The reality of an empty place in our nest from Robert's departure had soaked in, and our lives were back on track; at least, that's what I thought.

Franco Munez, the choreographer at New Amsterdam Theatre in Manhattan, had hired Robert as a background dancer the previous spring, after our son and Lizzie were engaged. Auditions for another musical at New Amsterdam Theatre had begun. Franco had chosen the lead male and female dancers, but the male broke his ankle and had to have surgery. The choreographer remembered Robert's exceptional talent and knew he'd had vocal and drama classes at Adelphi University of Performing Arts. Franco hired him as the lead male's replacement for the musical *Meeting in the Woods*.

I had followed Dr. Brugger's recommendations and was fitter than I had been ten years earlier. When I danced, my feet moved almost as fast as young Bird's had. I had plenty of dance experience from studying under Nadia and running my dance studio; my concern was that I had no singing or acting experience. I decided to call Robert and find out if background dancers had been chosen for *Meeting in the Woods*.

"The women have been chosen, Dad, and Franco will hold an audition for the men soon."

"With no acting or singing skills, guess I couldn't get an audition."

"The female lead and I do most of the singing and acting. Most background dancers aren't good in those areas anyway, and few have the dancing ability you have. I'll talk to Franco. Bet you'll get an audition."

To dance on stage was something that a boy from Greenstone, Missouri, had wished for long ago. Though that desire had never left me, I hadn't pursued it, but after having survived my heart attack, I wanted it more than ever. Trying to break into stage performance was a leap in the dark for someone my age, but I needed to see if I could do it. With my marriage solid and me not getting any younger, my chance at what I wanted was now or never. I hoped Robert could help me get my foot in the door.

Though fueled with anticipation, I decided against telling Alex about my conversation with Robert. Younger dancers were out there; the odds were against me.

Three days passed, and I hadn't heard from my son. Alex and I had finished our first class of the day at The Silver Slipper and were waiting for our next class to arrive. Robert showed up.

"Hey, Mom and Dad, caught part of your class from the doorway. You've got some decent dancers."

The expression on my wife's face gave away her surprise; with practices at New Amsterdam Theatre and teaching at Adelphi University, Robert only showed up at the studio on Saturdays to teach.

"What's up, Robert?" Alex said.

I didn't give my son a chance to respond. He was going to talk about a topic I hadn't discussed with Alex: whether or not the choreographer from New Amsterdam Theatre had agreed to give me an audition. And I wanted Robert to tell me in private.

"Students are here for our next class, Robert. Can we give you a call later?"

"Yeah. Sure, Dad. I can see you're busy."

"Okay, you two," Alex said, "what's going on?"

"There's something I need to talk with you about," I said, "but now's not the time; class is about to start."

"Is it something with your—"

Sure of what was about to pop out of Alex's mouth, I cut her off. Our kids didn't know about my heart attack. That's the way I wanted it, and Alex had agreed to keep it secret.

"It's nothing, really, Alex."

"Dad?" Robert took a step forward toward me, turning his back to Alex. We locked eyes, and my son knew his mother had no clue why he was at The Silver Slipper.

"You audition at eight a.m. tomorrow," Robert mouthed to me. "Catch you later, Dad."

Robert turned to face his mother and gave her a hug. "Got to get going."

Alex was a no-show for dance class, so I drafted a lady student to be my dancing partner.

My wife was waiting outside the door of the studio when I finished teaching. Her shoulders were back, her chest forward, and her expression spoke to me. I was entering hostile territory.

"Here's the thing, Ty; you kept your heart attack from me, until you got good and ready to tell me about it. So what's the secret now? And how is Robert involved? Let's talk in the office."

I followed Alex in and closed the door. She sat in the desk chair and I stood. She was giving me that "you're in the doghouse" look. I felt like a kid in the principal's office waiting to be reprimanded. I hesitated and didn't answer my wife's questions.

"Ty, what's going on? With Robert's busy schedule, he didn't come by just to visit."

"Robert came to talk about that dance performance he's in at New Amsterdam Theatre."

A sigh. Alex's eyes softened. "So there's nothing wrong with your heart?"

"No. My cholesterol's fine, and I'm not having chest pains. But there is a connection between Robert's visit today and my heart. Just not a medical one."

"What does that mean, Ty?"

"It means Robert put in a good word for me with his choreographer, and I got an audition. It means if I don't get cut, I'll be one of the background dancers in the musical *Meeting in the Woods* at New Amsterdam Theatre. With all the young guys that'll be auditioning, that's a big *if*, but I've wanted to dance on stage since I was that lanky kid from Greenstone, Missouri, and I'm not walking away from my chance at it now."

Alex looked stunned. She'd had no clue I ever wanted to dance on stage. Seconds ticked away, then her expression changed; my wife understood what the audition meant to me. She gave me one of her sweet smiles. "I'll keep my fingers crossed that you get chosen. Students for our next dance class are arriving; we need to be in the ballroom."

Chapter 74

I was early. Nerves had me in high gear. Twenty-one other guys showed up at New Amsterdam Theatre to audition for eight spots as background dancers. I knew Franco Munez would have no problem finding the dancers he was looking for; the other men were twenty-plus years younger than me.

Franco, a lean, muscular man with deep lines carved into his forehead, picked eleven men from the group and told them to take the stage. I was not among them. The remaining eleven of us sat in the theater seats.

"Make two lines, one behind the other," the choreographer said, "six dancers in front, five in back."

A man assisting Franco gave each dancer a number to stick on the front of his shirt.

Then Franco said, "Dancers, follow my lead." He motioned to his assistant, now off stage. "Start the music."

To fast music, Franco performed a modern-dance routine. Three dancers in the front line kept up with him and had lines as crisp as his. They were outstanding dancers, and I was sure the choreographer would choose them to dance in a final audition. Then the music stopped.

"Dancers, switch lines," Franco said. "You five in back, move to the front, and everyone follow my lead."

Again, the music played. Four of the five men who were now in the front line were exceptional dancers, and the three who were standouts minutes before held their own.

Franco signaled to the man off stage to stop the music.

"Now you will dance, and I will watch," the choreographer said.

The man assisting Franco handed him a pen and clipboard, then started the music.

After a few minutes, the choreographer called out to his assistant, "Stop the music."

The dancers in group one waited in their two lines for Franco's assessment.

Franco walked to the back line, scratched his bristly goatee, and pointed. "You, you, and you, are chosen. The rest of this line is dismissed." Then, facing the front row, the choreographer told four of the dancers to stay. The other dancer in the front row was dismissed.

With eleven of us in group two left to dance in the preliminary audition, I figured I might as well go home.

There's no way I'll make it to the final audition. They're all young guys, I thought.

I got up to make a quick, quiet exit and saw Robert sitting three rows behind me. I forced a smile and sat back down.

"Group two, take the stage," the choreographer said.

Two lines were formed, as before, eleven men vying to dance in the final audition and have a chance to secure one of the eight spots as a background dancer. I was in the back row.

"Follow my lead," the choreographer said.

In my head, I was replaying the steps he had shown the other group, concentrating on the first move, a high kick.

The music started, but Franco hesitated. With his first step, I understood why. What I had committed to memory was useless. I followed the best I could, counting how many of each step the choreographer performed, noting when he transitioned to a new step. I memorized the new dance sequence.

The music stopped. "Switch lines," Franco said.

My row moved to the front. I was the dancer on the end, nearest the music.

"Dancers, follow my lead. Start the music," Franco said to his assistant.

First beat. I was in time, in step. The adrenaline was pumping and my heart was pounding. Some advice Pop had given me long ago, *"Keep your head clear of everything except the performance,"* revisited and steadied me. A tape was playing in my head, a speeded-up version of what I had seen just minutes before. This step, then that. My eyes were on Franco, but they didn't need to be.

Then the music stopped.

"Dancers, now I watch while you perform."

The man assisting Franco again handed him the clipboard and pen, then started the music.

I was in beat, didn't miss a step, and I thought my technique was good. The music stopped, and I didn't have a clue how the other dancers in my group had done. My concentration had been completely on my performance. The eleven of us in group two waited for Franco's assessment.

"No need to have a final audition," Franco said. "The seven dancers I chose from group one have a spot as a background dancer. And the eighth spot is yours," he said to me.

"Dancers, we begin the choreography tomorrow at 8:00 a.m."

The other dancers cleared the stage, and I began to leave, too, since it seemed Franco had nothing more to say. Bursting with excitement, I wanted to share my victory with Robert.

"Stop, please," Franco said.

With one foot on the stage, one on the first step of the stairs, I halted and turned to face him.

"You're Robert's father?"

"Yes."

"Robert came to me, asked if I'd give you an audition. He told me about your studio and your many years of dancing. But, I said to myself, this is a young man talking about his father. Robert convinced me that you were a good dance instructor, but I didn't think it possible that you were the artist he described you to be. I was wrong. Should you love performing, you will get other parts. See you tomorrow."

I made my way back to Robert. To my surprise, Alex was seated next to him. "Ty, you were wonderful."

"Yeah. The best one up there, Dad. You're in, right?"

"I'm in." I wasn't a kid anymore; a lot of years had passed since I'd won that dance contest in Wakefield. But in that moment, young Bird's energy rushed through me. Wrapped up in my excitement, I couldn't imagine what this new twist in my life would come to mean.

Chapter 75

Because of my practice schedule at New Amsterdam Theatre, Alex had to recruit male students to be her dance partner, till I arrived after lunch for afternoon classes at The Silver Slipper. I could tell my wife was stressed, but performing on stage was more important to me than lightening the workload Alex was carrying.

The infrequent times my daughters were at home, I wasn't. And though Robert and I were in the same theater performance, I rehearsed with the background dancers; he practiced with the lead female dancer, so he and I didn't cross paths. I loved being part of the dance ensemble at the theater, but I was feeling less and less a part of my family's lives.

Except for my attendance at dinner, the spirit of Christmas had come and gone without my participation. Rehearsals with the complete cast were in session for the musical, requiring more of my time. Sore muscles, aching joints, and exhaustion were a way of life. Franco had driven us for perfection in the choreography, and now we had the director, Saul, to deal with as well, barking out directives for the singing and acting. The leads did most of the heavy hitting in those areas, but I'm sure I contributed to Saul's fits of anger.

With practices running longer at New Amsterdam Theatre, I'd show up, tired, at The Silver Slipper and help Alex with the last two classes of the day. Except for conversing while teaching, interaction between us was like walking into a meat cooler—extremely cold.

By that February of 1996, with the performance date of *Meeting in the Woods* approaching, Franco and Saul were driving the cast to perfect the musical. Exhausted, I stopped helping Alex at The Silver Slipper. Running the studio alone, Alex looked more worn-out than me, but all I thought about was being part of the dance company and proving I could keep up with those younger guys.

At the theater, Robert and I spoke a few words between run-throughs of the musical, but at home, fewer words passed between Alex and me. My wife didn't complain about my absence from her; she didn't grumble about me not helping more at our dance studio, but the special way she'd always looked at me was gone. I feared losing her more at that time than I had when she and I were younger, when she was in that dark place called depression.

Unsatisfied with our performance this particular day, Franco and Saul had scheduled a second practice that evening at New Amsterdam Theatre. The house was dark when I got home. A cold wind whipped through my aching bones as I put the key in the door. I was tired, sweaty, hungry, over-practiced, over-coached, feeling not so full of myself as a dancer, feeling less full of myself as a husband and father. I opened the front door quietly, then tiptoed upstairs to go to bed. The streetlight shining through the top of the drapes exposed Alex's form. I watched her chest rise and fall as she slept, her rhythmic breathing calming, but electrifying too. Her arm moved ever so slightly, and I wanted to lie down, press my body against hers, and feel her warmth. I missed her. My wife returned to a lifeless pose. I got in bed, closed my eyes, and wondered if Alex still loved me.

Chapter 76

It was early; the girls and Alex were still asleep. My body felt like I'd done battle with Goliath and lost, and I dreaded going to rehearsal. I made my way to the bathroom. When I washed my face, I saw my reflection in the mirror. My eyes were a spider's web of red threads woven this way and that. I dressed and made my way to the kitchen to get the coffee going. It was Saturday; employees had the studio covered, and Alex didn't have to go in. At the kitchen table, I downed cup after cup of black coffee, trying to make sense of the mess I'd thrown my wife into, the mess I'd made of my relationship with her. I wanted to tell Franco to get another dancer, but there was no time for someone new to learn the dances; we opened the next weekend. *Meeting in the Woods* had an open-end run, meaning if ticket sales were good and critics' reviews were favorable, my contract would obligate me until ticket sales dropped. I wanted out of my obligation. The question was how could I make that happen?

I left my house in Washington Heights and boarded the number-one train at 181st Street, my destination the Theatre District of Manhattan off of Times Square. How I wished I could go back in time. What was I thinking that day at The Silver Slipper when I told Alex I wanted my shot at performing on stage? I'd chosen my path, a good one with a wonderful wife, children, and a dance studio. Alex could never be replaced, nor could my children, and the road I'd taken to own the studio, I knew I'd gladly take again. I'd worked at getting fit after my heart attack, but I was aging. My body couldn't keep up with the crazy life I was living. The bottom line was that I didn't want theater life; I wanted my sane life back, the one I knew with Alex. *I'll tell Franco today that I don't want to be in the musical,* I thought.

I got to New Amsterdam Theatre early. Punctuality wasn't my concern; I was stressed. I sat in the audience seating area, thinking, trying to choose the right words to tell Franco I wanted out of the performance. The stage lights were on. I hoped that as usual, it was Franco who had arrived early, that he was the only one in the office backstage. My sense of what I wanted out of life was clear, but to let Franco down after he had given me a chance, after he praised me, attacked my sense of responsibility to him. And yet, another weight rested on me, a legal one that allowed Franco and Saul to hold me to my contract. The lights in the seating area came on, and I squinted. My eyes adjusted to the brightness, but no vivid words for telling Franco I wanted out of the musical had come to mind. Franco walked onto the stage and other members of the cast were arriving. I got up, thinking I'd approach him before rehearsal started. My body was sleep deprived, and my empty stomach was crying for fuel. I didn't want to be there. I climbed the stage steps to talk to Franco, but then the director, Saul, came from behind the curtains.

"Take your places," Saul said.

Too late, I thought.

"Ty ... get in position," Franco called out.

I took my place behind the forest scenery and decided I'd speak to him after the first act of *Meeting in the Woods.*

The character of Geno, played by my son, Robert, and Adina, played by the lead female, Taylor, opened the first act with dialogue. The two lovers from different ethnic backgrounds were seated on a downed limb in the woods, distraught about their parents' refusal to give their blessings for the young couple to marry.

The music heightened in intensity, and the lovers began to express their agony through dance. The animals of the forest came out of hiding and formed a circle around them, dancing to express their compassion.

Dressed as a fox, I missed the first beat, but then got in step with the circular weaving formation. We animals broke into a series of leaps, chanting, "Lovers, break away and marry." Then the dance move and formation changed, and thoughts of my family and what they meant to me disturbed my concentration, and I was out of step again. The music changed, got faster, louder.

What's next? I thought as I focused on the dancer in front of me, dressed as a rabbit. I tried to follow the rabbit's lead, but I couldn't. Moving a step closer to the front row, I hoped to hide my missteps behind the rabbit, hoped Franco and the director, Saul, wouldn't see my bumbling effort to perform. Then the rabbit changed direction, making a quarter turn to the left. It followed with a high left-leg kick to the side. My muddled brain froze; my body stayed front and center. The rabbit planted a left foot into my chest, knocking me backward, and I felt myself falling toward the floor. The dancer to my right, a squirrel, was finishing his left-leg kick. He came down and landed on my right forearm. There was a loud pop. The dancers and the music stopped. I was flat on my aching back, staring up at the bright overhead lights that looked like they were moving from side to side. A steady throb pulsed at my temples, and I was dizzy. But the pain in my forearm made my other complaints minor concerns. Then I heard his demanding voice.

"Ty, what have you done?" Franco was standing next to me.

"I've messed up my life," I said, knowing he wouldn't get my true meaning.

Franco called Robert and told him that I was taken by ambulance to Saint Luke's Roosevelt Hospital.

That there'd be no confrontation with Franco about my responsibility to dance made my broken arm seem like divine intervention. I only hoped that divine intervention would salvage my marriage, and my wife would give me a second chance.

I didn't know that Robert had called his mother. The doctor in the emergency room had just given me the news that my arm would be in a cast for seven weeks, and then Alex walked in. Her eyes were filled with tears. "Are you happy now?"

"I've been a fool. I'm done with that theater nonsense. Thought I wanted it, needed it. But believe me, all I want or need is you and us the way we were. I've been miserable. Today was the day I was going to quit. Honest. Do you believe me?"

Epilogue

A little over eight years has gone by, and I celebrated my fifty-fourth birthday May 21. That broken arm in 1996 healed fine, and though it took me a week and a half of eating humble pie, Alex and I not only survived my selfish whim about dancing on stage; our union became more solid than it had been before. Today we're continuing life's journey together, running The Silver Slipper. And I couldn't imagine being more content doing anything else.

Dad still manages Pop's & Charlie's soda-fountain shop in Greenstone, Missouri. He's become quite the dancer and helps Emma Jean and the rest of the instructors with swing-dance lessons. Once in a while, Dad gets Mom out on that checkerboard dance floor too.

Bruno had heart bypass surgery in 2000 and came out of it fine, except that his doctor took away his cigars and restricted his diet. Giving up his stogies was bad enough, but my mother-in-law, Michelle, had to really put her foot down concerning Bruno's Italian taste buds. After Bruno's surgery, I told him and the rest of my family that I'd had a heart attack in 1995. I think that might have been the special connection that finally won my father-in-law over. Since then, he's had a better attitude toward me, his non-Italian son-in-law.

In 2001, Grandma Margaret passed on the twelfth of September. The loss of life and destruction the day before in New York City and Washington, DC, had caused a wave of sorrow across the nation, and Margaret's death added another layer of mourning for my family and me.

Robert and Lizzie have blessed us with three children. The oldest, Tyler, was born July 6, 1998. Had he arrived one day later, Tyler would have been born on Robert's birthday. How off base I was in '95 when I thought Lizzie and Robert were rushing into marriage because they had a baby on the way. Glad I didn't stick my foot in my mouth and ask that *why* question back then. "My little man," as I call Tyler, calms down his three-year-old twin siblings, Marcus—Markie, as I call him—and Mindy when they get rambunctious. Tyler's a miniature Robert in more ways than one. After "my little man" came along, I took my son, Robert, aside. We had a talk about the trying schedule Robert was keeping with his stage performances. I have to give my son credit; he and Lizzie had already discussed the matter. Robert stopped performing and has since been a full-time dance instructor at Adelphi University of Performing Arts.

And my twin girls have made me so proud too. Angela, a graphic artist, married her boss, Andrew Bartfield, in 2002. And Andrea, whom I now go to for legal counsel, married a widower, Tom Warden, a year later. He owns a restaurant that serves the best salmon I've ever eaten, and he's brought two more grandchildren to our family, Sarah and Sam. How rich a man I am.

On the sly, I like to watch my grandchildren play when they come to visit. I sit and chew a wad of bubble gum and try to imagine how their lives will turn out. A vision comes to me: a winding stream behind the church in Greenstone, Missouri, trying to get where it needs to be. And from my own journey, what I've learned is this: just as no stream's path runs in a straight line, each of *us* wanders in pursuit of our destination. The tricky part is recognizing when we've arrived at the place we were meant to be.

The End